TILL DEATH DO YOU PART

A hair-raising scream ripped through the house. The music stopped. No more laughing. No more conversations.

Sylvia whispered, "Oh my God," then took off in the direction of the scream. I followed, with Kate close behind me.

Sylvia was about three feet ahead of me, but had ditched the high heels since I last saw her and was snaking through the crowd with ease, headed toward a closed room on the other side of the foyer.

When she reached the double doors, she pushed them open but then stopped in the entry.

Unable to get past her, I stared over her shoulder.

Megan was sitting on the floor by a fireplace, ivory satin puffed around her like a soft cloud. Her father's head was in her lap, a huge, vicious Merlot-colored stain damning that beautiful dress. . . .

More praise for Leann Sweeney's
Pick Your Poison

"A dandy debut that will leave mystery fans eager to read more about Abby Rose."
—Bill Crider, author of *We'll Always Have Murder*

"*Pick Your Poison* goes down sweet."
—Rick Riordan, Edgar Award-winning author of *Cold Springs*

A WEDDING TO DIE FOR

A YELLOW ROSE MYSTERY

Leann Sweeney

A SIGNET BOOK

SIGNET
Published by New American Library, a division of
Penguin Group (USA) Inc., 375 Hudson Street,
New York, New York 10014, USA
Penguin Group (Canada), 90 Eglinton Avenue East, Suite 700, Toronto,
Ontario M4P 2Y3, Canada (a division of Pearson Penguin Canada Inc.)
Penguin Books Ltd., 80 Strand, London WC2R 0RL, England
Penguin Ireland, 25 St. Stephen's Green, Dublin 2,
Ireland (a division of Penguin Books Ltd.)
Penguin Group (Australia), 250 Camberwell Road, Camberwell, Victoria 3124,
Australia (a division of Pearson Australia Group Pty. Ltd.)
Penguin Books India Pvt. Ltd., 11 Community Centre, Panchsheel Park,
New Delhi - 110 017, India
Penguin Group (NZ), 67 Apollo Drive, Rosedale, North Shore 0632,
New Zealand (a division of Pearson New Zealand Ltd.)
Penguin Books (South Africa) (Pty.) Ltd., 24 Sturdee Avenue,
Rosebank, Johannesburg 2196, South Africa

Penguin Books Ltd., Registered Offices:
80 Strand, London WC2R 0RL, England

First published by Signet, an imprint of New American Library,
a division of Penguin Group (USA) Inc.

First Printing, January 2005
10 9 8 7 6 5

Copyright © Leann Sweeney, 2005
All rights reserved

1

My daddy always said that if you want to round up some liars head to a wedding or a funeral. So as I sat in a back pew at Seacliff First Baptist, I got to wondering how many liars were in attendance this afternoon. Seeing as how I'd been invited to the rehearsal dinner for this little shindig, I believe I'd already met a few candidates.

Thanks to a frigid wind sneaking between every door crack and window sash in the old church, my teeth were chattering like dice in a crap game. The building sat a few blocks from Galveston Bay and a blue norther had barreled through last night, leaving behind a genuine taste of winter.

Most of the hundred people in attendance, including me, still wore their coats, and I shoved my hands in my pockets. Leaning toward my sister, who had reluctantly agreed to come with me, I said, "Remind me never to get married in January."

"You *did* get married in January," she whispered.

"That never really happened," I shot back.

"Oh, I forgot. Denial is Abby's best friend."

"Denial's the perfect friend once you discover you married a greedy, womanizing alcoholic," I answered.

Before she could respond, the gentle organ music abruptly crescendoed.

A bridesmaid swathed in Christmas green rustled down the aisle so fast you'd have thought she was trying to catch her own echo. This would be Courtney, a cousin of the bride. The one who liked margaritas. And wine. And studly groomsmen. Next came the other cousin, Roxanne, a stripped-down model of her sister—pallid as the moon, skinny as a bed slat, and suffering from a very bad hair day. She looked ready to cry, her spider mum bouquet trembling at her waist. *If I had hair like that, I'd be ready to cry, too.*

The maid of honor, Margie, looked, well . . . *happy* in contrast to everyone else, including the nervous lineup of tuxedoed men waiting near the altar. The groom kept pulling at his coat sleeves and even from where I sat, I could see sweat glistening on his forehead. He'd better watch out or it might freeze right there.

From the corner of my eye I caught a glimpse of a woman in a beige wool pantsuit wearing this retro chocolate brown cloche hat. She tiptoed into the church and sidled behind the bride and her father, carefully avoiding Megan Beadford's train. After the woman slipped into an empty pew on the groom's side, I realized she had not signed the bride's book on the lectern.

Didn't she know you had to sign in at weddings? Ordinarily this detail wouldn't have bothered me, but I had been assigned to oversee that book, a small task I suppose Megan felt I could handle after so far failing at what she'd hired me to do. The bride had wanted her biological mother here today, but though I'd been successful with several other cases in my new profession as an adoption PI, I still had no decent leads on Megan's background.

So why am I an adoption PI rather than the mean-street variety? Because some things change you forever, lead you down the road you're supposed to take. The events of last summer did that for me even though they nearly shredded my heart. Those wounds make my ticker beat a little faster, a little harder, and a little more urgently now. It all started when my gardener was murdered. I'd wanted to find out why. One thing led to another, and in the end I discovered that my adoptive daddy lied to Kate and me about our biological parents up until the day he died, learned that our birth mother had been murdered when she'd tried desperately to find the twin baby girls (me and my sister) who had been stolen from her. My daddy didn't do the stealing, but he didn't ask enough questions about the babies he was adopting, either.

And then there were the betrayals. We had a slew of those. Our aunt Caroline knew the truth and never spoke up. A dear family friend helped daddy with our illegal adoption and never came clean until I confronted him. But my ex-husband was the biggest liar and cheat of all, even more worthless than I'd realized when I divorced him. He had blackmailed my adoptive father, killed the one person who wanted to tell me the truth about our mother's death, and then tried to murder me when I figured out exactly what he'd done. And all for money. That's all I had ever meant to him—money.

But as horrible as all those things had been to endure, they had led me here today, to my new job as an adoption PI, to a real sense of purpose for the first time in my life. I might have come to this church as Megan's friend, but the job she'd hired me for still hovered in my brain like a hummingbird buzzing in the background. She would get her truth if I had anything to say about it. People deserve the truth.

Just then the latecomer dropped her handbag, the long leather clutch bag falling with a thump onto the old oak floor.

"Is she carrying rocks to throw at the bride and groom rather than rice?" I whispered to Kate.

"Shhh," answered my sister, who was staring over her shoulder.

Making a mental note to corral the lady in the hat after the ceremony, I followed Kate's gaze and focused on Megan. She had seed pearls woven into her fine blond hair, and a cathedral-length veil billowed out behind her. The dress was ivory silk, an A-line devoid of sparkle or beads. This elegant simplicity suited her personality, and by the admiring smile on Kate's face I guessed she agreed with me.

We had become friendly with Megan and her fiancé, Travis, in the last few months. Who couldn't be friends with folks as sweet and innocent and full of hope as those two? When I'd first met Megan, I figured she was about sixteen, but she came to me with a copy of her birth certificate proving she was twenty years old. That piece of paper had been my only clue in the adoption search, mainly because Megan was adamant that her adoptive parents not know she'd hired me. Besides being sweet and innocent, she was also as stubborn as a two-headed mule, a trait we happened to share.

Kate and I tried to convince her not to keep secrets, arguing that maybe her parents would understand Megan's need to find out about her past and would then help us with valuable details about the adoption. But Megan wouldn't budge, saying she knew it would hurt their feelings. When her parents had told her she was adopted—they'd waited until she was a teenager—they requested she not look for her biological mother. But asking a teenager *not* to do something is sort of like asking a gator not to bite you. She couldn't stop thinking about a reunion and finally hired me without their knowledge.

I may not have delivered on Megan's request in time for the wedding, but we talked every week. When she mentioned that the woman who was supposed to do the wedding book delivered a premature baby last weekend, I volunteered to fill in. That's how I'd ended up at that disaster of a wedding rehearsal dinner last night and this chilly affair today.

Mendelssohn's overture began. Everyone rose to face Megan and her father as they slowly walked toward the preacher and groom. Once they reached the altar, the balding, stern-faced James Beadford kissed his adopted daughter and placed her satin-gloved fingers into Travis Crane's outstretched hand. The bride and groom stared into each other's eyes, then turned to the preacher.

Here's where the lying starts, I thought to my cynical self.

Thirty minutes later, I did the driving while Kate directed us to the reception at the Beadford house. She was using the tiny map insertion from the invitation. The lady with the hat had gotten away from me during the crushing exodus after the ceremony, but I assumed there would be others besides her I would have to catch up with to sign the book—those folks who skip the ceremony and just show up for the booze and the food. I knew about those types because of my own January wedding several years back, the one I hadn't really forgotten. The one I could only hope to forget in time.

I maneuvered my Camry through a sparsely populated upscale neighborhood ever closer to the ocean and finally came upon parked cars lining both sides of a dead-end street. Folks who had dragged their dress-up winter coats out of mothballs were walking up the hill to a monstrous white house at the end of the cul-de-sac. We'd found the spot. I turned the car around and parked down the block so we could make a quick getaway after we'd made nice with all these strangers.

My sister knew Megan almost as well as I did since she'd done a psychological profile on her, something Kate does on all my clients. Kind of handy having a shrink for a sister. Texas's Central Adoption Registry requires a similar screening before they hook up long-lost relatives. Since Texas is a closed adoption state, all records are sealed by the court, but the registry offers a legal means for adoptees and their biological relatives to meet if both sides independently send in paperwork expressing their wish for a reunion. Once the registry finds a match, they interview both sides and arrange the meeting, thus avoiding a lengthy court petition to unseal records.

Kate's psychological profile of Megan confirmed what I had already decided—that she was stable enough to handle bad news if it came to that. I'd gotten a firsthand taste of her maturity already. She'd dreamed of a private meeting with her biological mother after the reception, maybe at a hotel in Houston before she and Travis took off on their honeymoon to Hawaii. But when I told her last week I still couldn't get anywhere in my document searches, she didn't go off the deep end. She just calmly told me to keep trying.

As Kate and I trudged up the hill toward the house, she said, "How did Megan explain your presence at the rehearsal dinner last night? Has she changed her mind about telling her parents who you really are?"

"No. She introduced me as a new friend she'd met at the health club."

Kate laughed. "It's a good thing they don't know you like I do."

"Hey. Since Jeff and I have been together, we run a couple miles two or three times a week, so I'm more fit than you think." Jeff Kline, whose cologne still clung to my pillow this morning, works Houston Homicide. He'd investigated the death of my yardman, the one who'd been unlucky enough to get in my ex-husband's way, and we'd been spending plenty of time together since last summer.

"You're more of *everything* since you hooked up with our cop friend. Don't let go of that guy if you can help it."

"Believe me, I won't." My nose started to run and I sniffed. The wind off the bay was cold enough to make a lawyer put his hands in his own pockets.

Kate offered me a tissue. "So am I allowed to be your sister once we get inside this place? I'm sure you and Megan will want to have a consistent story. We wouldn't want to alert the relatives that she hired you."

"By your sarcasm I'm guessing you're still convinced Megan should have told her parents."

"Keeping secrets from your family is never a good idea." Her coffee-colored shoulder-length hair was practically horizontal as she bowed her head against the wind.

"Maybe not, but Megan shouldn't have to learn the same way we did about our past. No one should."

"It's not like her parents lied to her, Abby."

"Okay, so they didn't lie like Daddy did, but they waited way too long to tell her the truth and then made her feel like she'd be betraying them if she tried to learn about her past."

"Are you substituting your judgment for theirs?"

"Guess that's not fair," I mumbled. "I just don't feel comfortable at weddings and it's reduced me to whining. What say we go for some food, a little small talk, then get the hell out?"

"Now, there's a plan I won't argue with," she said.

We approached the wide stone stairs leading up to the house, and the sounds of stringed instruments drifted out through the open front door. Just as we reached the steps, the limo carrying the bride and groom arrived. Travis helped Megan out of the backseat, and Roxanne appeared in all her greenness from out of nowhere. She eagerly lifted Megan's gown to keep it from dragging on the pavement. They all went inside to a round of applause.

Not only was the wedding photographer busy doing his job, the hat lady was standing right behind him snapping her own pictures. Seeing her reminded me of my mission: to seek out all guests and get their signatures and well wishes in the embossed book clutched at my side. Not exactly a job for Superman, but I felt obligated. "Come on, Kate. I have to catch up with that woman in the brown hat."

But before we reached her, she disappeared into

the throng following Megan and Travis inside. When we reached the front door, Megan's mother stepped out to greet us.

"Thank goodness you're here," said Sylvia Beadford. "I see you have the book." She nodded at the album under my arm.

An apple-shaped, overly made-up woman, she wore a turquoise silk suit that complemented her dusky pink complexion. But Sylvia's ruby lipstick was smeared and her rose corsage was already wilting. The frosted hair hadn't wilted though. She had enough hairspray on those beauty-shop curls to put a new hole in the ozone layer. From her tense demeanor, I guessed she was having far less of a good time than those inside whose laughter nearly overpowered the music. Note to self: Never have girl babies who put you through wedding torture.

I held up the album. "I missed a few people and Megan said she wanted—"

"I'll handle that." She took the book, saying, "Meanwhile, I could use your help."

"Sure—and by the way, this is my sister, Kate."

"She can help, too." Sylvia grabbed my wrist and pulled me inside; then despite her dyed-to-match spike heels, she bulldozed through the guests lingering in the foyer.

I caught a glimpse of twin staircases with white wrought-iron banisters flanking the foyer on both sides. Beyond was a great room filled with guests. A balcony above that huge center room was also packed with people holding wineglasses and plates of food.

Megan's mother led us down a hallway, past a spacious dining room. We ended up in a kitchen worthy of a television chef and found ourselves surrounded by caterers in black and white uniforms. Seems the lady who delivered the baby too early had only half-finished one of her jobs. Kate and I set to work putting handfuls of birdseed in small squares of netting and tying each packet up with ivory ribbon.

"Birdseed is a good choice," Kate said, already getting busy. "More environmentally friendly than rice."

"That's what Megan said," Sylvia agreed, before hurrying off. But two glasses of champagne arrived beside us a minute later. Tying ribbons and drinking champagne? I could handle that.

The breakfast area where we sat and worked on our task overlooked a screened porch complete with umbrella table and chairs for balmier days. A family room could be seen through the double doors straight ahead and huge picture windows dominated the far wall. The Gulf of Mexico was an angry green, the sky a grouchy gray, while the strings played on, their music calming and gentle above the din of crowd noise.

Silver trays of canapés kept leaving the room on the raised arms of the waitstaff. I managed to snatch some finger sandwiches and a few pastry puffs stuffed with shrimp salad. Kate munched on two of her favorites, broccoli and carrots, sniffing them first as if her practiced nose could actually discern whether they were organic.

We were nearly done with our job when the best man, Holt McNabb, came into the room gripping a longneck beer, his other arm around bridesmaid Courtney's waist. The tattoo on her back right shoulder, a cobra ready to strike, clashed with the strapless taffeta gown. Before Holt spotted us in the breakfast alcove, he planted one on Courtney, a kiss that left no doubt saliva was being exchanged. She in turn grabbed his well-toned butt during this semipornographic moment. It ended when he opened his eyes and spotted me.

He lifted her chin and smiled at her. "Hey, Courtney—could you get me a plate of those baby-back ribs? Meanwhile, I'll give these ladies a proper thank-you for all their help."

Courtney hesitated. "You'll be waiting here, then?"

He smiled. "Maybe. And that's final."

"You're kidding, right?"

He gripped her shoulders and turned her in the direction of the dining room. "Yes, I'm kidding. Now, get going."

She left.

Kate hadn't had the honor of meeting the rest of the rehearsal dinner crew, if you want to call it an honor. I'd met Daddy James, Momma Sylvia, the gruesome twosome cousins/bridesmaids, best man Holt, and Uncle Graham—the one who had tried all last evening to outdrink his daughter Courtney. I think Graham won.

"Good to see you again, Abby." Holt set his beer bottle down on the table. But though he was addressing me, he focused on Kate. His pale blue eyes seemed to like what they saw, but then who wouldn't be mesmerized by Kate's classic Audrey Hepburn look?

"Hello, Holt," I said. "Nice wedding."

"Care to introduce me to your friend?" he asked.

"My sister, Kate Rose," I said.

He placed both hands on the table and leaned toward her. "Thank the lord the stepsister brought Cinderella to the ball. Where did I put that glass slipper?"

"Make that twins, not stepsisters," I said.

"Twins? Are you kidding? She's got three inches on you and the nicest smile south of Dallas. Say, you doing anything later, Miss Kate Rose?"

Kate leveled him with a look that could have melted the cupid ice sculpture on the buffet table in the dining room. "You want me to join you and Courtney?"

Holt raised his hands and stepped back. "No crime to appreciate females. Happens to be a weakness of mine. And if you're not interested, I respect that."

The awkward silence that followed was broken by Travis's appearance in the doorway.

He said, "Holt, we're cutting the cake and you're supposed to say something first."

Holt nodded and flashed a *GQ* smile. "Ladies, it's been a pleasure."

I laughed when he was gone. "Does he like himself or what?"

"The nice thing about someone like him is that he doesn't have much time to talk about anyone else. He's too busy being consumed with himself."

Since I'd seen plenty of cake cutting in my time, and Kate didn't eat anything with white sugar, we stayed put. But I was as hungry as a goat on concrete, so I had a friendly waiter fill me a plate with boiled shrimp before he took the platter into the dining room.

Kate continued making the little net pockets and seemed to be doing a damn fine job, so I took my time peeling the shrimp and enjoyed every single one of those critters. About thirty minutes later Kate announced she was finished and went to the sink to wash her hands. Licking the remnants of cocktail sauce off my fingers, I followed suit, dodging several waiters on the way.

Kate told me she would arrange the little birdseed treasures in the crepe-lined basket Sylvia Beadford had provided if I wanted to find Megan and say hello. "And good-bye," she added with emphasis.

"Good idea. Much as I hate to agree with Holt, I do kind of feel like a Cinderella relegated to the back of the house for menial tasks."

I wandered out into the family room, my drink in hand. The string quartet had been set up in here, but most folks were in the adjoining great room to my left. The musicians had taken a break, and the noise of multiple conversations in both rooms filled the air. A fire crackled in the fireplace and a champagne fountain with golden liquid bubbling out of pitchers held by cherubs sat on a table perpendicular to the windows. Plates filled with slices of the now-mutilated tiered white cake surrounded the fountain.

I noticed Roxanne speaking with the violinist in a corner to my right. I knew he was the violinist because he had his instrument clutched to him like a life jacket. Roxanne's stringy brown hair made me wonder if she'd sprayed her head with Pam rather than Final Net, and the violinist's body language brought the image of a treed possum to mind. Nothing pretty about that scene.

But James and Travis had them beat. The new father-in-law and son-in-law were outside on the deck that overlooked a covered oval swimming pool. Either the wind had stung their faces an angry crimson, or both their blood pressures were sky-high. James kept poking his finger into Travis's silver-vested chest.

Then Travis glanced back toward the house, took hold of his father-in-law's elbow, and led him toward the other end of the deck.

I immediately scanned the room for Megan, feeling protective all of a sudden. No bride should have her wedding day ruined by some silly family dispute that probably could have waited until the appropriate time. That's what Thanksgiving and Christmas are for, right? I soon spotted her talking to her uncle Graham in the next room.

I made my way around clusters of guests engaged in animated conversations or playing with their digital cameras. I reached Megan and her uncle in time to hear Graham Beadford loudly proclaim he was related to Thomas Jefferson by way of a different mother than Sally Hemmings, a "damn prettier" slave girl, according to him. For Megan's sake, I hoped no one was videotaping this embarrassing moment. Uncle Graham was so drunk he'd probably grab a snake and try to kill a stick.

Megan blushed and said, "Hi, Abby. I was hoping to convince my uncle to try the coffee. We rented this huge silver urn and it's filled to the brim, but no one seems interested."

"Maybe he and I could sample the coffee together,"

I offered, setting my champagne glass down on a small side table near the wall.

Graham attempted to focus on me, his head wobbling with the effort. "Don't I know you?"

"We met last night at dinner. Abby Rose."

"That's right. Megan's little rich friend. So you want to force-feed me some caffeine? I'll bet you could ante up for a whole Starbucks. Gold mine, those Starbucks. Who'd have thought us Texans would willingly pay five dollars for steaming coffee in our ninety-degree summers? Shoulda got in on that action when they first came to town."

"Uncle Graham, forgive me, but there are guests I haven't even spoken with yet," said Megan.

He gulped the last of whatever he'd been drinking and slid the rocks glass on the table, nearly tipping over my champagne flute. "Well, forgive me for monopolizing you."

But Uncle Graham didn't move and Megan seemed reluctant to leave him, though if I were in her place I would have done so in a heartbeat.

I took Graham's arm. "Let's you and I chat."

Megan mouthed a thank-you once he seemed willing to depart with me.

I wasn't simply being a Good Samaritan. He'd called me the "rich friend," and I wanted to know how he'd learned about my financial circumstances, considering I hadn't mentioned my background to anyone last night. I hadn't even told Megan. Despite being well-off, I charge for my services, using everything I make to support a home for unwed mothers in Galveston—a home I have a special interest in. Kate and I were born there.

"So, Mr. Beadford," I said, my hand on his upper arm. I guided him in the direction of the dining room. "What's your line of business?"

"Not computers like you, that's for sure. Computers are getting to be like goddamn cars. Too much maintenance to love 'em, but you can't live without 'em."

Had I still been working for CompuCan, my late daddy's company, I might have said he obviously needed one of our computers. But I'd spent the last several months shedding myself of anything but minimal involvement, deciding I was never cut out to be a CEO. But obviously Graham Beadford thought I still worked there.

"So what do you do, Mr. Beadford?" I repeated.

He stopped in the middle of the room, his square chin raised. "Plenty. I do plenty. I've owned my own business and I've worked with my brother, James, on the oil equipment supply side. But if you need a computer man, I can do that, too."

"Sorry, but I've changed jobs. Can't help you there. I'm in . . . social services now."

"Really? The Internet is behind on their information, then." It was his turn to pull me toward the dining room. "But even so, you inherited some big bucks, Ms. Rose." Graham made a sudden weave to the right and slammed his shoulder into a woman wildly overdressed in black sequins and a mink stole.

Graham was a small, burly man, similar in stature to Megan's father—and he hit the lady square on the collarbone. When he failed to offer an apology, she shot him a "go directly to hell" look, readjusted the dead animals around her shoulders, and resumed her conversation.

"Excuse him," I whispered as we passed, wondering what else this guy had turned up on me. There were plenty of news stories to be found considering the home I'd recently vacated in ritzy River Oaks had become a crime scene after the gardener was killed. But why was this man plugging my name into some search engine in the first place?

I must have looked concerned because Graham patted my back. "Don't worry. I won't say anything about your little brush with death at the hands of your ex-husband or mention your mountains of money."

"Who says I'm worried?"

He stopped in the dining room entry and lifted my chin with his index knuckle. "Uncle Graham knows people. I'll bet you're scared I'll blab to all these upper-middle-class schmucks about how filthy, stinking rich you are. And you're afraid if I do, people will be hanging on you like snapping turtles. Asking for favors . . . donations . . . handouts. I had money once. I know what it's like. Royal pain in the ass."

He didn't slur one word, and I realized then that Graham Beadford might not be as drunk as I'd thought—though from the smell of him, he was well on the way.

The coffee urn that looked like it could have provided enough java for a cruise ship breakfast sat on one end of a shiny teak table. The now-weeping ice sculpture rested in the center surrounded by silver platters of cold crab, pâté and crackers, boiled shrimp, cubed cheeses, marinated mushroom caps, and cherry tomatoes stuffed with something swirled and yellow. The chubby photographer, his camera strapped behind him, was parked in a corner sucking the meat out of a crab claw.

I held up two fingers to the waitress manning the urn and she filled scalloped china cups and handed them to me.

When I gave Graham his, he pulled a pint of Southern Comfort from his pocket and spiked his coffee, sending liquid sloshing onto the saucer. After restashing his bottle, he lifted both cup and saucer to his lips and slurped off the top.

"Starbucks could learn a thing or three from me," he said. "Make a bigger killing if they had more than those sissy-ass drinks on the menu." His bald, freckled head glowed under the crystal chandelier hanging over the table.

I drank half my lukewarm coffee, then glanced back over my shoulder to make sure Megan wasn't close by and still subject to him reinserting himself into her line of vision. She wasn't. "Listen, Graham, I need to get home. Maybe I'll see you again when I visit with Megan."

"I live in Dallas, so I doubt that. But why not stay and keep me company a little longer? I could get to like you, little lady."

"Sorry. I came with my sister and she has a client waiting." Small lies are sometimes necessary. I reached over and set the cup and saucer on a tray by the wall an arm's length away.

"She works on Saturday?"

"She's a shrink. Crazy people sometimes don't know if it's Saturday or Wednesday."

"That sounds like an excuse. Have I upset you? Because I could sure use some intelligent conversation. Every idiot here belongs to my brother. *His* clients. *His* line of credit. *His* wonderful life. Besides, Megan wanted you to take care of me—as I'm sure you noticed."

His tone told me more than all his previous words or actions—bitter noise from a guy whose blood-to-alcohol ratio was probably permanently off-kilter. Having learned my lesson about alcohol abusers the hard way, I said, "Sorry, Graham, but I can't stay."

I turned and walked toward the kitchen just as the music started up again. Beethoven's "Ode to Joy." I sure hoped Megan and Travis had some of that joy in their hearts, because so far, this reception was proving to be devoid of happiness and warmth.

When I arrived in the kitchen, Kate was handing her artfully arranged basket of birdseed packets to the bride's mother.

That's when a hair-raising scream ripped through the house. Kate and Sylvia lost their grip on the basket and all those pretty little pouches scattered over the tile floor. Some of the netting opened, sending tiny seeds bouncing in every direction.

The music stopped.

No more laughing. No more conversations.

Sylvia whispered, "Oh my God," then took off in the direction of the scream.

I followed, Kate close behind me.

We pushed by people who looked frozen in time, their collective silence almost oppressive. Maybe it was the adrenaline rush that heightened my senses, but the mix of seafood and booze and flowers seemed like an ocean I had to swim through. No one but us seemed to be reacting to what every single guest surely must have heard. But that's how it often happens in an emergency. The more people around, the less response. Everyone expects someone else to do something.

Sylvia was about three feet ahead of me, but had ditched the high heels since I last saw her and was snaking through the crowd with ease, headed toward a closed room on the other side of the foyer.

When she reached the double doors, she pushed them open but then stopped in the entry.

Unable to get past her, I stared over her shoulder.

Megan was sitting on the floor by a fireplace, ivory satin puffed around her like a soft cloud. Her father's head was in her lap, a huge, vicious merlot-colored stain damning that beautiful dress.

2

Megan reached out to me with blood-stained hands and pleaded, "Abby, help him. Please help him."

I wasn't sure why she'd turned to me rather than her mother, but that question caused no hesitation on my part. I squeezed by the still-immobile Sylvia, hurried over, and knelt beside Megan.

James Beadford's dilated eyes stared up at the ceiling and a wicked gash to his temple had bled enough to completely mask his right ear. I lifted his hand and felt for a pulse, not going for the carotid. His messy head and neck would have made that difficult.

So much blood. And it was still seeping into Megan's lap. Beadford's skin was warm, but I felt nothing, not even one tiny beat of his heart in that thick, limp wrist.

I sat back on my heels, heard and felt a crunching sound beneath my feet. The brick hearth was right behind me and I leaned against it, realizing I was crouching in small pieces of glass. A couple of feet behind Megan lay the scattered remnants of a leaded crystal vase, the jagged base glittering like a giant diamond in the light from the window.

Meeting Megan's anxious gaze, I shook my head. "I'm so sorry. He's gone."

She stared down at her father's face, then bent at the waist and collapsed over him, her strapless bodice heaving with sobs.

I looked over at Sylvia, who hadn't uttered a sound, hadn't moved an inch. She stood rigid, fists at her sides, a tinge of gray around her crimson mouth. Kate's pale face loomed behind her.

"Kate, call nine one one."

But before Kate could react, Sylvia Beadford swayed and then toppled like a felled oak, taking Kate down with her to the wood floor. Megan must have known her mother would crumble. Probably why she reached out to me for help first.

I started to get up, ready to assist Kate and Sylvia, nearly tearing my angle-hemmed skirt when I started to rise. But Megan's cold, sticky fingers gripped my forearm. "Don't leave us. Please."

Then Graham appeared, looking downright sober. He assisted Kate to her knees so she could minister to the passed out Sylvia before flipping open a cell phone to make the 9 1 1 call.

Not long after, noise again filled the Beadford house. Chaos bred from fear makes plenty of noise—raised voices, the sound of a distant siren, people shouting and wanting in the room. Didn't matter poor Sylvia was laid out like a trussed turkey in the doorway. Kate was fanning the woman's face with someone's handbag and I swear those so-called friends of the family would have stepped right over Sylvia to get a better look at the body.

With the help of a calm, rational Holt McNabb—maybe he was an okay guy after all—Graham pushed all the guests back, telling them to find a place to "park it." They did let Travis pass. I wasn't sure even *he* should come in, but we'd already messed up the crime scene plenty. Besides, I needed my arm back. Megan's grip had my fingers going numb and Travis seemed the right person to help alleviate that problem.

Meanwhile Holt and Graham assisted a dazed Sylvia to her feet and led her away, leaving me and Kate alone with Travis and Megan.

Megan had stopped crying. She was probably numb

with shock now. Travis gently pulled her from beneath her dead father. Once she was on her feet, he wrapped his arms around her small, trembling frame and rocked her, smoothing her hair, not letting go for dear life. "I've got you, hon. I'm here," he said over and over.

I moved away from them and whispered to Kate, "I need your phone."

She lifted her black silk shirt and pulled it from her matching skirt pocket. "You calling Jeff?" she asked.

"You betcha." I took the phone and dialed his cell.

"Kate?" he answered, sounding puzzled. Must have recognized her Caller ID.

"No, it's me." I turned my back on Megan and Travis. "Remember that wedding?"

"Yeah?" Wary now. He probably heard the tension in my voice.

"It just turned into a funeral," I whispered. "Father of the bride got whacked with a very large vase."

Shrieking sirens sounded so close I figured the police were pulling in front of the house. I missed his reply.

"Repeat that," I said.

"Where are you?" He was all cool and collected now. A freaked-out girlfriend might be trouble, but murder? Comfortable territory. I could hear the rustle of paper. He was unwrapping a stick of Big Red gum, no doubt.

"In Seacliff." I gave him the address.

"Galveston County. Out of our jurisdiction. But I'll be there anyway."

He disconnected.

Jeff may be a man of few words, but he's great in the action department.

He didn't arrive for another hour, probably because Seacliff is well south of Houston, and half the trip is on two-lane roads rather than freeway. In the meantime, plenty of other cops showed up, not only from

Seacliff, but from several surrounding towns. A county
sheriff patrol arrived on the scene, too. And then
there were the fire trucks. And the ambulance. Everyone in small Texas towns makes an appearance for
the 9 1 1 calls. By the time I was commanded to my
"holding area" by the female plainclothes officer who
seemed to be in charge of the investigation, I was
beginning to wonder if Graham Beadford had mentioned al-Qaeda when he'd called.

Kate and I had been separated. I didn't particularly
like this, but reasoned the lady in control knew what
she was doing. Everyone who had entered the room
or saw the body was being guarded by their own special cop until he or she could be interviewed. Mine, a
uniformed officer from a nearby town, took me to the
laundry room. We sat in wooden folding chairs facing
each other, crammed in with the washer, dryer, and a
wheeling clothes rack. He resisted all my attempts at
conversation, just sat there coldly staring past my right
shoulder. I swear if we were cremated together that
guy wouldn't have warmed up.

Finally a Seacliff cop rescued me, informing Officer
Subzero that his help was needed with all the cameras
and video recorders gathered from the guests.

Cameras. Wow. I hadn't thought about them. Folks
had been snapping pictures like crazy, and who knows
what they'd inadvertently captured. The new cop and
I walked through the house. Most people had been
cleared out, and those who remained stood in small
groups in the great room talking with uniformed police officers taking notes.

I was escorted to the formal living area off the
foyer, a room I hadn't even noticed when Sylvia am-
bushed us for kitchen duty. Reminded me of my old
digs in River Oaks with its uncomfortable-looking Vic-
torian couches and artistically draped window—one of
the few windows that looked out on the street rather
than the water.

Jeff sat on the largest gold brocade sofa and was

leaning toward a thin brunette sitting in one of several teak dining room chairs that had been brought into the room. He didn't seem to notice our presence. The woman looked to be in her late twenties and wore a gray wool suit and open-collar blouse—the same person who had sent me to babysit the Maytag. Jeff had on a faded denim shirt that matched his eyes and had gotten a haircut since I last saw him this morning. He always kept his blond hair short, but this time the barber had left little more than stubble on his head.

My cop escort cleared his throat and said, "Uh, ma'am?"

The woman looked up and Jeff stood, his jaw working his ever-present gum.

"Hey, how you doing?" he asked, coming over to me.

"I still have a pulse—unlike someone else here—so I think I'm in good shape," I said.

He gripped my upper arms and kissed the top of my head. "You've had a rough day, kid."

I felt the tension in my neck muscles melt a little when I smelled the combination of cinnamon gum and aftershave unique to him. He took my hand and led me to the sofa. I sat, grateful for even a less-than-adequate cushion for my sore patoot.

I smiled at the woman and said, "Hi. Bet you've had a tough day, too."

She did not return my smile. Her crossed legs were long enough and her features attractive enough that she could have been working a catwalk in New York rather than sitting here ready to interview a witness. "Thanks for your patience, Ms. Rose. Jeff tells me you were employed by the bride."

Jeff? I thought. *They'd certainly gotten friendly in an hour's time.*

He must have read my expression and quickly offered an explanation. "Quinn is an old friend. She honed her skills in Houston PD before taking the top job here."

"Great," I said. "So is that Captain Quinn or—"

"Sorry." She reached over Jeff and offered a hand in a greeting. "It's Chief Fielder. Seacliff PD. Quinn is my first name."

Chief? Wow. She looked so young.

I gripped her slim fingers and offered a firm handshake, one I hoped said "I can throw a horseshoe with the horse still attached," even though that was not how I really felt. I felt small and . . . well, scared. But my daddy always told me to never show weakness when I was afraid, that it would only make things worse.

Fielder had a yellow legal pad on her lap and several pages were already turned back. "Jeff tells me Megan Beadford hired you to find her biological mother."

"That's right."

"So you didn't know the rest of the family?"

"Actually, I only just met them last night at the rehearsal dinner."

"I'm not sure I understand. Did you attend last night and today in your capacity as an investigator?"

"No. I was a last-minute replacement for the wedding book-slash-birdseed handler, the one who went into labor a month early."

She smiled, which softened her features, made her already attractive face prettier. "That's what your sister told me." She then made note of my answer on her yellow pad. "And by the way, we let your sister leave. Apparently a patient of hers was in some sort of crisis. She took your car and said you should catch a ride home with Jeff. Now, to the issues at hand. You had been making inquiries about Megan's biological mother, correct?"

"Yes, but our professional relationship is not common knowledge. I'm here as a friend."

"Not common knowledge?" She tilted her head and raised her eyebrows.

"Megan wanted my inquiries kept private. She felt

her family would not be happy about her wish to find her birth mother."

"Really?" She scribbled some more. "There was tension in the family?"

"Maybe some."

Jeff said, "Any conflicts at the rehearsal?"

"The rehearsal itself went fine," I said. "But once the wedding party and families bellied up to the open bar before dinner, everyone on Megan's side suddenly seemed to have *issues*."

"Issues?" Fielder said.

"The cousins weren't speaking—I know because I sat between them at dinner. And the best man, Holt McNabb, brought in a TV and set it in front of him on the table to watch some college basketball game. That pissed off Mr. Beadford. He and McNabb went to a corner and Mr. Beadford seemed to be raking him over the coals. This upset Sylvia and—"

"I get the picture. But these sound like minor altercations. You didn't witness anything more serious? Perhaps a fistfight? Or threats?"

"No. Nothing like that."

"And you're not here in any official capacity?"

Did she think I was lying? "You mean did I find Megan's birth mother at the last minute and bring her here? No. And I'd appreciate it if you don't upset anyone by telling the rest of the family how I came to know Megan."

"I'm not in the business of telling witnesses anything. *They* tell me. Moving on, you are licensed, correct?"

Not even an hour's worth of absorbing the odors of Tide and Downy could make me feel "mountain fresh" pleasant about her patronizing attitude. "Provisionally," I replied evenly. "But I specialize in adoption searches for someone who is licensed."

"And your supervising PI's name?" she asked, pen poised.

"Angel Molina," I said. "But what does—"

Jeff placed a gentle hand on my knee. "Bear with Quinn. She's just doing her job."

"And this Molina has an agency in Houston?" Fielder went on.

"He does," I answered. "Is that important?"

"This is all routine, Abby," Jeff said.

Fielder glanced at Jeff's hand, which had moved up to my thigh. "I'll check out the agency later." I saw her fingers flex several times, saw her nostrils flare a little when she took in some extra air.

Jeff, good detective that he is, noted these subtle indicators, too. He promptly assumed a less intimate posture by leaning back, his arms spanning the sofa's arched back.

So he wanted her to feel more comfortable, huh? He *cared* about her. Oh, I was picking up on the signals, all right. These two probably had a history that was more than just professional—and from the way she kept looking at him, she wished it wasn't history.

"Tell me exactly what you saw when you walked in on Megan and her father," she said.

"I saw a very distraught young woman with her father's bloody head in her lap."

She laid the pad and pen down. "Sorry. Guess I should be more specific."

"Guess you should."

"You, Ms. Rose, do not have an emotional wall to climb when it comes to remembering what you saw in that room. After all, you hardly knew the dead man. I consider that rational distance important in reconstructing a crime scene that was seriously compromised by several factors."

"You mean those gung-ho paramedics doing CPR on an obviously dead body? Why did they do that, by the way?"

"Wouldn't you want them to do everything possible if it were your father?" she replied.

"Not if his skull was exposed and gray matter was in my lap," I shot back. "Besides, my father's already dead."

Jeff rested a hand on my back. "Abby, it's okay." He addressed Quinn. "Abby's father had a heart attack and the paramedics were called and . . . well, you understand."

I stared hard at him, saying nothing. What the hell did he think he was doing telling her my personal business?

"I'm sorry if I upset you, Ms. Rose," Fielder said.

"You didn't upset me," I said evenly, summoning a calmness I did not feel.

"Good. Now, can you tell me the exact position of the body and where Megan Beadford was sitting? I also need to know which direction her father's feet were pointing and where the broken glass was in relationship to them."

"Can I draw it for you?" I said.

She picked up the pad, tore off a clean sheet of paper and offered it to me along with her pen. I made the sketch, indicating that Beadford's head had been parallel to the fireplace on the left wall, his feet toward the back of the room. Megan was sitting on the dead man's right side facing the fireplace. "You want my impression on how they came to those positions? See, I've had plenty of time to think about exactly that."

"Okay, sure," she glanced at Jeff. "I'm always up for *impressions*."

Was that a smirk? Maybe I should clam up and let her go with her own assumptions. But since the last thing I wanted Jeff to think was that I was selfish and immature, I stifled the urge to rebel.

"I saw blood on the corner of the fireplace hearth, here." I circled the spot. "I think he hit those bricks when he went down after getting smashed from behind with the vase. He was probably facedown and Megan simply rolled him over onto her lap."

"Thank you for your astute observations, Ms.

Rose." She took the paper and slipped it to the back of the pad behind the unfinished pages.

"So there was more than one wound?" Jeff asked, looking at Fielder, not me.

I answered anyway. "He had a nasty mess at the back of his head. I saw a paramedic take a big shard out of his hair when they were moving him onto the backboard to do CPR."

"You really saw quite a bit." She nodded her approval. "Jeff said you'd be a tremendous witness."

Smug bitch. If I ever needed an artificial heart I'd be sure and call her up. "Thanks so much," I replied, pasting on my best fake smile.

"And who else entered the room aside from the professionals?" she asked.

"My sister . . . Travis . . . and Graham Beadford came in with the paramedics. Holt McNabb—he was the best man—"

"I know who he is."

And please make sure I know you know. "Anyway, he was around," I said. "The cousins—you've met them, right? Courtney and Roxanne? They wanted in to see their uncle, but their father kept them out."

"And Mrs. Beadford never entered?"

"No. She'd passed out," I said impatiently. "But I'm sure you know that, too."

Jeff squeezed my shoulder in a reassuring gesture before placing his elbows on his knees and leaning toward Fielder. I might have liked this tiny bit of support an hour ago, but not now. It was obvious he was uncomfortable showing affection toward me in front of her.

"What else about the room?" Fielder asked. "Anything strike you as out of the ordinary?"

I closed my eyes, picturing the scene. "Glass on the floor. Big chunks. And tiny pieces crunching underfoot. Wood floor with several Oriental rugs. Plenty of gifts on display—china, silver, candleholders, picture frames—and lots of unopened gifts, too."

"Anything else?"

I held up a palm in her direction, my eyes still closed. "Two tapestry wing chairs with a table between them over by the bookshelves on the right side of the room. And glasses on the little table. Three, maybe four?" I opened my eyes and gave Fielder a questioning look, wondering if this jibed with what she knew.

She just said, "Is that all?"

"A beer bottle, maybe? Or two? One on the gift table and—"

"You sure?"

Was I? "Maybe not. A lot went down in a few short minutes."

"Now about this wedding book," she said. "That could prove helpful since we believe some guests left the reception prior to the discovery of the body. Where did you put it?"

"Mrs. Beadford took it from me when I came in."

Fielder pursed her glossed lips. "We haven't found it."

Did she think I stashed the stupid thing somewhere to make her life more difficult? My neck muscles knotted up again. "So ask her where she put it," I said, hoping I sounded civil.

"Can't ask her. She's under sedation at the hospital." Fielder sighed. "Okay, describe this book. Exactly what are we looking for?"

As I told her, I couldn't help but think about the woman in the brown hat. "There was at least one guest at the church who didn't sign it. And who knows how many people only attended the reception and had to sign it at the house. If Mrs. Beadford didn't get their names, there's no way of knowing who all came and went."

"We have hundreds of pictures, Ms. Rose, and more to come, so we'll eventually know who was here. If I showed you some photos, would you remember who signed the book and who didn't?"

Jeff, who had been chewing his gum and making sure he kept his hands off me, spoke. "Seems like the long way around, Quinn. Are there any obvious suspects you could zero in on and—"

"You know I can't discuss how to handle the case in front of *her*." She said *her* like I was a piece of roadkill stuck to her shoe.

Okay, that does it. I rose. "Maybe I'll just leave you two alone."

Jeff touched my elbow. "Abby, I'm sure Quinn didn't mean—"

"Actually, Jeff," Fielder said sweetly, "I think Ms. Rose has had enough questions for one day. But I could use your advice. Would you excuse us?" She arched those perfectly penciled eyebrows at me. She had eyes the color of cane syrup, but there was nothing sugary residing there.

"Certainly." I left the room feeling both their stares on my back. If I'd had my own car, I would have driven home with the radio blaring so I wouldn't have to think about all this. But I had to wait for a ride.

I paced in the marbled foyer, trying to deal with the green-eyed monster in a rational fashion. Fielder had a job to do. She needed all the information she could get and I had seen quite a bit. But though she had asked me plenty of questions about the crime scene, she'd asked me nothing about what I had seen or heard at the reception *before* Beadford's death. I smiled. Serious oversight, baby.

Of course, the exchange I'd witnessed between Travis and his father-in-law may not have been an argument over anything more important than what time the bride and groom would leave the reception. I had no way of knowing what transpired between those two.

I walked in circles, my dress pumps torturing my feet and my head throbbing from the day's stress. I was trying not to think about Jeff and his extended consultation with Fielder—it's damn hard not to think about something—when Megan came down the right-hand staircase.

She had changed from the stained dress into blue jeans and a coral sweater. When she saw me, she ran over and embraced me. "I'm being punished," she said into my shoulder. "That's why this happened."

I moved back, held her at arm's length. Fresh from the shower, I assumed, what with the wet hair and scrubbed face, she looked like the child I'd thought she was when we first met.

"What do you mean?" I asked.

"I went behind my father's back and hired you. And now I'm being punished. I never meant to hurt him."

"Hold on. Did you tell him the truth today? Did you two argue about that?" I didn't want to believe Megan could have struck her father, but she *was* the one sitting there with his battered head in her lap.

"No. But I wasn't truthful, either. And that's as good as a lie."

"Still, you and your father were fine today, right? No problems?"

"The last time I saw him alive was when we d-danced. And . . . and he said he wanted me to be happy and . . . and . . ." Her eyes filled.

I hugged her again, rubbed circles on her back all the while thinking about my own adoptive daddy. He, too, had claimed to want only my happiness. But he'd made more than one mistake in that department, and mistakes born of love still hurt just the same. "I'm here for you, Megan. Call me for anything. Anytime. And I again apologize for not finishing the job."

This time she drew back on her own. "You sound like you're quitting. You're not quitting, are you?"

"I didn't plan on it, but if you want to take this up later, I'll give you every cent of your retainer back."

"Please don't quit, because even though I feel guilty about keeping the truth from my dad, I still want to know my birth mother. Now more than ever."

I was wondering if that need to know had anything to do with what had appeared to be her rather distant relationship with Sylvia, but didn't think this was the right time to ask. Then Jeff emerged from his little conference, and while he was offering his condolences to Megan, I went after my coat, which I found in the kitchen where I'd left it. My pockets were turned out, either from the cops checking them out or Kate searching for my keys. My small handbag had been tucked in one sleeve but the clasp was open and my phone/computer nearly slipped out when I grabbed the purse. The low battery warning was beeping so I powered the phone off, then put on the coat.

After I gave Megan another reassuring hug and a whispered promise to follow through on her request, Jeff and I walked out into the bitter cold evening. Normally I would have huddled up to him, but not now. After all, Fielder might be watching us out the window and I wouldn't want to upset her.

On our way to his truck, he exchanged high-fives with two other cops manning the scene and then introduced me. One guy had worked HPD vice with Jeff way back when and the other was a former Harris County Sheriff's Deputy who had testified at a vehicular homicide case Jeff worked a few years ago. Seems Quinn Fielder wasn't the only city cop who wanted to escape to the bay.

We walked down the hill and I stepped up into his nonpolice-issue white Chevy truck after he opened the door for me. He then got in and revved the engine. Before we pulled away, he shoved several sticks of Big Red in his mouth. Neither of us said a word until we passed Space Center Houston and were closing in on the freeway.

"What did she tell you?" I asked.

"What did *who* tell me about *what*?"

Typical man. If the conversation doesn't flow continuously you better have that CNN ticker tape running across your forehead for frequent updates. "What did your friend Quinn need you for so badly? Can't she do her job alone?"

"I can't tell you what we discussed."

"This isn't your case, so why keep secrets?" My voice was hard. The green-eyed monster didn't want to be contained.

"Any information I have concerning an ongoing investigation is off-limits. This is no exception."

"Fine. Be that way." I folded my arms.

He took out another stick of gum while I turned my face to the window. This might be an extra-long ride home.

3

Lying in bed the next morning, I thought about what happened between Jeff and me last night—our first fight since he and I started getting serious a few months ago. Problem was, he didn't seem to realize we were having an argument. When we reached my house and I suggested he go on to his own place, he looked at me as if we'd been playing a friendly game of poker and I'd pulled a fifth ace. Then his beeper went off and a double homicide on the southeast side took him away with hardly a good-bye.

So I spent the night with my calico cat, Diva, in the chilly house. She had climbed beneath the quilt at some point and now purred at my feet. I'd recently bought this place, a three bedroom brick-and-stone bungalow near Rice University. It was built in the fifties and needed a new furnace among other things. The steps creaked and the wallpaper looked like something from Archie Bunker's house, but I loved my new home, loved its smallness compared to the mansion I'd grown up in. Aside from a college dorm room, this was the first time I'd truly been on my own, despite more than thirty years on earth. My late daddy had decided that living in the lap of luxury with him was how he was supposed to take care of his girls. But Daddy had been wrong. He'd been wrong about a lot of things. In the months since I'd learned exactly how wrong, I'd almost forgiven him for his lies.

I laced my fingers behind my neck and thought about Megan, wondered how she was doing and if the loss of her father would mimic mine—a wound that never quite heals. I'd seen a profound sadness in her eyes when I left her house yesterday. It was probably the same look I wore the day Daddy died.

The phone rang and I saw from the Caller ID that it was Kate.

"Traitor," I said when I picked up.

"I'm sorry I had to leave you there, Abby, but one of my teenage patients attempted suicide, so—"

"Okay. The guilt ball is back in my court. I was just kidding, anyway. Is the kid okay?"

"She's fine. Her parents are transferring her to a private facility this morning. By the way, Terry and I dropped off your car late last night."

"Thanks. Might need that today. So Terry helped you with your patient?" Terry Armstrong, also a psychologist, is Kate's significant other.

"Yes. He met me at the emergency room."

"You two should go into practice together," I said.

"Living in the same house is more than enough time spent in each other's company. Not that I don't adore him, but there's such a thing as too much togetherness. So what happened after I left last evening?"

I filled her in, excluding my own issues with one snarly police chief.

"So Megan still wants you to find the birth mother?" she asked, sounding surprised.

"Yes, but I'm consulting with Angel as soon as I can. Should have asked for his help when I came up empty in the first place. I guess pride isn't so hard to swallow if you chew on it long enough."

Diva emerged and blinked her amber eyes several times. I rubbed under her chin with my free hand.

"Sure you still want to do this job? Megan's a sweetheart, but the rest of the family? I don't know, Abby. Graham smelled like a bar at closing time, Holt kept looking at me like maybe we could get together after they got that inconvenient body out of the way, and the sisters? I think they have serious identity issues."

"Not all that pretty, huh?"

"Not."

"Can you tell me about Sylvia?" I asked. "I was holed up in the laundry room with a guy meaner than a rodeo bull and about as talkative. I didn't see what happened to her."

"She woke up pretty quick after fainting, but then started crying and carrying on—which is understandable. I heard from one of the paramedics that she got so hysterical they had to give her IV Valium in the ambulance."

"And she seemed like such a take-charge person. Guess not."

"You can never predict human behavior, Abby. Especially during times of stress."

"Okay, Doc. I bow to your superior knowledge."

She laughed. "And so you should. Seriously, it may simply have been seeing all that blood that got to her. I'm not too good with blood myself. Anyway, I called only to explain why I ran out on you yesterday. Terry's up and hungry, so before he starts talking about kolaches or doughnuts, I better get some fruit and bran into him. Call me later."

She hung up. Poor Terry. A man who loved to eat as much as he did had no business getting mixed up with my sister. She juiced everything imaginable, even ears of corn, and bought seeds and nuts and vegetables no ordinary person had ever heard of. But Terry surely had psychoanalyzed himself enough to understand his unconscious motivation to subject himself to torture.

Phone still in hand, I checked the clock. Eight A.M. Angel would be awake. I had his home number on speed dial and he answered on the second ring.

"You get up this early, huh?" he said once we exchanged greetings.

"Not usually. But that last case you gave me has proved tougher than I thought. And now there's been complications. Any chance we could get together at your office and discuss it?"

"I have a few rules about the office. I never go there on the Lord's day. You work as long as I have, you can make some rules."

"Tomorrow, then?" I asked, unable to hide my disappointment. If he helped me out today, gave me some hints on how to start this thing over, I could get busy Monday morning.

"Hey, I didn't say I don't work on Sunday, I just avoid my damn office answering machine. Meet me at the pancake house—you know which one. Say, eleven o'clock after Mass?"

"Okay." I hung up, smiled, and settled back under the covers, Diva purring on my chest. I could sleep for two more hours.

But not five minutes later I heard the doorbell. Who in hell was ringing my doorbell at this hour on a Sunday morning? Unless Jeff forgot his key. Or maybe this visitor was from the Seacliff police and they wanted to discuss something about the murder.

Gosh, I hope it's not Fielder, I thought, catching a glimpse in the dresser mirror on my way out of the bedroom. With the light-socket hair and dark circles under my eyes, I could have scared a maggot off spoiled meat.

I put on my pink chenille robe and hurried down the stairs, but after looking through the peephole, I stepped back. Damn. I thought I'd permanently parted ways with my aunt Caroline, yet there she was on my doorstep.

She tried knocking and I crossed my arms, considering whether to answer. I hadn't returned any of her phone calls and was hoping that once I'd moved from the old neighborhood, she couldn't find me. But Kate still had contact with her, and she's a whole lot more forgiving than I am. Aunt Caroline probably had an easy time wheedling my new address out of her.

Daddy's sister, Caroline, and I never got along even before I learned she'd taken money from Daddy to keep silent about my illegal adoption. I mean, her nose is so up in the air she'd drown in a storm. But after I found out about how she'd lied for years, lied out of pure greed, I couldn't stomach the sight of her.

But now she'd found me, and knowing her, she wouldn't give up until she had her say.

Might as well get this over with.

I unlocked the dead bolt and opened the door.

If this had been a year ago, she would have marched right in, but she didn't. She just stood there. "Thank you for answering, Abigail. I know you don't want to see me, but I have missed you. Missed you very much."

Was this early-morning pilgrimage to seek my forgiveness her substitute for church this morning? I gestured with my head for her to follow, and we walked toward the kitchen, Diva leading the way.

Going through the house was like navigating an obstacle course on a reality television show, and Diva had her usual fun, leaping alongside us from one packing crate to another. Though I had moved in more than a month ago, boxes sat untouched everywhere. We reached the kitchen, where my small stack of cookbooks sat on one chair and clean but unfolded laundry took up the other. I moved the books.

After taking off her cashmere coat with the fur collar, she placed it on the back of the chair. Aunt Caroline then sat and set her Gucci bag by her feet. She wore a fuzzy peacock sweater with some kind of gaudy beaded strands decorating the neckline.

Still saying nothing, and hoping the silence would make her squirm a little, I fed the cat and started the coffee. Only then did I toss the clothes off the other chair into an already overflowing basket near the door to the laundry room. Most of them ended up on the tile and I checked Aunt Caroline's reaction, considering this a test. She flinched a little, but offered no criticism.

Was this newfound restraint an act?

"I had a hard time locating you, Abigail," she said, fingering one strand of beads.

"Kate tell you where to find me?" I asked.

"No. Your policeman friend led me here. I hear you're involved with him."

"Is that right?" Instant anger burned in my gut. I could cope with jealousy—after all that was my responsibility—but if Jeff had been talking to Aunt Caroline behind my back, then—

"And he didn't tell me anything, if that's what you think. I had *him* followed since following Kate seemed . . . invasive."

I blinked. "And following Jeff *isn't* invasive?"

She smiled one of her face-lift afflicted smiles. "He'll understand. He's probably used to it."

"Right, except *he* does the following," I said.

"Same difference. Anyway, I did learn a few things after what happened last summer," she said. "I may have been less than honest with you in the past and—"

"Less than honest? I swear you'd lie even if the truth sounded better." Was I being harsh? You betcha. After a few decades of deception I figured I owed her about as much respect as a coyote owes a jackrabbit.

"Can I finish?" she said.

"Go on."

"I'm willing to work on those . . . less than desirable aspects of my personality." She said the last few words so fast I nearly didn't catch them.

"And so you have Jeff followed to accomplish that goal?"

"Yes," she said quietly. "The detective I hired said there's nothing wrong with following people. Can you forgive me for my past mistakes?"

"I don't know." I chewed on a cuticle, already feel-

ing myself weakening. Heck, she was pushing seventy.
And grudges made you run even if no one was chasing
you. I didn't want to run.

"Please consider the possibility," she said, her
eyes moist.

I stood abruptly, a tiny, unwelcome lump in my
throat. "Coffee?"

Her features relaxed as much as the Botox would
allow. "I'd love coffee."

We sipped and made small talk about her latest
charity event. Then Aunt Caroline said, "I'm aware
you left CompuCan. They miss you."

Kate had told me my aunt still sat on the board of
Daddy's old company. "Right," I said. "They miss me
bumbling around like I knew what I was doing. I have
a new job."

"Doing what?"

"I find people," I replied, avoiding eye contact. I
had a working person's job now, not a token appointment from an inherited business. I was guessing she
wouldn't approve and for some stupid reason, her approval still seemed important. Old habits die hard.

But she surprised me by actually sounding interested. "So tell me more. Is this a computer job? Because despite your protestations, you're very good
with computers."

"The job does involve plenty of Internet searches,
but actually . . . I'm a private investigator specializing
in adoption."

She slowly nodded. "I see. And have you had
much work?"

"A few cases so far, but I have to build my reputa-
tion and—"

"I could help. Give me some business cards and tell
me where your office is. I have plenty of friends who
would be more than—"

"That's not necessary, Aunt Caroline. In Texas, you
have to—how do I put it?—apprentice with a licensed investigator."

"So you're an intern? You're not even getting paid?" Ah, the old Aunt Caroline hadn't completely disappeared after all.

"I *do* get paid," I snapped.

She held up both hands. "Sorry. I'm being judgmental and I vowed not to do that. Do you work downtown?"

"Angel's allowed me to work out of my home with my own little branch of his agency. It's called Yellow Rose Investigations, though technically I'm employed by him. He's sent me a few clients and I'm advertising on my own as well."

She looked around. "You work *here*?"

"I have an office in the front of the house in what was supposed to be the formal living room. I'm done with formal anything, Aunt Caroline. This is what I want." I spread my arms and nodded around the room, hoping she understood this was a warning. I didn't want any of her snooty society friends sending me business.

"This place is, well, very *like* you," she said, nodding again. "But if you plan to redecorate, remember the traditional look never goes out of style."

"I'll remember." This visit was dragging on way too long.

"And if you're at peace with this new lifestyle, that's wonderful."

At peace? I wondered if I'd ever be at peace with her, but running away wouldn't solve that problem. I'd accept her back into my life if only to quit running from the past. But that didn't mean I'd ever forget how she'd betrayed Kate and me.

Angel Molina mopped a hefty bite of blueberry pancakes through the puddle of syrup on his plate. I'd finished my omelet and was nursing a mug of coffee while he worked on his second stack. Angel's a strapping, soft-spoken man with steel-colored hair pulled straight back into a ponytail. He usually wore white

shirts that looked fresh from the dry cleaner and today
was no exception. A longtime Texas Ranger who went
private, he took me under his wing after Jeff arranged
for us to discuss my future as a PI.

"Now, fill me in on this case," Angel said after swal-
lowing a mouthful of pancakes. "The client's that
sweet little girl I sent to you, right?"

"Yes. Megan Beadford." I explained what had happened yesterday, then said, "I thought she'd forget
the whole mother hunt after her adoptive father was
murdered, but she wants me to keep looking. Trouble
is, I've got next to nothing to go on."

Angel dabbed at the corner of his mouth with a
paper napkin and checked the pristine shirt for traces
of breakfast. Satisfied he hadn't spilled anything, he
said, "You brought the file?"

I handed a thin folder across the table. We were
sitting in a back booth of Angel's favorite twenty-four-
hour restaurant. Sunday's after-church crowd, replete
with screeching, whining children, filled every table.
Another throng of adults and toddlers swelled out the
door waiting for their turn at breakfast mania.

Angel thumbed through the meager pages of Me-
gan's file and stopped at one sheet. "No match at the
Central Adoption Registry. Too bad." He looked up.
"But I see no court filing to open the adoption file.
That's the next logical step."

"Megan nixed that suggestion. She believed a court
case would be hard to hide from her family."

He shook his head, tight lipped. "Secrets. Everybody with their damn secrets. Keeps us working,
though, huh?"

I smiled. "Sure does. That's why I couldn't contact
the lawyer who handled the adoption. I have a name—
Caleb Moore—but since he was hired by James Beadford he would have been obligated to notify Megan's
father before talking to me."

"That's true. So now you've learned something
about the PI business if nothing else. It's about pulling

rabbits out of sombreros." He continued thumbing through the file. "What's this?" He held up Kate's psychological profile of Megan and the summary of their counseling session.

I told him about partnering up with Kate and my reasons for doing so.

"Smart girl. But that doesn't help you find people, especially those who don't want to be found. And I see that in this case you've got the birth certificate and little else. Pretty challenging."

Our waitress passed by, slipping a new carafe of coffee onto the table and nodding when Angel pointed at his empty plate to indicate he wanted another stack.

I poured more coffee. Bad coffee. Weak and ineffective, like I felt.

Meanwhile, Angel took a lipstick mirror from his shirt pocket and removed a molecule of blueberry from between his front teeth.

A lipstick mirror? Who said *Vanity, thy name is woman*? "Did you just have those teeth bleached?" I asked.

He grinned. "Friday. Do I look good?"

"You smile like that again and I might need to put on my sunglasses."

He held the mirror eye level and bared his teeth. "So it's a bad job? Too fake?"

I laughed. "You're good-looking enough to make a glass eye blink."

"Wiseass." He tucked the mirror back in his pocket and returned to the folder, this time pulling out my copy of the birth certificate. He studied it for several seconds. "At least you got the hospital name, but where is Kingston Bay?"

"Right across from NASA, a town with only about a dozen streets. There's a good-sized medical facility, though. St. Mary's. It serves the astronauts and the Clear Lake area."

"You went there, I assume?"

"Sure. But the administrator I spoke with said their birth records only go back twenty years."

Angel huffed a sarcastic laugh. "Really? Hospitals do not destroy birth or death records, my friend, so I suggest you return and find someone else to talk to."

"But why would that man . . ." I didn't finish the question because I knew the answer. Why does anyone lie? Because it creates less problems for them than the truth.

Angel nodded sadly, reading my expression. "You see? Everybody lies. But as I tell my son, the truth is worth hunting down. Each nugget you find is like a treasure from God. Our job is to collect those tiny pieces and pass them on to the client. Sometimes those little nuggets turn out to be priceless jewels."

I smiled. "You have a way with words, señor."

"One more thing. The birth certificate is a lousy copy. Have you had a good look at the client's state-issued document?"

Texas does not issue original birth certificates but rather certified copies with the state seal. The last time I saw it was when I scanned Megan's copy for my files. "No. I thought since all I needed was the hospital and city of birth, then—"

"Get another look at hers." He stared at me with an intensity that made his velvet brown irises seem almost black. "A *good* look."

"Okay. But did I miss something?"

"We all miss things." He tapped a manicured finger to his temple. "To see the answers you need a clear mind, but a clean copy doesn't hurt."

I laughed. "So I *did* miss something."

"I do not know, Abby. I can tell you only what I would do if I were you."

"Then that's good enough for me."

4

I arrived back home around one P.M. and had a message from Quinn Fielder. Sounding polite but authoritative on my machine, she informed me my assistance was needed with some photos taken at the reception. She gave the address of the Seacliff Police Station and told me she expected me by four P.M. at the latest.

Great. Thanks. I poked the delete button. Felt good to delete her. But of course I had to comply. This was about helping Megan, not about my own ego.

I went to my office to put away Megan's file and found Diva asleep on my desk. She knew the most pleasant spot in this house of chaos, maybe even sensed my new office was where I felt most at home.

The room had been shipshape since the day after I moved in. My work space. All mine. I had moved in Daddy's computer desk and it took up most of the room, that and his worn red leather wing chair, which I now reserved for clients. I'd mounted his gun case and added my own two handguns to his collection. Since I hadn't been to the shooting range in over a year, that's where they belonged. Daddy always said you shouldn't carry a weapon if you're not trained or you're out of practice, and he was right.

I sat on my standard issue but comfortable office swivel chair and lifted Diva into my lap. She tolerated me for twenty seconds before jumping away and hopping onto the windowsill. She inserted herself between the vertical blinds and did some window-shopping for the many birds and squirrels that populated the neighborhood.

After turning on the computer and checking my e-mail, I did a search for Caleb Moore, the attorney used for Megan's adoption. I wanted to be prepared to act should she change her mind about contacting him. Most firms had a Web site these days, but since Megan was twenty years old, this guy could be retired or dead. Sure enough, when I got a hit on Moore it was for the man's death notice in the *Galveston Daily News* archives two years ago. More searching found him to be the attorney of record in the bankruptcy of a local manufacturing plant, but that was all. Literally a dead end.

I sat back, wondering what I should do next. My Internet options were limited. Maybe after I worked at this job for a while, I'd have more courage to deal with the underground searchers, those less-than-legal resources who can gain access to private information in exchange for considerable money. Hacking into closed adoption files was not a good idea for someone working toward a PI license. There had to be a less risky way to get what I needed.

I glanced at the computer clock and decided to let the detecting go for now and head for my meeting with Fielder. But when I reached the kitchen and pulled my car keys from my purse ready to head out the back door, I glanced down at what I was wearing. Jeans and a Houston Rockets sweatshirt. New, expensive jeans since I trimmed down to a size six, but still jeans.

I had to change. And comb my hair. And—wait a minute. What the hell was wrong with me?

I left dressed as I was, before the green-eyed monster had me hunting through boxes for one of my old low-cut, sequined prom dresses.

The sand-colored brick Seacliff Police Station sat on a side street off Highway 146 several blocks from the bay. Sago palms flanked the double glass doors and inside a pockmarked young man wearing the tan uniform I had become so familiar with yesterday after Mr. Beadford's murder sat at a dented metal desk to my right. The speckled vinyl tile bore grayish mop streaks and untouched grime had collected in every corner. The place smelled musty even though dry hot air blasted from a ceiling vent.

The young man stood. "Can I help you?"

"My name is Abby Rose. Chief Fielder wanted to see me."

"Yeah, she said to—" His desk phone rang and he picked up, listened for a second, then said, "The chief has no comment. This is an ongoing investigation." He replaced the receiver gingerly, still staring at the phone. "Reporters have been calling all day. Last murder we had was five years ago, and it was nothing like this. Vietnamese fisherman got into it with his partner and stabbed him right through the gut with this old shark spear. Only had two calls from the press on that one. But this here? I can tell you—"

"Thanks, Officer Henderson," came Fielder's voice from a hallway straight ahead. "I'll meet with Ms. Rose in my office."

She gestured from the shadowy corridor for me to follow her, and I left Henderson sitting at his desk doing nothing, probably because that's what he was good at. That and running his mouth.

Dark wood paneling, circa 1970, lined the hallway and the worn dingy carpeting was probably about the same vintage. Fielder disappeared through a doorway to my right and I came in on her heels.

The old world ended and the new millennium began inside her office. The wood floor gleamed, her huge oak desk commanded the room, and an air purifier hummed in one corner. I caught a hint of lemon polish and above me an antique brass and walnut ceiling fan looked as if it was hot off the assembly line.

On the wall to my right hung a massive framed

photograph of a man wearing the Seacliff uniform,
only with a lot more brass than I'd seen on Henderson
at the front desk. The man in the portrait looked to
be in his sixties and an engraved metal placard confirmed this: "Chief Quinton W. Fielder, 1940–2002."

*So policing was a family business, huh? Was that
how she'd landed the top job at such a young age?
Probably.*

"Thank you for coming, Ms. Rose," Fielder said.

"No problem." To my left photos were spread on
a conference table and the map I'd drawn yesterday
was tacked to a bulletin board on the adjacent wall.

Fielder's eyes bore shadows beneath, evidence of a
sleepless night. She wore blue trousers and an aqua-
striped oxford shirt, the buttons strained thanks to her
more than adequate breasts. Badge and gun were
attached to her belt. Maybe she was going straight from
here to compete for a spot in a "Girls with Nightsticks"
Playboy layout. Good thing I was wearing a sweatshirt.
Sweatshirts hide even what you don't have.

She had walked over to the table. "I hope you can
help me with something."

"Sure." I joined her, deciding that being polite and
cooperative were the order of the day for Megan's sake.

She held up a picture, one taken on the front steps
of the Beadford house. It showed the bride and groom
entering, the crush of guests in their wake and the
professional photographer snapping away.

"This was taken about the time Kate and I arrived,"
I said.

"Good. Now, here's the same photo." She slid an
identical 5 by 7 across the table, but this one had
grease pencil cross outs on all the people in the picture
but one, the woman in the beige pantsuit and brown
hat. She was standing alongside the photographer and
looking down into the viewfinder of a digital camera
pointed at Megan and Travis.

Fielder tapped the unmarked face. "Did she sign
the book?"

"No. She came late to the church. Mrs. Beadford might have gotten her signature, though. Have you found the book?"

Fielder reached into a file box under the table and produced the album. "Mrs. Beadford tucked it away in an upstairs bedroom for safekeeping. But after interviewing her—"

"Is she okay?"

"She's doing better. Came home from the hospital last night. But she claims everyone at the reception signed or made congratulatory notes except for her." Fielder nodded toward the picture. "Neither Mrs. Beadford nor anyone else in the family knows who she is. And if she came inside after taking her photos, no one remembers seeing her. How about you?"

I mentally scanned the room where the strings played, then searched my memory bank for images of the great room. Nothing. But I was certain that if I had seen her, I would have remembered her because of my failure to get her to sign the book. "We never crossed paths in the house, but I spent most of the time in the kitchen with Kate and the caterers. She could have come and gone by the time I had a chance to mingle with the guests."

"Maybe," said Fielder.

"James Beadford could have invited her," I said. "Or she could have been someone's escort." But another possibility popped into my head. Had the questions I'd asked a few weeks ago at the hospital where Megan was born or even Megan's request to the adoption registry flushed a bird from cover? A *mother* bird who couldn't resist a wedding?

"I've considered those obvious possibilities," Fielder said. "You didn't see anyone with this woman at the church, did you?"

"No. She was alone." Shoving aside my excitement at the possibility the mystery woman could be Megan's mother, I said, "Maybe she was a reporter for the local paper? The Beadfords seem well-off and the newspaper might have wanted to cover the event for the society page."

Fielder's eyes narrowed and I surmised from the twitch in her jaw muscle that she didn't appreciate I may have come up with something she hadn't considered.

"I know this town, Ms. Rose," she finally said, her tone as frosty as the air outside. "Number one, I doubt she works for the paper. Number two, unlike where you come from, we don't have a society page."

Unlike where I come from? Was she referring to Houston in general or had Jeff told her about my former life as a do-nothing heiress while I had been imprisoned in the laundry room yesterday?

"I need more information from you, Ms. Rose," Fielder went on, her demeanor controlled, her voice devoid of emotion now. She walked over to her desk and sat, gesturing at the armchairs across from her.

I took a seat.

"I'd like to hear more about the rehearsal dinner," she said.

"I told you what I know."

Fielder leaned toward me, fingers intertwined on top of the desk. "Are you sure?"

"As I said before, I noticed lots of bickering, but I got the feeling the family was pretty much acting as they always do, or at least that's what Megan indicated."

"I want facts, not guesses," she said.

I pictured a scarlet A for "Attitude" embroidered on her shirt. Trying not react to my emotions, I said, "I already told you about the tension concerning the TV that Holt brought with him. And I noticed Travis and his new father-in-law engaged in a lively discussion at the reception."

"They argued?" She pulled a legal pad toward her. Patches of new color spread beyond her blush.

"That would require an assumption," I said.

She looked down at her pad, jotted a few notes.

"Anything else you saw or heard that might be important?"

"No," I replied.

"You're free to go," she said abruptly.

"Gee, thanks," I said, "but I was always free to go."

Since I was already in Seacliff, I swung by the Bead-ford house to see Megan, hoping I could also pick up the birth certificate as Angel had suggested. I parked the Camry on the Beadford's cul-de-sac and slid from behind the wheel, deciding I would keep my specula-tion about the mystery woman to myself. Megan had enough on her plate right now.

The setting sun tinged the horizon beyond their house a deep orange, seagulls squawked above me, and the smell of dead fish hung in the air. The crime scene tape had been removed, but one forgotten strip on a front hedge blew in the breeze like an enemy flag. I grabbed the remnant and stuffed it in my jeans' pocket before I knocked on the door.

Courtney Beadford answered. Unlike the day of the wedding, both earlobes were cluttered with rhine-stones and metal studs. She also had an amber stone embedded in one side of her nose, and a small gold ring pierced an eyebrow. Her blunt-cut hair of mid-night black looked uncombed, and her pasty face was powdered unevenly with makeup too dark for her skin. Bloodred lipstick completed the attempt at mod-ern art.

"Oh. It's you," she said tonelessly. "She's in the kitchen."

Leaving the door open, she turned, shuffled through the foyer, and started up the left staircase. She was wearing an orange middrift T-shirt and low-rise jeans that had slipped down past her protruding pelvic bones. *Anorexic?* I wondered. *Or just too busy abusing substances to eat?*

I made my way to the kitchen and found Megan and Travis hovered over Sylvia, who sat at the table with documents, several sets of gold cuff links, and a row of men's ties before her. A woman in a peach jumpsuit with *Enchanted Occasion Caterers* embroidered in coral on the pocket stood near the sink stacking trays and plates onto a wheeling cart.

Some enchantment here yesterday, I thought.

"Hi," I said quietly. "Decided to drop by since I was in town."

Megan looked up. "Abby. Thanks for coming."

I walked over to Mrs. Beadford, whose eyes were swollen from crying. "How are you today?"

She stood, took my hands, and squeezed. "I'm better. Really. I heard you were wonderful yesterday. You and Graham stepped up and I am so grateful."

"And I am so sorry for your loss," I replied.

She bit her lower lip, looked down. "I still can't believe he's gone."

Megan patted Sylvia's back. "Mother, you need to decide on a tie for Dad while I talk to Abby." Megan then came around the table, pulling Travis along by the hand. "Maybe she can decide if we leave her alone for a few minutes." She started for the hall, her new husband in tow.

"Glad you're feeling better," I said over my shoulder before I followed Megan and Travis out of the kitchen. But Sylvia, fingering a navy blue tie, didn't seem to hear me.

"Sorry, Abby," Megan said, once we were halfway to the foyer. "But I worry the more she sees you, the more likely she is to ask questions about our friendship."

Travis squeezed Megan's shoulder as we walked. "Meg, you know she's bound to find out."

"But not now," Megan said. "I don't know what she'd do if she found out right now."

We passed a stripped-clean dining room and stopped in the foyer. Megan and I looked up at Travis. *Great-looking guy,* I thought. He was clean shaven with deep brown eyes and bed-head hair. But the way he stared at Megan revealed the most about him. I saw a vulnerability in his expression, the kind only love creates.

Travis placed his palm on Megan's cheek. "You worry so much about everyone else. You need to take care of yourself."

"He's right, Megan," I said. "I'm thinking I should put the investigation on hold. It's too much to deal with right now."

"No, it's not," Megan said, all her stubbornness showing in her jutting chin. "I'll keep my mother focused these next few days, and that will help us both. Meanwhile, you do what you can. Do you need more money? I know Mr. Molina gets a percentage, so—"

"Slow down." I took her hand between both of mine. "You're talking fast enough to confuse God."

Travis smiled. "Wait until she really gets going."

She punched his arm playfully. "Shut up, you."

He bent and gave her a quick kiss. "I will when you do."

She grinned, and then it was as if she decided she had no right to be happy even for a second. Her eyes filled and Travis read her distress instantly and brought her to him, pressed her head to his heart.

"I do need one thing if you're certain you want me to continue the job," I said.

Megan pulled away from Travis and produced a crumpled tissue from her jeans pocket. She wiped under her eyes and said, "Sure."

"Can I trouble you for the original copy of your birth certificate?"

Her brow furrowed. "But you scanned it. I saw you."

"Humor me. I need the state-issued one."

She cocked her head. "Okay." She hurried through the foyer and up the right-hand staircase.

When she was gone, Travis said, "Wish she'd do as you suggested and put this mother search on the back burner."

"Have you known all along about Megan's adoption hunt?" I asked.

"Nope. She told me Friday night after I asked her why she picked you to help out. I mean, no one, including me, knew about your friendship."

"I think Megan wanted me to meet the family."

He smiled. "You got that right. She hoped you'd see exactly why she wanted to find her mother. She and her father were pretty close, but it's been hard for her with the others. She rarely sees her cousins, and Sylvia has a big heart but—"

"I did notice a distance between Megan and Sylvia," I said.

"Megan denies it, but I think that's because she always felt guilty for favoring her dad over her mother. Megan was a daddy's girl, and though she and James never shared blood, she's as tough as him underneath that beautiful skin."

I nodded. "She needs that strength now. A murder investigation is not like on television, over in an hour. It will take its toll."

We turned at the sound of a door closing off the balcony and seconds later Megan appeared, rushed down the stairs, and handed me an envelope.

"Here it is," she said. "And I'll call you once we have all this funeral and legal stuff under control." Her eyes still glistened with tears. "I hope you don't think I was rude dragging you out of the kitchen. I am so grateful for—"

I pulled her close and hugged her. "No need for explanations. Call me anytime. I mean that."

"Thanks," she whispered.

Travis put a protective arm around her as I opened the door and left.

I picked up a Subway sandwich on my way home and then ate in front of the television. I spent the rest of the evening in the living room unpacking boxes of knickknacks and pictures while the complete Beatles collection provided musical accompaniment. I used the remote to skip my least favorite song, the one about how all you need is love. There are lies and there are damn lies. That song was a damn lie.

Diva and I had just settled into bed around eleven when I heard Jeff's truck pull into the driveway. I tensed. Things had shifted between us as they inevitably do in relationships, my jealousy having created the tipping point. My fault. How I hated when things were my fault.

So make this right, idiot. Apologize for being such a twit on the way home yesterday.

I lifted the quilt and sat, slipped my feet into my slippers, then couldn't seem to move. I leaned forward, palms over my face, my heart beating double time. I took a few deep breaths to get control of my emotions. *How dumb is this, Abby? You're thirty years old. . . . You've been married before, and yet you're acting like—*

"Hi," Jeff said from the bedroom doorway.

I raised my head, met his gaze. He had loosened his burgundy tie and held his tweed sports jacket over his shoulder.

"Hi," I said quietly.

"Can we talk?" he said.

Now those are words guaranteed to make any woman go liquid, especially coming from a guy who could make me melt just by licking his lips. I kicked off the slippers, sat crossed-legged on the bed, and patted the space next to me. "Do you even know what we need to talk about?"

"No, but I sure as hell hope to find out." He tossed the jacket on the chair in the corner, carefully removed his gun and badge and placed them on the tall dresser. After plumping a pillow against the headboard, he sat down beside me. "What's got you so upset?"

"You and your damn girlfriend," I said.

"My girlfriend? I think that's you, last time I checked."

"You've slept with her, haven't you?"

We both looked straight ahead and a long silence followed.

"That obvious, huh?" he finally said.

"I can read you with one eye tied behind my back," I said.

"You're scary."

"No. I'm a good detective."

"So you are. Anyway, it was a long time ago. Ten years. Big mistake. Back then all that mattered to me was what a girl looked like. I'd just started in Homicide and though lots of guys turn to booze after they've worked a year of scenes, I turned to women. I met Quinn through her dad—he was chief of police in Seacliff and—"

"I know that, too."

"That I'd worked with her dad?"

"No. Knew he was police chief. Go on."

"Did you research Quinn on the Internet or something?" he asked.

"I'll tell you how I found out about him later. Right now, we have more important stuff to discuss."

"Okay." He took a deep breath and reached for the gum in his shirt pocket. He had two sticks of Big Red working before he went on. "I met her when I gave some expert help on a manslaughter case in Seacliff. Quinn's father told me his daughter wanted to get into the academy, asked me if I could pull some strings."

"And then pretty soon you were pulling her strings," I said.

"Yeah," he said. "That's about right."

"I can understand your interest. She's . . . very attractive."

"On the outside. And like I said, back then that's all that mattered. Anyway, I broke it off after a couple months. She was too intense for me, not to mention too young."

"You broke it off? How did that go over?"

"Not so good." He chewed his gum faster. "Let's say she didn't let go easily."

"You two seemed to have forgotten about all that from what I saw yesterday."

"It's old business, Abby," he said. "She has a job to do and isn't afraid to ask for help, which means she's matured."

"I'm not afraid to ask for help, either. But when I asked what you discussed with her, you wouldn't tell me."

He moved in front of me, mirrored my cross-legged position, now chewing far more languidly. "So this isn't just about Abby being jealous. This is about Abby's insatiable need to know everything and maybe dip her toes in some dangerous water."

His blue-ice detective stare worked like it probably does on every suspect he interrogates, and I made myself stare right back even though I wished I had a trap door in the mattress to escape through.

"Is that a crime?" I asked.

Putting his index finger on my chin, he applied pressure and my head lowered. "Get your nose out of the air. Curiosity is not a crime for you—more like a lifestyle—and I obviously acted like an ass yesterday. But this business with Quinn? Well, you know I'm not so hot at mixing personal stuff with police business."

I smiled. "You are definitely not so hot in that department. But you are so good in other departments, it makes up for it. So let's get personal."

He smiled and ditched the gum.

5

The next morning, I traveled south again, switching the car radio station back and forth between NPR and a local talk show for entertainment. Some days I am easily amused. Forty-five minutes later, I pulled into the parking lot at St. Mary's Hospital and stepped out into more typical south Texas weather than the previous frigid days: temperature in the low sixties, gray skies, and enough humidity to make even big hair wilt.

After entering the St. Mary's lobby with my leather attaché in hand, I stopped at the information desk situated in front of a floor-to-ceiling aquarium and was given directions to the baby ward. I rode the elevator alone and soon found myself staring through picture windows at five clear bassinets holding infants wrapped up like sausages in their white receiving blankets. I was looking at three boys and two girls from their color-coded knit caps.

A woman in fuchsia surgical scrubs, maybe mid-fifties, spotted me and smiled broadly. She came around through a door to my left and said, "Which sweetheart do you belong to? I'll bring the baby closer to the window for you."

"Though I would love to belong to one of these sweethearts, I came about a baby who was born here many years ago. Can I ask you a few questions?" I took out a business card, the one identifying Yellow Rose Investigations as specializing in adoptions.

I handed it to her, and while she read, I noted the picture ID hanging from a lanyard identifying her as C. Worthington, R.N.

"If this is about an adoption, I can't talk about it," she said kindly, handing the card back. "All patient records are confidential."

I opened my attaché and produced the notarized release of information letter Megan had addressed to the hospital, the one I used the last time I came here and spoke to the administrator.

She looked, but didn't touch. "Did you go through administration, Ms. Rose?"

"Yes. Worked with a Mr. Hansen." I didn't add that I had bypassed him today. Before she could question me further, I exchanged the release letter for the birth certificate. "This young woman hired me to help her find her mother. Megan Beadford was here once, just like those cute little kids beyond the window."

The nurse shifted her gaze to the bassinets, her eyes softening. "They are so precious when they sleep. So wonderful." She refocused on me. "But as much as I'd like to help, I don't see how I can, Ms. Rose."

"How long have you worked here?" I asked.

"Ten years, and from the date on the birth certificate, your client made her entrance into the world long before I arrived on the scene."

"Okay, but maybe you know someone who's worked here longer."

She squinted in thought, then said, "No. And if you got no help from Sister Nell, then—"

"Sister Nell?"

"The medical records administrator. But I assume that's where Mr. Hansen directed you first."

A baby started wailing—the boy in the middle crib. The nurse glanced back at him and smiled her loving, unruffled smile.

I said, "You probably need to take care of him, so—"

"Darien's had everything I can offer," she said evenly. "Fed, burped, changed, rocked. He's fine."

I looked uneasily at the wide-mouthed Darien. The kid was into a rhythm and getting louder and more red faced by the second. But since Nurse Worthington wasn't responding to his screams, I went on. "I visited with Mr. Hansen several weeks ago. When he could find nothing during his computer search, he said he would contact medical records and get back to me."

"And did he?" Her crossed arms and amused features told me she knew plenty about Mr. Hansen—stuff I obviously did not.

"I had to call him back."

She nodded knowingly.

I said, "He told me medical records only had baby charts that went back twenty years."

"Really? I suggest you speak directly with Sister Nell. She's been here since they opened St. Mary's doors."

"Sister Nell. Does she have a last name or—"

"Everyone knows Sister Nell. You'll find her."

More noise erupted from the peanut gallery, but the nurse remained unperturbed, despite my sincere belief that Darien, who'd woken the rest of his buddies, was about to burst a blood vessel in his head. I had to get out of here. "Thanks. Is medical records on the first floor?"

She nodded and gave me a little wave, then turned and walked back into the nursery.

Meanwhile I hightailed it to the elevator. If this job would be taking me to more maternity wards in the future, I wasn't sure I could stay in the business.

Back downstairs, the open door to medical records revealed an office with a fatigued-looking receptionist wearing a white shirt as pale as her face. Her desk was piled with file folders. There were doors on either side of her desk and one behind her.

"My name is Abby Rose and I'm looking for Sister Nell." I put the business card on the woman's desk.

She glanced at it just as the phone rang, then waved me in the direction of the door behind her before she picked up the receiver.

I followed a tile path around the desk and stopped in the entry to what I assumed was Sister Nell's office. Though the receptionist's desk had been piled ominously high, every available square foot in this room was stacked with books, binders, and manila file folders. Apparently the front desk was the first port of call and everything eventually ended up here.

A graying kinky-haired woman sat at a desk against the left wall staring at a computer screen, her back to me. The monitor was not elevated, and she had to crane her neck and hunch her shoulders.

"Bet you go to bed with a backache," I said.

She jerked around, hand to her heart. "Mercy, young woman, you scared the bejesus out of me."

She wore a navy blue sweater, white high-collar blouse, and a charcoal-colored skirt. So where was her nun's veil?

"Sorry if I startled you," I said. "But your monitor is too low. That can cause back pain." *Weird image,* I thought. Nuns and computers just didn't seem to go together.

"Oh, you're the technician. Every time I turn around they've got someone new." She rolled her chair away from the desk. "Have at this evil machine. I cannot seem to make it do my bidding."

"What's the problem?" I came around cardboard file boxes filled to overflowing with documents.

"I keep losing the network and I have files to upload, files to download, files to scan, files, nothing but files. And forgive me if I make it sound like a Shakespearean tragedy, but it's the God's truth." She took a deep breath, fingering the crucifix hanging around her neck.

"Hmmm. Could be something simple." I got down on my hands and knees and checked the network cable running beneath her desk to the wall jack, saw the problem, and looked up at her. "I think you have a furry friend, one who likes to gnaw."

"The mouse?" She had joined me on the floor. "I've been trying to catch that little bastard for a week."

Little bastard? I smiled to myself. I might just like Sister Nell. I pointed to tiny teeth marks on the cable. "He'll zap himself if he takes a bigger bite, but my guess is he's learned his lesson. All you need is an undamaged line and you'll be fine."

She steepled her hands and raised her green eyes to the ceiling. "Praise God they sent me someone with some common sense this time."

I stood and offered her a hand up, which she gratefully accepted. She was a lean, fit-looking woman, but I did hear her knees crack when she rose.

"I may have common sense, but I don't work here," I said.

"Really?" Her eyes crinkled with delight. "Perhaps I should buy an extra lottery ticket then, since this seems to be my lucky day. Of course I'd share the ten million with you if I knew your name."

"Abby Rose," I said. "I came to ask you a few questions."

"Hang on a sec, Abby." She picked up her office phone and dialed four numbers. "Roger, I need a new cable for my computer."

She listened, then said, "How would I know—"

"You need an Ethernet cable," I said.

She relayed this information with a satisfied smile and hung up. "You are quite a useful, young woman. Quite competent. What can I do for you?"

I glanced around. "Can we, um . . . sit?"

"Oh, God forgive me, yes. Don't have many visitors aside from doctors and they never sit." She wove her way through the clutter—reminded me of home—and opened a closet door on the far wall. Several thin boxes fell from a shelf and hospital stationery spilled everywhere. A broom toppled as well. "Jesus, Mary, and Joseph," she muttered before returning with a padded folding chair. She left the fallen items where they lay.

Once we were seated with her swivel chair facing me, I handed her my card. "I'm helping a young woman find her birth mother and not having much luck. Maybe you can help."

After glancing at the card, she put it down, pursed her lips, and closed her eyes, wagging a finger. "If it's a medical record you need, let me assure you they are like a nun's dreams—not to be shared with the public."

"I understand, but could I explain? That might give you a better idea on how you might help me."

"Well, you've certainly helped me out, so if I can do a damn thing—make that a *blessed* thing—I will."

I told her about the case, including my conversation with the nurse today. The more I talked, the more tight her features grew.

When I finished, she said, "Let me see your confidentiality release and the birth certificate."

I removed the birth certificate from the envelope and handed it to her along with the release. After returning them, she sat back, lips tight with anger. "I am not without fault, won't ever be nominated for sainthood, but I don't abide liars."

Liars? What the heck was she talking about? "Have I done something wrong?"

"Not you, dear. Him."

"Him?"

"Our administrator. But I suppose when you mix the healing arts with business, you should expect that kind of behavior. Mr. Hansen told you the records went back only twenty years?"

"Yes."

"That's a damn lie and he knows it. He was simply too lazy to follow through on your request."

Whoa. Obviously there was more about Mr. Hansen she'd be willing to share, but I tried to get her back on track. "I returned to pursue this, so it's okay."

"It's *not* okay and he will hear about this. And then

he better get his fat ass to confession." She crossed her arms and leaned back. And then unexpectedly grinned. "Of course, I'll be right alongside him, don't you know?"

I laughed, felt myself relax. "Bet you will."

"Now," she said, "let's get to work on your Megan." She put her hands on the keyboard, then stopped. "Damn. Where's Roger with that cable?"

She picked up the phone and dialed the four numbers again. "Roger? When did you think you'd get that stupid cable over here? Next year?" She put down the receiver without saying good-bye and smiled at me. "I tend to annoy people. That's why I work alone."

"I call it the broken-record technique," I said.

"I like that. And broken records are actually good for something. They get results."

Seconds later the man who I assumed was Roger scurried in carrying the cable. Sister Nell rose and backed away from her desk, bumping into a filing cabinet when she did. She clutched her elbow and winced, but if she swore this time I didn't hear her.

Once Roger made the switch, she returned to her computer and booted up.

"Hand me the certificate again," she said.

After I gave it to her, she checked the date and gave it back.

I was about to return it to my briefcase, but then realized I'd never looked at the copy after Megan gave it to me, not gotten "the good look" Angel suggested.

I stared down at it now and noticed a small difference in the darkness of the type in spots. The hospital name definitely seemed lighter than both Megan's and her adopted parents' names. And I noted a smudge beneath "U.S.A." in the country of birth box. Did this mean anything? Or—

"Here we go," said Sister Nell. "Got the year pulled up."

I was sitting at an angle, unable to see much of her screen, but she appeared to be scrolling down a list.

"Something's wrong," she said. "Read me the date one more time."

After I did, she said, "Hmmm. Let me check the day before and the day after. Perhaps someone made a mistake."

"What kind of mistake?" I scooted my chair closer to look over her shoulder.

"Move away," she snapped. "These are confidential records."

"Sorry." I sat back, feeling like I had in first grade when I was sent to the principal for showing my underwear to a boy in the cafeteria.

Sister Nell absently patted my knee, her gaze still on the monitor. "Sorry to be short with you. Did I mention I annoy people?" She put her face closer to the screen. "Let me try one more run through this list. Perhaps a baby was entered as a medical or surgical patient that day by mistake."

"You mean you can't find her?" I said.

She didn't answer, just stared a few seconds longer, shook her head, and turned off the monitor. "Very puzzling. Of course, I would not have found a child named Megan Beadford, since her adoptive parents no doubt named her, but I did expect to be able to pursue this on my own after I had the names of any girls born that day. Maybe contact a possible birth mother candidate and convince her to contact the Adoption Registry."

"But you can't do that?"

"No," she said, "because despite what it says on that birth certificate, no baby girls were born here on that date, just two boys. No babies were born at all on the day before. And one single boy was born the day after." She raised her eyebrows. "So what does that tell you?"

I looked down at the birth certificate still in my hand and blinked several times. "It tells me that either Megan Beadford had a sex change or this case just made a hard right turn down a very different road."

6

Once I left the hospital and got into the Camry, I called Megan's house on my cell. I wanted to tell her about my visit to Sister Nell and what I'd learned. There could be a simple explanation—maybe a clerical error—but if Megan and I could go to the Bureau of Vital Statistics and get a reissued certified copy, we'd know if the state database information matched what was on Megan's current copy. If so, St. Mary's obviously made a mistake somewhere down the line in their data entry.

When Roxanne answered, I asked for Megan.

"They are shopping for funerary boxes," Roxanne said. "I have been delegated to stay home and receive sympathy calls should they come in. Is this a sympathy call?"

This girl went beyond weird. "It's Abby Rose. If you remember, I was there the day Mr. Beadford died. Could you have Megan call me when she gets home?"

"Oh, it's you! I'm so glad you called. My sister, Courtney, did not make the trip to pick out a casket. She hasn't been here all day. I'm extremely concerned."

And exactly why did I need to know this? But I couldn't just click the off button. I felt obligated to respond. "What's worrying you?"

"You have a sister. I saw you two together after Uncle James was . . . dispatched."

Dispatched? Sounded like he'd been sent to the hereafter via FedEx.

She wasn't done, though. "If your sister was involving herself with evil and immoral acquaintances, you'd do something, right?"

I wanted to tell her *I* was the twin who could have had *Most Likely to Get Herself into Deep Shit* written under her name in our high school yearbook, but instead I replied, "Certainly I'd help her. Or try to."

"Courtney will find herself dead one of these days," Roxanne said. "She'll be laid out on some filthy mattress with a needle stuck in her arm."

"Have you talked with your sister about her problem?" I asked.

"Have you ever tried to have a rational discussion with someone under the influence?"

Indeed I had, but I wasn't about to discuss my marital history with Roxanne. "I'm sure Courtney will come home. But if she doesn't arrive by nightfall, call that nice Chief of Police Fielder. She'll help you. And please, tell Megan I need to talk to her when she gets home." I rattled off my cell number, said good-bye, and disconnected as fast as I could.

Whew.

But my relief was short-lived. When I arrived home, Fielder had left a message to call her, and I feared Roxanne had wasted no time contacting her about her grown-up sister, Courtney, who had been missing for all of half a day.

No use putting this off, I thought, reaching for the receiver. "How can I help you today?" I said once I was connected to Fielder. Communicate like you have the upper hand, I always say.

"I have a request." She sounded almost nice.

Obviously she hadn't spoken with the potential leech Roxanne or she would have sounded less than nice. And her word *request* implied I might refuse if I so chose. "Go ahead," I said.

"The only other photo we've found of the woman of interest was taken from the upstairs balcony. Not useful for an identification."

"But it does establish her presence inside," I said almost to myself.

"Yes it does. Do you think you could remember her face well enough to assist me in creating a composite?"

"I'm not sure I remember her all that well. Maybe if you told me why this woman is so important, it would jog my memory." I knew damn well why she was important to Fielder, but she could be important to my client, too.

"And how would that help *jog your memory*?" she replied coldly.

"You know, Chief, I sense a lack of mutual respect here. I mean, I'm in the PI business, a professional like you who helps people and—"

"I forgot about your . . . *profession*." Her tone left no doubt she lumped me in with vagrants, prostitutes, and sex offenders. "And," she continued, "I may continue to forget about your professional relationship with the victim's daughter when I speak with other members of the family—as long as I have your cooperation in this matter."

Man, was she slick. But though I liked the little swap she was willing to make—my help in exchange for her keeping Sylvia in the dark about the birth mother hunt—I wasn't all that sure I could come through with enough details for a composite. So I said, "The woman wore a hat into the church, one of those cloches that comes down over the ears. I noticed the hat more than her face, so I'm not sure I could offer much."

"But you saw her outside the house taking pictures, right?"

"You know I did."

"And got a better look at her face?"

"Maybe."

"So you may recall more about her than you realize. Please meet with the sketch artist?"

Ah. The P word. She must be desperate. "I guess I could try, but is this a genuine sketch artist, not someone with some fancy software?" I was remembering Jeff's rant about how sketch artists were becoming extinct because of technology, even though a good artist did a far better job with composites than a computer ever could.

Fielder said, "Yes, a trained sketch artist who works on contract. We have software to produce composites here in Seacliff, but unfortunately the only person proficient with the program left us several months ago. Rather than bother one of the other local police departments for help, Jeff arranged for me to contract with this artist in Houston who needed work."

So she'd called her buddy Jeff. No surprise there. And I was beginning to read her subtext pretty damn well. She probably had no intention of letting her local police friends know she had an expensive software program she didn't know how to use.

But if this would help Megan and her family, that's all that mattered. "Do I make an appointment with the artist or do you?"

"Because of the urgency of this investigation, I've taken the liberty of calling him. He'll be in his studio until six tonight."

You've taken plenty of liberties, I thought, but she was working the case and that's all anyone could ask for.

After jotting down the artist's name and address, I hung up and filled the time waiting for Megan's return call by whipping up a stir-fry. Thanks to Central Market, the vegetables, chicken, and sauce were packaged in one oh-so-convenient container. I was just wiping the remnants of teriyaki from my lips when the phone rang.

"Hi. You called?" Megan asked.

"I did. We need to make a trip to the Bureau of Vital Statistics in Houston first thing tomorrow. I have a possible—"

"I don't think I can go," she said, lowering her voice.

"Oops. Is your mother around?"

"No, but I still worry about people overhearing me. Anyway, she has to sign some documents at the medical branch in Galveston tomorrow, something about the autopsy. She wants me with her, and I'm not sure how long it will take."

"Maybe we should wait until next week to pursue this."

A short silence followed. Then she said, "No. If I have to make time I will. So—uh-oh. Wait." Another pause followed, then Megan said to me, "So nice of you to call. The obituary will appear as soon as we've finalized details about the service. We've chosen Forest Rest, but check the newspaper for dates and times. And thanks again."

The line went dead.

She'd probably call back . . . but when? I checked my watch. The artist's studio was only twenty minutes away. Might as well get this little chore over with and catch up with Megan later.

Mason Dryer's studio, an apartment above the double garage of a house near the Galleria, happened to be his home, too. Dryer told me as much as we ascended the stairs, and I immediately wondered why Fielder said he'd be in his studio until six when he was in his studio all the time. Did she want to make sure I complied with her directive tonight? Probably.

Following Dryer up the stairs, I noticed smears of yellow, red, blue, and orange paint on the thighs and back pockets of his black jeans where he'd obviously wiped his hands many times. He hardly had any butt to use as a wiping board though. The man was so skinny he might need worming.

We entered the apartment, one large room cluttered with stacked canvases, easels, and plastic crates holding paint supplies and brushes. A Futon was partially obscured by a draped easel, and a small refrigerator and microwave sat alongside. He'd also managed to squeeze in a desk and a card table. Two walls had good-size windows, offering plenty of natural light. The room smelled like McDonald's and sure enough a half-eaten Big Mac and ketchup-drenched fries rested on the table.

"I've interrupted you," I said. "Are you sure you want to do this today?"

"You bet I do. Easy money, as opposed to my other job." He thumbed at the covered easel.

I walked toward it. "Can I see?"

"I think my work would be a distraction." A muscle above one generous, dark eyebrow began to twitch. He reached up and pressed a paint-darkened index finger against the spot. "Damn thing's been doing this all day."

"My sister says drinking tonic water cures those spasms."

"Some pocket change might cure my tension better. Let's get to work." He swept up the unfinished meal and tossed the food in a trash container, then unfolded a second chair so I could join him at the table.

But rather than the expected sketchbook, he drew out a notepad from a crate below the table. "I want you to concentrate on your first impressions. Really hone in on this person with your mind's eye."

"I'm not sure I remember much."

"Extroverts are very visual. You guys make good observers, so trust yourself."

"I'm an extrovert?" I said.

"I know you are," he said with a smile. "You've been taking in the room, asked to see my painting, and your voice, well, no one would accuse you of being shy, Ms. Rose. Now close your eyes."

I complied, settling back as much as you can settle in a folding chair.

He said, "Go back to the time you first saw this woman—a woman, right?"

"Yes, but I saw her twice."

"Excellent, but we'll focus on the first time, because that's when your brain recorded the most valuable information." He'd taken on a tone both soft and commanding, which I found soothing.

"Take yourself back to where you saw her," Dryer said. "Where was that?"

"At a wedding."

"Where specifically?"

"In a church."

"And what was your first impression of her physical appearance?"

"Sort of . . . sneaky. See, she came late and—"

"Those impressions are important," he said gently. "But let's focus on her physical features."

I nodded. "Okay. She was a small person."

"Small in frame? Small in height?"

"Height. Not overweight. Not thin either, though. She had on a beige wool pantsuit. And . . . wait. Do you know what I'm seeing?"

"What?"

I squeezed my eyes tighter. "This is so weird. I can't believe I remember this, but it's just like she is sitting right across the aisle from me again."

"Go ahead."

"Her suit jacket had one of those tiny plastic thingies sticking out from the left cuff and the store tag was still attached. Looks like a Nieman Marcus tag."

"Focus on her face, please."

"Sorry, okay. Tanned face. Doesn't look like bottle tan, either. Maybe electric beach tan? And then there's the hat."

"What kind of hat?"

"A cloche . . . dark brown felt."

"Ah. So it fit snug. What shape was her head?"

"Her skull was more prominent on the top than the back."

"You're doing great. Did her hair cover her forehead?"

"Hmmm. Her hair. Something about her hair. I'm seeing wisps peeking out around her face. Pale brownish gray."

"Good. Go on."

"She still wore the hat when I saw her later on. More hair revealed. Gray streaked."

"Could you see her face better?" he asked.

I took a deep breath, exhaled, and closed my eyes again. "Yes. Her cheeks were bright from the wind."

"Tell me about the shape of her face."

"Oval."

"And could you tell how old she was?"

"She moved like a young person, but there were lines on her forehead and around her eyes. Blue eyes, but a dark blue." The more I concentrated, the better I could visualize her. This was amazing.

"Crow's-feet?"

"Not that severe, but she did have age lines. And frown lines. Made her look . . . sad. Yes. She looked sad. I'd guess she was in her forties."

"Eyes close together, far apart?"

I reached up and felt the bridge of my nose with thumb and index finger to gauge the space. I'd never thought about these little things when I looked at people before. "Maybe a half inch farther apart than mine," I said.

I went on to describe the thin-lipped mouth, the straight nose, the slightly hollow cheeks, and even the freckles where her throat met her collarbone.

"And she never smiled? Showed her teeth?"

"If so, I didn't notice. Of course we were all focused on Megan—she's the bride. She looked so wonderful and she had on this lace coat over her wedding dress when she got out of the limo, sort of a 1940s look and—"

"Abby, please move your mental camera to the woman. If it helps, think about where she was standing in relation to the bride."

"Sorry. She was waiting on the steps near the professional photographer, but sort of off by herself. And she was focused on her own camera, trying to get a shot of the bride and groom as they arrived."

"Ears are very distinct. Did the hat cover them?"

"I could see the lobes but not much more. She was wearing pierced earrings—small pearl studs."

"Okay. I think I have enough to go on."

I stood. "So do I come back tomorrow or—"

"This will take about fifteen minutes and I still need your help." He was digging around in the crate again and this time pulled out a sketchbook along with a box of charcoal pencils.

"Only fifteen minutes?"

"I can work as fast as the computers stealing what used to be a decent side income. Don't get me started, though." He flipped open the book and chose a pencil from a tennis ball can seconding as a brush and pencil holder.

I dragged my chair beside him, and for the next quarter of an hour we worked together creating the composite. The guy was unbelievably talented, and soon we were both staring at the woman in the church.

Dryer pulled a spray can from the crate. "This is fixative. Not good stuff to breathe in, so you might want to step back."

I stood and moved about three feet away. While he sprayed I kept staring. Something about the picture made it impossible for me to stop looking at the face I had pulled from my memory. What was it? But then the cloud of fixative hit me and I turned my head and had a minor coughing fit.

Dryer, meanwhile, retrieved a camera case from under the Futon and snapped several shots of the drawing with his 35mm. He then opened a drawer in the desk, removed a large manila envelope, and carefully placed the drawing inside. "Chief Fielder wanted this by tomorrow at the latest."

"Is she coming here to pick it up?" I asked.

"She said Officer Henderson would come when we were done."

"She's paying you on delivery?"

"No. Some city official has to cosign on the check, so she's mailing me the money."

"Then you wouldn't care if I delivered it? Because I'd be happy to drop the composite off." Since Kate had seen the woman, too, I wanted her to have a look, see if she had the same feeling I had that this face was familiar.

"She might not contract with me again if I don't follow her directions," Dryer said. The eye must have twitched because he pressed the heel of his hand against his brow.

"If I could get the drawing to her more quickly than waiting for Henderson, then she'd be happy, right?"

"Yes . . . but, she'd have to okay the arrangement and—"

"Let's just forget it." Fielder might not okay anything that had to do with me, even if it benefited her.

But he picked up a cell phone from the desk and dialed a number off a scrap of paper he took from his jeans pocket. "She said to page her as soon as we were done, so I might as well ask her." He listened for a second, then punched a few numbers and disconnected.

"While we wait for her to call back," I said, "can I see what you're working on?"

He smiled. "Are you sure you're interested?"

His cell trilled. If that was Fielder, either she had no life aside from her job or she needed the composite in the worst way.

It *was* her, and after Dryer explained he extended the phone in my direction. "She wants to talk to you."

I took the phone. "This is Abby."

"How soon can you bring me the drawing?" she said curtly.

"When do you need it?"

"Tomorrow morning. Megan and her mother will be home until around nine thirty and I wanted to show it to them."

"I can meet you there. I need to talk to Megan anyway."

"Okay . . . and thank you." She disconnected.

A please and a thank-you all in one day? Well, slap me naked and sell my clothes.

Dryer and I spent the next half hour looking at his paintings. No gentle landscapes or country cottages for Mason Dryer. He'd painted ballerinas on tightropes suspended in fluid skies, monkeys and cats in vivid color riding through clouds in an old-fashioned motor car, jesters dancing on domes. I loved his stuff. So when I left, I was carrying not only the envelope, but the monkeys and cats, too.

I pulled into my driveway twenty minutes later, and Kate showed up just as I was taking my new painting from the trunk. I'd called her on my way home since I wanted her to look at the composite. Would she see what I thought I was seeing in that face?

"You didn't waste any time getting here," I said, lifting out the canvas.

"I was leaving my office when you phoned, so I wasn't far away." She stared at the covered canvas. "But I thought you said you visited a sketch artist. I didn't realize they painted their subjects these days."

"Funny. Get the back door for me, would you?" I tossed her my keys.

"So where'd you get the painting?"

I told her about Dryer's day job as we went inside. After I turned on the kitchen lights, I tore the brown paper off the canvas and showed her my purchase. She seemed less than impressed, but Kate's tastes tend to lean toward the comfort of Monet or Renoir.

"Tell me about tonight," she said after offering a polite comment about my cats and monkeys. "I always wondered how a person could create a picture from someone else's memory."

"Dryer's good. Almost like a hypnotist. I mean, I was sitting in that church looking at the woman again."

"Okay, so let me see."

I carefully removed the pencil drawing from the envelope. "Is this how you remember her?"

Kate stared at the picture. "Wow. That's her all right. He did this in fifteen minutes?"

"Yup. There is something special about this face. He captured her accurately, but . . ."

"I know what you mean. She looks . . . kind of familiar, but maybe that's only because we saw her Saturday."

"Take a longer look—especially at those eyes and the shape of her face."

"My God, Abby, she looks like—"

"Megan," I finished.

7

When the alarm went off the next morning I resisted the urge to hit the sleep button. I had to get an early start to be in Seacliff by nine A.M. After I showered, dressed, and fed Diva, I rummaged through boxes until I found my digital camera. I took several shots of the composite, downloaded them to my computer, printed 8x10 and 4x6 copies and added them to Megan's file. The more I stared at the drawing, the more of Megan I saw in the woman's features.

Kate and I might be putting too much stock in the likeness, but what if Megan's mother had secretly kept track of her daughter? And what if the wedding drew her out of the shadows for an event no mother would want to miss? But this was still speculation, and I wasn't about to present this theory to Megan. Not yet, anyway.

I arrived at the Beadfords by eight forty-five, and this time Roxanne admitted me to the foyer. She wore oatmeal-colored sweats, no makeup, and a thick red fabric headband that revealed a patch of blemishes on her forehead. In my khakis and off-the-shoulder blue sweater I looked like a supermodel compared to her.

"You didn't have to make the trip here, though I do appreciate it," Roxanne said. I must have looked confused because she added, "She came home."

"Who came home?" I said.

"Courtney."

How could I have forgotten our strange conversation yesterday? "I'm glad she returned safely," I said with a smile.

"Perhaps I fret too much," she said. "But with Uncle James quitting the earth in such a horrible turn of events, I suppose I overreacted."

Quitting the earth? Turn of events? I decided Roxanne had been spending way too much time reading gothic novels. I was saved from further pained conversation by someone ringing the bell. I turned and opened the door to find that Chief Fielder had come to my rescue. Now there was some black irony.

"Good morning, Ms. Rose . . . Miss Beadford." Her gaze rested on the large envelope in my hand.

"Good morning." I handed her the drawing once she crossed the threshold, wondering if she would pick up on the resemblance to Megan.

"Are you satisfied with the composite?" Fielder asked.

"Very," I answered.

"Composite of what?" Roxanne asked.

"I'll fill you in later, Miss Beadford," Fielder said. "But for now, I'd like some time with your aunt. Can you tell her I'm here?" Fielder sounded about as pleasant as I'd ever heard her. Guess she saved up her best stuff for the victim's family—and I couldn't argue with that approach.

"Certainly," Roxanne said. Then she lowered her voice. "Aunt Sylvia's upstairs preparing for her trip to Galveston. The medical examiner will be performing a postmortem examination on Uncle James's remains, and she must complete the paperwork for the eventual release of his body."

I swear she almost smiled before she walked through the foyer and made a slow ascent up the right staircase. Hmmm. Maybe someone forgot her medication today.

I caught Fielder rolling her eyes. Then she said, "I appreciate you coming down here, Ms. Rose." She wore black trousers and a herringbone blazer, but even her expertly applied makeup couldn't hide her fatigue. Definitely puffy around the eyes.

"I'm much more comfortable with Abby," I said.

"Certainly." She forced a smile.

The awkward silence that followed was broken by Sylvia and Megan's appearance. Megan had on the same clothes she'd worn yesterday, but Sylvia was dressed in a throat-high black knit dress that made her look like she was already headed for the funeral.

We exchanged greetings, and before Fielder escorted Sylvia into the formal living room off the foyer, she told Megan to wait, that they'd only be a minute or two.

Keeping her voice low, Megan said, "Sorry I had to hang up on you last night. Why do we need to go to the Bureau of Vital Statistics? I thought the Adoption Registry was a dead end."

"I've been digging deeper, and you may not have been born at St. Mary's," I whispered. "Maybe a new copy of your birth certificate will confirm this."

"Not born at St. Mary's? But—"

"I don't think this is the best place to talk," I said.

"You have a real lead?" she asked, eyes bright.

"Could be the break we're looking for," I replied.

"Okay. We go today."

"But Fielder wants to show you the composite. And you said you had to take Sylvia to Galveston."

"Travis will fill in for me with Mother."

"She won't mind if you bail?"

"Oh, she'll mind," Megan said. "But Travis is good with her. He'll think up a decent excuse—like I need some time away from everything, which happens to be true."

"Okay, we're on," I said.

The living room door opened and Sylvia came out. "Chief Fielder would like to see you now, sweetheart."

Megan brushed past her mother, and Sylvia's sad

gaze followed her daughter as she entered the room and pulled the door shut after her. The weekend events seemed to be taking their toll on everyone.

"How are you, Mrs. Beadford?" I asked.

She glanced at the closed door. "I'm upset."

"I think Megan's handling this situation as well as anyone could under the circumstances."

"That's not what I'm talking about."

"Is it something the chief said?" I asked, curious now.

"The chief's doing a fine job. Seems to be working hard on this horrible murder. But she showed me that drawing, and I never saw that woman before. Why would a stranger invade our home, destroy our beautiful wedding, and kill my husband?"

"Did the chief tell you that the woman in the composite is the killer?" I asked.

"She wouldn't say. But it seems the only logical explanation."

Not the only explanation if that stranger came here to see her child get married. But I certainly couldn't offer this insight. "Maybe there are other possibilities," I said. "The chief may find some other clue to Mr. Beadford's death once she's sorted through all the evidence—and there seems to be plenty of that to go around."

Sylvia's eyes flashed. "Do you know something I don't? Has that policewoman been discussing my husband's death with—" She stopped, closed her eyes, and pressed a shaky hand to her forehead. "I am *so* sorry, Abby. I've been snapping at everyone today. First Megan and Roxanne this morning at breakfast and now you. There's just so much to deal with and . . ." Tears filled her eyes.

I put an arm around her shoulders. "No need to apologize, Mrs. Beadford. I understand. By the way, is that coffee I smell?"

She nodded.

"Could I bother you for a cup?"

"Certainly. Yes. Coffee would be good."

We went to the kitchen together with her tottering on yet another pair of ridiculous shoes similar to the ones she'd chosen for the wedding—pointy with one-inch narrow heels—throwbacks to foot binding, in my opinion.

The kitchen had far more to offer than coffee. A silver tray filled with breakfast pastries sat on the counter beside platters of cookies, covered sheet cakes, and a huge fruit basket.

"The neighbors have been so supportive," Sylvia said, gesturing at the food. "Help yourself while I get your coffee."

I chose a raspberry kolache and sat at the kitchen table. Sylvia placed a white mug of steaming brew in front of me and sat down with her own cup.

After my daddy died, I'd wanted to talk about him in the worst way, but had little opportunity. People seemed almost afraid to say his name in front of me. So maybe Sylvia needed time to talk about her husband. "Tell me about Mr. Beadford. I met him only once, at the rehearsal dinner, but he seemed to command the room."

She smiled and her whole body seemed to relax. "He could grab your attention, couldn't he?"

"And he owned his own business, right?" I bit into the kolache, the pastry so rich I figured I was about to consume enough fat calories for a week.

"Built the company from the ground up twice. There was no quit in that man."

"Twice?" I said around a mouthful of berry heaven.

"The first time we went bankrupt. Not through any fault of James, mind you. Running a small business is tough, and supplying equipment for the oil business is very competitive in Texas. James thought he'd do better here than in Dallas, and as it turns out, he was right."

"So you're not from this area originally?" She definitely seemed calmer and happy to talk about her husband's accomplishments.

"We came south for a fresh start, a move that also allowed James to put some space between him and his brother, Graham. They'd been in business together, but it's very difficult working day in and day out with family members."

"I understand," I answered, wondering if Graham had something to do with the first failure. That might explain the animosity between the brothers.

"Graham stayed in Dallas," Sylvia went on. "His wife had a decent job and supported the family for several years, but when she passed on from breast cancer—horrible time for Courtney and Roxanne—Graham never seemed to recover. He's lost one job after another."

"So he and his daughters are only staying here because of the wedding?"

She nodded, her chubby right hand working the fingers on the left. "They arrived two weeks ago. Graham is at the Surfside Resort, thank goodness, but the girls wanted to be near Megan, so they've been with us. Having relatives underfoot day and night, well, I'm not coping very well, Abby. Not with James . . . not with the—"

"I think you're doing fine," I said quickly, hoping to abort a round of tears.

"Tell me more about yourself, Abby," she said. "Megan met you at the health club, right?"

Before I could answer, someone rapped on the back door. Saved again, thank goodness.

She rose to answer, and a second later Graham entered carrying a case of beer. "Saw you were running low and—" He stopped, nodded my way. "Nice to see you again."

"I'm not sure we need more beer." Sylvia backed away from Graham like he'd brought in a keg of dynamite.

"*We* may not, but I do," he answered. "They charge

five dollars for one beer at the damn hotel, and I bought this whole case for ten bucks.''

He carried his treasure chest over to the refrigerator.

"Will you excuse me, Abby?" Sylvia said. "I have to see if Megan is ready to head for Galveston."

She hurried out of the kitchen and down the hall, leaving me to deal with her brother-in-law.

After Graham stacked as many beers as he could in the already overloaded refrigerator, he grabbed two sausage kolaches and joined me at the table. Somewhere upstairs, a radio or stereo blared, heavy metal music now our muted background noise.

Graham looked up at the ceiling. "Christ, I'm glad Courtney's staying here and not with me." The whites of his eyes were bloodshot, and his breath smelled like the beer he'd probably had on his way here.

"Um, Sylvia tells me you're from Dallas. Very different than Houston, huh?" I was hoping to move on to a safe, nonfamily related topic. Where the heck was Megan when I needed her?

"Both places are damn hot in the summer and damn ugly in the winter. But with your money, you probably take plenty of vacations when the weather turns nasty." He chomped into a kolache.

I had no intention of talking to him about my private life, so I changed the subject. "You sure did come to the rescue the other day after your brother died," I said. "I know Megan and Sylvia are grateful for your help."

He cocked his head, squinted as if considering this. "My brother. Funny to hear you refer to him as my brother. He would have liked to forget, that's for sure." The little hitch in his voice added enough sadness to cancel out his attempt at sounding smug. He stood abruptly and walked over to the refrigerator, but rather than choose a beer as I would have expected, he started rummaging around for something else.

Thanks to our conversation at the reception, I'd already assumed Graham and his brother weren't best buddies. If the bankruptcy had created bitterness between them, if they'd hardly spoken over the years, I could understand why Graham was staying in a hotel rather than here, even though this house could have handled plenty of guests. Chief Fielder would be wise to take a good long look at brother Graham.

I heard a small rustling sound and turned in the direction of the family room, where the string quartet had played during the reception. Megan held up a sheet of paper with the words *Meet me at the Kroger parking lot in fifteen minutes* printed in black marker. She disappeared an instant before her uncle turned around holding a carton of orange juice.

I stood. "Good talking to you, Mr. Beadford, but I need to be going."

"It's Graham. James was the only Mr. Beadford in this family."

"Okay, Graham it is," I said. "I'll probably see you at the funeral."

"Right," he said distractedly, opening one cupboard after another, now apparently looking for a glass.

I slipped out the back door and felt my tight neck muscles ease the minute I started down the wooden deck stairs. Even today's dreary weather seemed brighter than that house of gloom.

From where I'd parked at the Kroger lot on the main highway, I'd watched Travis barrel by with Sylvia in the passenger seat of his Ford Explorer ten minutes after I'd arrived. Megan pulled up alongside me shortly after. I quickly explained about my visit with Sister Nell and what a new copy of her birth certificate might tell us.

We then made the trip to downtown Houston in separate cars and after we arrived at the Bureau of Vital Statistics near Reliant Stadium, we received visitor badges from security. Megan and I waited in line to make her application, and once she'd turned in her paperwork, we sat on one of the long wooden benches in the center of the waiting area. Nothing happened in a hurry in places like this. We'd be here awhile— Megan, me, and the cultural rainbow that is Houston. Browns, blacks, white and yellows, old and young, they were all here en masse, a steady flow coming and going, coming and going.

Megan sighed heavily and closed her eyes. "This may sound uncaring, but I feel relieved to be out of the house and away from my family."

"You don't sound uncaring to me. Right after Daddy's funeral, my sister and I took a long weekend in California. Helped a lot. I suggest you reschedule your honeymoon as soon as you can. Where were you going, by the way?"

"Travis and I wanted to go to the Caribbean, but Dad handed us two first-class tickets to Hawaii before we could even make plans."

"And how did Travis feel about your father making the decision for you?" I was remembering the argument I witnessed between father and son-in-law at the reception and wondered if that had been the source of their disagreement.

Megan said, "Travis is so easygoing, he had no problem with Dad stepping in. I had my heart set on snorkeling in Grand Cayman, but Travis said a sunny day was the same anywhere as long as we were together." She smiled, then dropped her gaze to her lap and twisted her shiny gold wedding band. "I can't imagine celebrating our first anniversary. It will seem like I'm betraying Dad if we enjoy ourselves."

"Time will help." I fell into silence, troubled by her describing Travis as "easygoing." I hoped Megan wasn't in for the kind of surprises my former husband had served up not long after we were married. The ex had added new meaning to the phrase *love is blind*. I think blind, deaf, and plain stupid more aptly described me.

"You and Travis seem very much in love," I finally said.

"He's the best thing that ever happened to me."

"How did you meet?"

She smiled. "On a blind date I set up for Margie—you remember Margie?"

"Maid of honor?" I said.

"Right. Anyway, Holt McNabb works for my dad, and one day when I visited the office, Holt asked me out. I'd never been attracted to him, but Dad thought I should give him a chance since Holt had expressed interest in dating me. I suggested Holt set up Margie with one of his friends and we could all do a movie or something. Margie's blind date turned out to be Travis, and the rest is history."

"So Travis scored points with you when Holt couldn't?"

"Yup. Travis and I couldn't take our eyes off each other the whole night."

"Bet that bruised Holt's over-the-top ego."

"He did pout some, but he and Travis go back a long way and apparently Holt was usually the one stealing girlfriends. Travis figures they're even now."

"Ask me, you made the right choice."

"You don't like Holt?" she asked.

"Don't know him all that well," I said.

"He can come across as self-centered, but he's been great for the business. Dad said Holt's a born salesman."

"Really? From the way he tried to sell himself to my sister you'd have thought he couldn't sell Pepcid to a commodities trader."

She laughed. "You always cheer me up, Abby. I'm so glad Travis convinced me to get help to search for my birth mother, because otherwise I never would have met you."

This piece of news sure grabbed my attention. "So Travis convinced you to look for your mother?" I felt a small tightness in my stomach. Travis clearly told

me the other night he found out who I really was only
after the rehearsal dinner.

"When we first fell in love, I spilled out all my
secrets," she said. "I told Travis I'd been dreaming
about meeting my birth mother ever since I'd learned
I was adopted."

"So he knew I was working for you when I showed
up for the rehearsal?"

"Sure. Why?"

"No reason." I decided it was time for a quick
change of subject. I might have to discuss this little
inconsistency with Travis later. "So when you met
with Chief Fielder, did you recognize the woman in
the drawing?" I wanted to add, "And do you think
she looks like you?"

"No, and I never caught so much as a glimpse of that
woman at the reception," Megan said. "I've never seen
her before in my life. Who could have invited her?"

So she didn't notice the resemblance. No surprise.
I once stared at a photo of my own birth mother un-
aware of who she was. I never picked up on our similar features even though they were literally as plain
as the nose on my face.

Megan went on, saying, "Or was she even invited?
The engagement picture in the newspaper appeared
right before Christmas and had all the ceremony details, so I guess she could have crashed the wedding
and followed people to our house afterward."

"That seems an odd thing to do," I said. "But
maybe people crash weddings all the time and I've
just never heard about it."

Megan sat up straighter. "Abby, could she have possibly come to the wedding to kill my dad? Could they
have known each other?"

"Maybe, but why pick a day with a house full of
witnesses to kill him?" I replied.

"Doesn't seem logical, does it?"

"And I would think that if you were planning to
kill someone, you'd bring a weapon, not count on

there being a room full of leaded crystal. I'm thinking
your dad's death resulted from an argument."

"Yeah. Guess you're right," she said.

"When you talked to the chief this morning, did she
mention whether she'd found anyone else who had
seen this woman inside the house?"

"No, but she showed me a picture taken from the
balcony and the woman was clearly visible, so today
I gave her the names of the two people I recognized
in that same photo. The chief said she'd schedule in-
terviews with them this afternoon to see if they have
any idea who the woman is."

"Maybe Fielder will get lucky, but I saw a whole
lot of photographs in her office. Hundreds of them.
It's almost like she has too much to sift through. Plus
she's investigating possible motives. That's a lot on
one cop's plate." Fielder was probably delving into
Sylvia and James's relationship, too. And though
Megan seemed to think Holt was a favorite of James,
those two sure weren't happy with each other at the
rehearsal dinner.

"The chief certainly acts like she knows what she's
doing," Megan said. "She assured me she'd find the
killer."

"And she will," I answered, sounding more confi-
dent than I felt.

"You want a Coke or something?" Megan asked.

"Sounds good."

We went in search of a machine, and when we returned and sat down with our drinks, every preschooler
in the waiting area decided we were worth staring at or
clinging to—probably hoping we'd share our sodas.

Two very long hours later, after we'd been drooled
on, kicked, and witnessed a few temper tantrums,
Megan's number flashed above window nine and an
electronically generated voice called out the same
number over the PA system. We walked up to the
clerk together.

"So sorry to keep you waiting, but I never did an

adoption certificate before," the young woman said. She was Hispanic, with flyaway dark hair and giant half-moons of sweat spoiling her burgundy shirt. Definitely frazzled. But she had apologized, and apologies in places like this, where tempers grew short after thirty minutes of waiting and reached the boiling point after two hours, did not come often. We weren't about to complain.

"You're very busy. I understand," Megan replied.

"We will have to assess a search fee," the clerk said, cringing like she expected one of us to smack her. "It's because you gave us inaccurate information and—"

"Inaccurate?" I said.

The woman addressed Megan when she answered. "Since you were born in Jamaica, you—"

"Jamaica?" Megan sounded stunned, and I was damn surprised myself.

"Yes. Kingston, Jamaica. Is there a problem?" the clerk asked.

"No," I cut in, clutching Megan's arm and squeezing hard. I hoped to convey the message that I would handle this. "She just lost her father a few days ago. That's probably why she got confused and wrote Kingston Bay rather than Kingston, Jamaica."

"I am so sorry for your loss, ma'am. Anyway, you must request a certified copy in person in Austin because you were adopted from a foreign country. We can only process certificates for Houston, Kingston Bay, and Brewster at this location."

"Is there any other information that would speed up the process when we get to Austin?" I asked.

"Well, I'm pretty new here, and I've never worked in Austin, so—"

"Maybe the hospital name?" I turned to Megan, who had gone pale as bleached bones. "Do you remember the name of the hospital, Megan?"

She shook her head no, thank goodness.

The woman turned back to the computer. "This may not help, but it's Duchess of Kent Hospital."

I stood on tiptoe—the counter separating us was high—and looked at her computer monitor. "You have everything right there, huh?"

"Yes, but we cannot generate—"

"Oh, we understand. You've been wonderful," I said.

The woman smiled with genuine relief. "Thanks. Thanks so much."

After I paid the search fee at the cashier's desk, I guided a shocked Megan out of the building and into the adjacent parking garage. When we entered the empty elevator, she finally spoke.

"What the hell does this mean, Abby?"

"It means we might finally get some answers."

8

We left the elevator and walked to our cars in the garage adjoining the Bureau of Vital Statistics. Megan had said nothing for several minutes, no doubt still trying to make sense of what she'd just heard.

"I don't understand this, Abby," she said when we reached our cars. "Why did my parents change the birth certificate?"

"We don't know if they did," I said.

She blinked twice, not understanding. "Who else would have done such a thing?"

She was still reeling and this wasn't a discussion for a parking lot. "I live about fifteen minutes away. Let's pick up something to eat, sit down at my place, and think this through."

Megan looked at her watch. "But I have to get home and I have to find out when they'll release Dad's body and I—" She stopped talking, and I could see she was fighting tears.

"Are you okay? We could go in my car and I'll bring you back here later."

"I'm fine. Really. And I guess I should be happy we found this out, but . . ."

I squeezed her upper arm reassuringly. "Hey, it's okay to be confused."

"I do need time to think before I go home or I won't be able to look my mother in the eye."

"There's a great bakery on the way to my place. We'll stop there first."

I didn't know about Megan, but my kolache calories had dried up long ago and I was starving. Megan had told me she wasn't hungry when we'd stood in line in the bakery/deli, but I bought her a turkey sandwich anyway. As for me, I couldn't wait to bite into my shaved ham and cheese on Italian herb bread.

Diva greeted us when we came in through my back door, and Megan knelt to pet her. I set the deli bag on the kitchen table and pulled two Diet Cokes from the fridge. We sat down, and Diva immediately jumped on Megan's lap.

"I'm still messed up about this, Abby," she said. "I don't understand."

"We can safely assume someone altered your birth certificate to hide the fact that you were born in Jamaica. This new information may lead us to the truth, but we need to find out who made the changes and why."

"Why is the big question. It doesn't make sense."

"You're right. But it's my job to find answers." I removed our sandwiches from the bag and slid Megan's in front of her. "Let's eat. You probably haven't had any real food since Saturday."

"I don't think I have." She touched her fingers to her forehead, making no effort to unwrap her sandwich. She stared at it for a second, then looked at me. "If my mother deceived me all my life, how can I go home and pretend nothing has changed? How can I grieve for Dad if he lied and—"

"Megan, listen to me. We can't be sure either of them lied to you. They could have been as much in the dark as you were."

"Did this . . . this alteration occur sometime between when I was born and when they adopted me?"

"It must have happened about the time of the adoption or after. Sylvia and James named you, and that was correctly entered in the computer."

"Oh. Right," she answered. But I could tell she still was having trouble processing this information. She'd been through too much in the last week.

Just then Diva lifted her head over the edge of the table, sniffed at the sandwich, and planted one mottled charcoal and orange paw tentatively in the direction of the food.

"I'll figure out what happened. That's what you hired me for. And now, if you don't eat, someone else will," I warned.

Megan smiled, opened the wrapper and pulled off a piece of turkey breast. She set it in front of Diva before picking up her sandwich.

While we ate, I convinced her this new information was exactly what we needed if we wanted to find her birth mother and that I would follow every lead as far as it would take me. Soon she was on her way home, but not before we stopped by City Hall to get new notarized authorizations for release of medical information and a letter stating that Abby Rose of Yellow Rose Investigations was acting on Megan Beadford's behalf in the matter of her adoption.

I returned home and went to my office after we'd parted downtown, hoping to handle a few inquiries by phone. I figured I could fax the authorizations to Jamaica if needed. But by the time I finished talking to the Adoption Board in Kingston, the Registrar General's office, the Duchess of Kent Hospital switchboard, and the American Consulate, I had a giant headache and exactly zero information aside from my sincere belief that every living soul in that country had inherited the "we don't know nothing, mon" gene. This pronouncement was always delivered with amazing goodwill and sometimes a laugh, but it still irritated the hell out of me.

I had just hung up after my fifth try at speaking

with the hospital medical records department when Jeff arrived.

"You look . . . stressed out," he said from the doorway of my office.

"Yah, mon. Maybe if I smoked some ganja like everyone else in Ja-MAY-cah, I could get unstressed."

"What are you talking about?" He leaned against the doorframe, his wary blue eyes indicating he was unsure whether it was safe to approach a woman whose sanity might be slipping away.

"Do you have police friends in the West Indies?" I said. "Anyone who might be capable of utilizing a telephone as a communication tool rather than a weapon of mass frustration? I mean, every single person I talked to acted like they wanted to help and then they'd just go away and never come back to the phone."

"New case?" he said, his expression relaxing into amusement.

"No, my ongoing case." I rubbed my tired eyes, then ran my fingers through my hair. "Sorry, but I have been on the phone for—" I glanced at the clock. "Four hours."

"So take a break."

"Good idea." I left the desk and went over to offer him a proper hello. After we kissed and hugged and kissed again, we went to the living room and sat on the only unencumbered piece of furniture, the green and red chenille sofa.

I quickly assumed the comfort position with my head in his lap. He began massaging my temples with his strong fingers, reminding me exactly how much pleasure this man could generate with only a simple touch—and I didn't even have to take my clothes off.

"I missed you last night," I said.

"Two homicides. One perp got away. This city is too damn big and too damn populated." Out came the gum.

"You've mentioned that before," I said.

"And I was so tied up, I forgot to tell you that Quinn asked me for help on IDing a suspect and I suggested she contact an artist I know to—"

"Mason Dryer?" I offered.

"Ah, she already called you." He stuffed his gum wrappers in his shirt pocket. "Did you meet with him?"

I nodded and told him about the composite, but decided not to mention I'd photographed the drawing. Better if we both remained ignorant as to whether this was somehow "interfering with an official investigation."

"So far," I said, "no one claims to know this woman, but Kate and I think she resembles Megan."

"Now, that's interesting," he said, switching from my temples and massaging my skull from the crown of my head to the nape of my neck.

I sighed and closed my eyes. This was so nice.

"But I hope you're not jumping to any conclusions," he added.

My eyes snapped open. "I remember your lecture on coincidence in murder investigations and—"

"Glad you were paying attention." He grinned. "But remember, Abby. People often resemble someone else. I'd be cautious about giving any physical similarities too much weight until you have some hard evidence."

I held up my right hand. "I, Abby Rose, do solemnly swear to temper all deductions with common sense and—"

"Shut up," he said with a laugh. "Let's move on to when I arrived and saw you nearly pull your hair out by the roots when I came in—an activity which, by the way, might allow you to grow out your hair."

I sat up and looked him in the eye. "Grow out my hair? I had no idea you liked long hair."

"I was talking about the color." He gently tucked a few of the chin-length strands behind my ear on one side.

"You don't like the color?" I'd recently gone from auburn to a more highlighted look at the urging of my wacko hairstylist. Goes to show you, you should never trust a man with jeweled teeth.

"Just kidding," Jeff said. "I love your hair."

But guys do not kid about hair or your hips or how you handle you checkbook, even when they smile and laugh and say they love you just the way you are. I'd consider a change. Maybe.

"I'm waiting to hear how your ongoing case has you talking to Jamaicans," he said.

"Big turn of events today." I told him about Megan's altered birth certificate and how many people I'd spoken to in Jamaica in an attempt to get some answers. "Do you understand my frustration?" I said. "How do I get anything out of those island people?"

"Beats the hell out of me. I interview most of my witnesses in person. I use the phone only to let the nice ones know I'll be showing up at their door. Not many nice ones, by the way. And now, I could use a drink. How about you?"

We both stood.

"Good idea. Rum and Coke, mon," I said, considering the possibility of a little business trip.

Jeff had to be in court the following day, so when we woke up, we jogged at the Rice University campus for an hour. I've dropped ten pounds in the last six months, thanks to hanging around with a man who has some discipline when it comes to exercise. We even lift weights together. My once pudgy thighs and less than toned arms are now more muscle than fat.

After our run we shared a shower and plenty of soapy playtime; then Jeff left for the courthouse. I immediately called my travel agent and asked her to investigate flights to Jamaica and hotels in Kingston. She gave me the options, and I chose a flight that left at ten the next morning.

I needed a new suitcase since mine hadn't survived

the last trip I took, so I spent considerable hours in department stores and leather outlets searching for what I needed. On my way home around six P.M., I dropped by Kate's place to tell her I'd be out of town for a few days.

She and Terry Armstrong live together in a West University bungalow even older than mine, which they had completely remodeled inside and out after Kate moved in. I pulled up close to the garage and Kate must have heard me, because she opened the kitchen door and called to me just as I got out of the car.

"Gate's open, Abby. Come on in."

Her border collie met me when I came through the narrow back hall leading to the kitchen. I gave Webster a scratch behind the ears and he wagged his tail, then ambled back to his blanket by the door. Herding dogs are supposed to be full of energy, but I'd decided long ago Webster either had a missing gene or he was just plain lazy. But no matter what, he was sweet and loyal and gentle—rather like Kate.

My sister was standing by the sink peeling steaming hot beets. Now on the one to ten "yuck factor" scale, I considered beets a twenty. Glad I'd had that pepperoni slice at the Galleria and could only hope I still had the receipt to prove I'd already eaten should Kate question me. She knows how much I hate vibrant vegetables.

"Hey, glad you came for dinner," she said, dumping the beets from the purple-stained cutting board into a saucepan. She turned and placed the pot on the island six-burner cooktop.

"No dinner. I came to ask a favor." I leaned against the angled granite-covered counter separating the kitchen from the small breakfast nook behind me.

"What do you need?"

"Can you feed Diva and give her some attention for the next couple days? Jeff is hardly ever around and—"

"Where are you headed?"

"Jamaica."

"A vacation? Did you tell me this already?" She now had her hands in what I recognized was a large bowl of bulgur wheat soon to be transformed into her rendition of "meatless loaf." I felt doubly thankful I had a valid excuse to escape soon. I had packing to do.

"No vacation. I found out yesterday Megan was born in Jamaica, not Texas."

She quit messing with the wheat. "No way. Tell me about this."

"I need wine first. Preferably white and cold. And not that organic crap, either."

"Yes, ma'am," she said, turning to the refrigerator.

Terry didn't like organic wine, either, so I knew I wasn't making an unreasonable request. Once I'd had a sip of a sauvignon blanc, I filled her in on our visit to the Bureau of Vital Statistics.

"How did Megan handle this piece of news?" Kate asked.

"How do you handle another bucket of possums? I don't think she was prepared to uncover a major and obviously illegal deception. But she still wants answers, and I plan to deliver."

"You two are a lot alike," Kate said.

"I think you're right, Doc. By the way, I spent some time talking to Graham Beadford, and there was no love lost between him and his brother." I recapped my conversation with Graham this morning and mentioned my theory that bankruptcy may have created the animosity

"Is Chief Fielder aware of that?" Kate asked, patting her wheat loaf into a glass pan.

"She should if she's been doing her job."

"But you could tell her." Kate removed her beet-stained canvas apron.

"You mean imply that Graham killed James?" I said.

"From what you've told me, sounds like Graham had years of pent-up resentment."

"Maybe so, but my take on Fielder is that she wants to handle this case her way without my help."

I heard footsteps in the hall leading to the kitchen and then Terry appeared in the entry. He stretched his arms over his head and said, "Hi, Abby." I swear his fingers touched the ceiling.

"Hey, Terry," I said. "You're looking especially . . . sleepy."

He walked up behind Kate and wrapped his long arms around her waist and kissed the top of her head. "I spent all last week and part of this one giving expert testimony in El Paso. I fell asleep about ten minutes after I got home this afternoon."

"You probably had too many fajitas and enchiladas while you were there. Those foods are directly linked to siestas, you know." I wanted to add, *And I hope you enjoyed your time away because the only tortillas you'll see here will be filled with alfalfa sprouts.* But since Kate doesn't always appreciate my humor, I kept my mouth shut.

Kate put her hands over his and said, "Sure you won't stay for dinner, Abby?"

I drained my wineglass. "No, thanks. If you visit Diva once a day while I'm gone, she'll be fine. I'll leave my itinerary on the kitchen table."

Kate came over and hugged me. "Have a safe trip."

As I left, Terry followed me out to my car. Before I got in, I said, "I tried to sneak you in a rump roast, but it wouldn't fit in my handbag."

He smiled. "Thanks for the thought. So you're taking a trip?"

"Kingston, Jamaica," I said.

"I went there once for a clinical psychology seminar. Got mugged right in front of the police station. Someone had told me that the tourists have to protect the cops from the criminals there and I knew it was no joke when I left. You be careful."

"I promise, big brother."

He bent and gave me a hug before I slid behind the wheel.

9

The next day I took a crowded flight on Air Jamaica that first stopped in Ocho Rios, a magnificent resort town I once visited with Kate and my father. It had been a high school graduation gift from him. We had climbed up the Dunn's River Falls and spent an afternoon playing with stingrays on a white beach. But those sweet memories were obliterated once we landed in Kingston. The instant I walked into the chaotic Norman Manley Airport terminal, I wished Megan had been born somewhere else. I might need a shot or two of spiced rum just to survive the trek to the taxi stand.

This is tourist season, I reasoned, rolling my bag toward the exit. *That's why all these people are shuttling to the U.S. with too much luggage.* But the tall women with waists about the size of dimes dressed in brilliant swaths of island fabric or every imaginable shade of spandex did not appear North American. So maybe the Rasta and ebony-skinned natives screeched and argued and laughed all day no matter what the time of year. And all to a reggae beat like the music coming from a far corner of the terminal. I felt crazy by the time I climbed into a lime green and checkerboard taxi manned by a driver who introduced himself as Jug.

"Where you go, miss?" he asked, steering out of the cab line.

"The Plaza." I tried not to look at the grimy seat beside me, knowing I was probably sitting on a cushion in similar condition.

"Ah, Plaza good choice, miss. Safe part of town." Jug—whose real name according to the faded license on his window visor was Thomas Anderson—laid on his horn. Why he was honking, I had no idea. Surely not for the ancient, diesel-smoking pickup a good twenty feet ahead of us. All the driver had done was tap his brakes.

But that was only the beginning. I was about to experience the most noisy, bumpy, and fascinating taxi ride of my life. And did I mention long? It took nearly an hour to travel about five miles because of the goat herds wandering the streets and the packs of wild dogs racing helter-skelter like the rabies-infested monsters they probably were.

By the time I made it to my very nice hotel room, thank you God, I felt dirty and tired and culture shocked. I may have loved the beautiful Ocho Rios, but this was like meeting her unshaven, potbellied father who was wearing nothing but boxer shorts. I had Jug's promise, however, that he would make my stay in Kingston as "trouble-free" as possible, or so he said. I hoped he was trustworthy, because he was picking me up at nine A.M. the next morning.

The hotel sat at the foot of the Blue Mountains, and from my seventh-story room, I had a spectacular view of a brilliant turquoise bay meeting a melon-colored horizon—all this provided free of charge by the setting sun. This vista was in such calming contrast to what I had just experienced on the streets of Kingston, I figured that's how folks maintained their sanity here. A walk on the beach below me could cure anyone's road rage in a minute.

After a fantastic room service meal of cod in white wine with onions and herbs, I used my computer/camera phone to connect to the Internet. I downloaded the address and a map for my trip to the Duchess of

Kent Hospital from a Jamaican health ministry Web site and then printed them out with my handy little travel printer. Then I made the mistake of lying down for a nap. I must have fallen asleep the minute my head hit the pillow, and the nap turned into ten hours of hard sleep. I had time only to shower, hop into some linen drawstring pants and a knit peach tank top, and grab two bananas from the breakfast buffet before meeting Jug outside the hotel.

"You rest good, miss?" he asked after I climbed in the backseat.

"Too good. I need to go to the Duchess of Kent Hospital. Do you know where that is?"

"Sure, miss, but if you sick, you can go to better place. I got a doc see you for cheap. Maybe ten bucks U.S." He had pulled away from the hotel and merged into traffic accompanied by a cacophony of blaring horns.

"I'm not sick," I said. "I'm trying to find a birth record."

"I know someone can make those, too. Paper like you need for them hard to come by, but this man— his name be Top Hat—he got a way to do anything, miss. Maybe cost you a hundred, U.S."

"Thanks again, Jug, but I don't need a new birth certificate. I need to find an old one." I smiled at him in the rearview.

"Sure thing, miss." His dark eyes glinted in the mirror with amusement. "Just remember everything in Jamaica cost you. You get what you want, but it cost you."

With that, the cab hit the largest pothole in the universe and I was catapulted to the cab's ceiling and hit my head. I slammed back into the seat where my tailbone made violent contact with the springs.

Jug seemed unperturbed by this bone-shaking experience, but I decided I might need the hospital for other things besides the birth record before this day was over.

*   *   *

An hour later—and I swear we traveled no more than two miles—Jug dropped me off in front of a dingy, stucco, two-story building that had to be a hundred years old. He gave me his card so I could call him when I'd finished my business and warned me that if I couldn't reach him, to take only a cab with a red license plate. These were apparently the "good guy taxis" registered in Jamaica.

I stood on the sidewalk, looking up at the weathered sign over the double wood front doors. This was indeed the Duchess of Kent Hospital, but the building looked like a neglected mission. Inside, however, I found no religiously garbed inhabitants but rather white coats, white nurse uniforms, white walls, and black people. And a volunteer wearing a striped apron who asked me how she could help. I produced a business card and handed it to her, but not one from Yellow Rose Investigations. This was one of my old CEO business cards from CompuCan. I no longer ran the company, but Kate and I were still majority owners, so the cards told a partial truth. I had decided to use this approach after my conversations with the Registrar General's Office. I was certain I would get absolutely nowhere with the government in Jamaica, but after visiting Sister Nell, I had learned all good things of value—like birth records—lie in computer databases. If this hospital had someone like her in charge of their records, I preferred to approach him or her directly for what I needed.

The lady with the striped apron had to make three phone calls to find out that they had a computer liaison with an office on the upper floor in what looked like a converted surgical suite—except the only surgery being done was on hard drives. The floor was littered with the guts of ancient PCs, though a few models were up and looked ready to go. Those sat side by side on a long brown folding table against a far wall. A man with messy bleached-blond hair and wearing a tropical shirt had his back to me. He was hunched over a keyboard, and though he switched off the monitor when I cleared my throat, I saw he'd been playing a video game.

"Hi," I said when he stood and faced me. "Are you the computer liaison?"

"Yeah. Dave. But if you're from Civil Registration, I'm still moving data. I told the last guy this is gonna take like a trillion years." Dave looked to be in his mid-twenties and his Valley-speak and freckled face marked him as American through and through.

"I'm not from Civil Registration." I walked across the white tile floor and handed him my CompuCan card.

He studied it so long you'd have thought he was reading a calculus textbook. "So? What's this mean?"

"Actually, you're not going to believe this, but I'm from a major computer software developer via my company CompuCan and I'm here to help."

As the unmistakable odor of marijuana permeated the space between us, his golden eyebrows pulled together. Apparently compound sentences triggered confusion in his pot-addled brain.

"Um, Dave? Could we sit and talk?" All monosyllabic words. Maybe they would do the trick.

"Sure. Whatever." He sat back in his computer chair, making no effort to find me so much as a stool.

I spied a straight-back chair resting against a wall behind a pile of ravaged PC towers, brought it over, and sat next to him. I then had to scoot farther away, fearing I might get high off the dope fumes emanating from his clothes and hair.

"As you probably know, the big cheese at the company, a man whose name I am not allowed to mention, has an estate in Grand Cayman," I said.

"You mean Bill?" he said.

"Yes." *If that name works for you, all the better.* "And after living near other less-affluent West Indies islands, he has decided to help the health care sector in these countries with a generous endowment. My company will be providing the technical support to see that his money is spent wisely, and I have arrived to assess various hospital computer needs here in Jamaica." Nice chunk of bullshit, even if I did say so myself.

"Cool," Dave said. "But maybe you should talk to an administrator."

"Do you think I would be here if that hadn't already happened?"

"Uh, I guess not." His freckled cheeks flushed.

Oh how I love the slow ones. "You must be from the states, correct?"

"Florida."

"And I see you're working under less than modern conditions."

"No shit," said Dave.

"What kind of network does this facility utilize?" I asked.

"Network? Are you kidding?"

"Okay, no network," I said. "What about the operating system? Unix?"

"Try Windows 2000," he answered, making a sweeping gesture around the room. "These machines are all donated, and most of them can't even support Windows Net Server much less the next generation."

I took out my computer phone, knowing that if this guy had any real geek in him, he'd start drooling the minute he saw it. "Mind if I check out the software? Make a few notes?"

He stared with undisguised lust at my phone. "Yeah. Guess that would be okay."

I held out the phone. "Do you have one of these?"

"No way. But I read about this model. You gotta charge them every day, right?"

"This one's ready to go. Want to play?"

"Wow. You mean it?"

I gave him the phone. "Meanwhile, I'll see what we need to do to improve the technology in this hospital."

"Hey. Go for it," Dave said. Unlike with Sister Nell and the U.S. government, privacy and confidentiality apparently meant nothing in this room.

I rose and went to the last computer on the table, booted up, and began exploring files on the hard drive. It was full of spreadsheets—hospital financial records dating back five years. If they had only five years worth in their databases, I was in trouble. But noting the PC was low on memory, I figured maybe this machine couldn't handle more than that. I moved to the next computer, and that's when I noticed a piece of masking tape stuck on the previous machine's tower. The word "billing" was written in black marker. If all the computers were similarly labeled my job just got a little easier.

The next computer tower was under the table and I bent and looked for its identifier. This one was marked "outpatient."

I glanced over at Dave. He was leaning back in his chair, eyes fixed on my phone, his hand moving the wand over the tiny keyboard. I swear he might have a techie orgasm any second.

I skipped the outpatient computer and moved on to the next one, which actually had a flat-screen monitor. When I looked below to check for a label, I noticed a landline Internet connection. Obviously this was the most modern computer in the room. And the label made me as eager as a dry steer scenting fresh water. It read *Births and Deaths*. Oh yes.

"Uh, Dave," I said. "I see you have Internet access here. What's that for?"

"I'm uploading a bunch of crap to Civil Registration. So far, I've reached 1995." He punched something on my phone and grinned, his eyes wide. "This is so awesome."

"And why are you sending these files to the government?"

He kept playing. "You know that bad-ass hurricane they had here about twenty years ago?"

"Gilbert?" Had to be. Everyone on the Gulf Coast knew about Gilbert and how lucky we'd been to be spared. The storm's hundred and sixty mile an hour winds had practically flattened Jamaica.

"Yeah. Gil Baby. Lots of records were lost. And more were lost when Ivan hit last year. Births, deaths, shit like that. Government's overhauling their vital stats and they want all the hospitals to send whatever they saved as far back as possible."

"I see."

"Took the guy who worked here before me about four years to enter stuff from old, practically unreadable medical charts. Some he could scan in, but most of them were in such bad shape he had to enter all the data manually."

"And now your job is to send the records to a central location?"

"Yeah, but if I had one of these babies," he said, caressing my phone, "shit, I'd be done in a month." He reluctantly held it out to me.

"Did you try getting on the Net?" I made no move to take the phone back.

"No. I only checked out the basics. Can't believe you have so much memory on this little thing."

I took the phone, entered my password, logged on, and handed it back. "It's satellite enabled. Surf away, dude."

He smiled and eagerly began to tap the keys again.

Everyone has their currency, I thought. I returned to the desktop computer and booted up. When the Internet connection screen opened, I hit connect and the PC dialed in. Meanwhile, I began searching the hard drive and soon found the file for the year Megan was born. I checked to make sure it contained demographic information on people who were born or died that year, then attached the records to an e-mail addressed to myself with the subject line "Lowest Mortgage Rates Guaranteed." That was in case Dave got curious when the message and attachment arrived on my phone in a few seconds. I hit send and the computer, circa maybe 2000, seemed to chug like a locomotive up a hill. I was used to high speeds and the latest software, and it seemed like a year later when I heard my phone ding, indicating an e-mail.

Dave offered a little Texas-Aggie-style "whoop" and said, "Hey, cool. You've got mail!"

No kidding, I said to myself, thanking those lucky Mary Jane leaves for providing me with this opportunity. Before I logged off, I went to the Sent Items folder on the ancient PC and deleted the e-mail.

Back at the hotel an hour later, I ordered a proper room service breakfast and eagerly opened the attachment I'd sent to myself—a large file containing text documents as well as scanned birth certificates. About five hundred of them, in fact, covering more than just the year Megan was born. Jeesh. This might take a while.

I decided to enjoy my breakfast first, something called bully beef served with johnnycakes. In Texas a johnnycake is a pancake, but these were more like fried biscuits. The meat tasted corned beef-ish spiced with herbs—thyme maybe?—and was mixed with tomatoes and onions. An unbelievably yummy combination. And the Blue Mountain coffee Jamaica was so famous for did not disappoint.

Once my belly was full and my brain was functioning on all cylinders again, I got to work. Unfortunately the file had not been organized chronologically. Not only were birth certificates scanned, but some entries were copies of pages from something called a "birth book." These entries were handwritten in a beautiful cursive. By early evening, after several breaks to rest my eyes and to walk off the stiffness in my back from hunching over the tiny screen, I had located all the birth records for girls born the same day as Megan. All three of them. Two were scanned certificates close to unreadable and one was from the birth book. I printed out all three.

Since nearly everyone in Jamaica, Rasta included, has British-sounding surnames, the mothers identified in these documents all sounded Anglo: Lucille Bodworth, Blythe Donnelly, and Mary Hanover. Didn't mean they were Caucasian like Megan. And fathers' names weren't included, so I feared that since twenty years had passed, I might have to spend a very long time hunting these people down.

I started with the easiest approach—the phone book in my nightstand—and decided to take the names alphabetically. An L. Bodworth was listed, so I dialed the number and a woman answered.

I said, "I'm trying to reach a Lucille Bodworth. Is she there?"

"I'm Lucy," she said in the cheerful Jamaican way I was becoming familiar with. Didn't mean I'd get anywhere with her, but she sounded pleasant enough.

And from her accent, she was probably as black as most of the islanders. I doubted she'd given birth to a blue-eyed blond baby. But I had to be certain, so I said, "My name is Abby Rose and I'm a private investigator. I'd like to discuss something with you and I was hoping we could meet for lunch?"

"Wait a minute, mon. Why should I meet up with some private cop? I didn't do nothing wrong." All her cheeriness had disappeared.

"Of course you didn't. I just want to ask you a few questions." I couldn't figure out a way to tactfully ask her what color her skin was. But even if she wasn't Megan's mother, she may have been in the hospital the same day Megan was born and that alone was worth exploring.

"So ask your questions," she said.

"I'd prefer to meet. I'm staying at the Plaza and they have a great restaurant. I'll send a cab for you and buy you lunch. How's that sound?"

She didn't speak for several seconds, then said, "You seem like an okay lady. Where you come from?"

"Texas," I said.

"Cowgirl? I never met a cowgirl. Guess it wouldn't hurt to talk, but I can get to you myself. Don't send no cab."

She told me she would be wearing a pink and yellow dress, and I headed to the lobby to wait. I paced around a grouping of chairs near a fountain wondering if I could be wrong. Maybe a Jamaican woman *could* give birth to a fair-skinned blond baby girl. *Yeah, and maybe rabbits will opt for birth control in the future.*

Twenty minutes later Lucy Bodworth arrived on the arm of a huge, lean man as black as she was. One question answered. But I still wasn't sure if this was the same woman from the hospital database. As far as I knew, the name Bodworth could be the equivalent of Smith in Jamaica.

"Are you Miss Rose?" said the man once I approached them near the front desk.

"Yes." I looked at the woman and smiled. "And you must be Lucy."

"True, and this is my brother Henry," she answered.

Indeed there was a resemblance. Same high cheekbones, same flawless, shiny skin. But I couldn't tell how old either one of them was. No stray gray hairs at their temples, no wrinkles either.

"Would you like to go to the restaurant now?" I asked.

"We're not hungry," said Henry in an accent far more on the British side than I had heard in Jamaica up until now. "We'd prefer the bar."

"Okay, that works for me." I was picking up on something I didn't quite like in his tone. Maybe it was him deciding for both of them about the hunger factor.

Once we sat down at a round table near a window, Lucy hit the plantain chips not a second after the waiter set the basket on the table. *I'm guessing she would have appreciated a meal, Henry,* I thought.

While we waited for our drinks, Lucy asked me where in Texas I was from and whether we had horses on the street and cattle in everyone's yard. She even seemed interested in my answers, but the serious Henry continued to unsettle me. Those dark eyes encircled by bloodshot whites never left my face.

Henry had ordered "aerated water," which I assumed was club soda, and Lucy opted for some concoction I'd never heard of. I chose Coke. When the drinks arrived, Henry rubbed the rim of his glass with a lime and said, "So what is this about?"

"I'm looking for a woman who delivered a baby about twenty years ago." I turned to Lucy. "Did you have a baby at the Duchess of Kent Hospital back then?"

Lucy started to open her mouth, but Henry put a hand on her forearm. "Why do you want to know?"

"Three babies were born that day and one was a white infant who was later adopted. I'm looking for that baby's mother and wonder if you might remember the other women who were there. My client wants a reunion." I directed this toward Lucy, hoping to show her that I was one of the good guys and just wanted to make a young woman happy.

"So you want to know what Lucy remembers?" Henry said.

"Yes." I folded my hands on the table and leaned toward Lucy. "Can you help me?"

But once again, it was Henry who spoke. "How much is this information worth to your client?"

Remembering Jug's words about how everything costs in Jamaica, I felt foolish for not realizing sooner why Henry had come with his sister. They were wanting money before I even knew whether they had information.

"Hmm," I said. "Maybe I could decide how much *after* you tell me if Lucy was in the hospital to deliver a baby that day."

"Sure she was. The young man is in school now or

we could bring him here and show you," said Henry, responding to my obvious displeasure with a smile—the first I'd seen from him.

Henry had slipped up big-time, though. The Lucille Bodworth I was looking for had given birth to a girl so this obviously was a con.

I stood. "Thanks for meeting with me, but our business is finished. I'll tell the bartender to give you another round on me for your trouble."

When I started to walk away, Henry's huge hand came down on my arm as I passed him. His grip was so tight and cruel I couldn't move.

"Lucy's got a good memory, mon," he said. "So don't go away so fast." His refined British accent had disappeared, and though he was grinning, his voice told a different story.

"Let go of me," I said loud enough for the few other patrons to hear.

The bartender slipped from behind the bar and headed in our direction. Henry must have seen him, too, because he released me and held up his hands in a surrendering gesture.

"Just trying to make a deal for both of us, mon," he said.

I mouthed a thank-you at the bartender as I made my escape. *Welcome to Jamaica, Abby,* I thought as I entered the elevator and headed back to my room.

The encounter had at first unnerved me, but then I got angry—and more at myself than at the brother-sister con team. *People lie all the time,* I rationalized as I made my way to the exercise room a half hour later. But I was still steamed and decided a little time on the treadmill might clear my head. After an hour of walking, I spent thirty minutes in the hot tub. Once I had relaxed, I was able to refocus on why I came to Jamaica in the first place.

I returned to my room, showered, and went back to the phone book to see if Blythe Donnelly, the mother written up in the birth book, had a listed number. She didn't, but these days finding anything unlisted is no problem. Still, finding her number turned out to be tougher than I thought. After several hours searching every Internet directory more than once, I finally came up with an unlisted number and street address.

But after this afternoon's encounter in the bar, I was now painfully aware the Donnelly woman might not be the person I was looking for. I'd be on the lookout for game players this time. My next move was to call Jug.

He didn't answer.

I considered waiting until tomorrow to pursue the lead, but I hadn't made the trip to sit around a hotel room, so I changed from my shorts and halter top into capris and a T-shirt, stuffed my phone and the address in my bag, hurried out of the hotel, and hailed the first cab that drove by.

The driver was nothing like my congenial Jug. This guy spoke in grunts, had matted long dreadlocks, and smelled like a curry factory. He also played reggae on the radio so loud you could probably hear it in Mexico. All my senses were grateful when we arrived at the address atop a hill on the outskirts of the city. I asked him to wait and he informed me in speech suddenly devoid of grunts that I would have to pay him the fare up to this point. Impatient idiot that I was, I handed over most of the Jamaican bills I possessed, figuring I could replenish my funds at the hotel when he took me back to the Plaza.

He promptly floored the taxi and pulled away. No red license plate, I noted before the car sped out of sight down the narrow gravel road. Too bad I hadn't remembered Jug's warning before I handed over the money. But I had Jug's number in my purse and hoped I could reach him once I was done here. Either that or I would be taking a very long walk back to the city.

The house was a one-story pink stucco with paned

windows and a low white rail fence. The yard, lush with palms, trees, and bushes, was dabbed with brilliant hibiscus-like flowers of magenta, fuchsia, and orange along the sloping backyard. Whoever lived here probably made a decent living—and liked their privacy. The nearest house was probably a half mile away.

Just as I opened the gate and started up the path to the front door, a porch light came on. It wasn't quite dark, so I assumed whoever was inside had seen me approach the door. But when I knocked and then knocked again, no one answered.

I made my way along a stone path through the yard and around to the back. I saw no garage, just a small shed and a cleared space where a car had obviously been parked many times if the numerous oil stains were any indicator. No car today, though. Maybe a child who was home alone had turned the light on and then thought better about answering. I knocked on the weather-worn back door, noting the paint was peeling all the way down to bare wood. Then I called, "Is anyone home? I need some help." I hated to exploit a child who might love to help me, but heck, I had no ride and plenty of time, so exploitation seemed in order.

But that didn't get any response, either. Damn.

I sidestepped to the window five feet to my right and pressed my nose against the pane. The madras plaid curtains were not fully closed and I stared into a tiny, neat kitchen. In a room beyond, another light cast a haze in the entry. And then I saw why. A timing device was attached to an outlet in the kitchen. The lights had been programmed to come on. No one was home.

I went back to the door and tried the knob. Naturally it was locked and when I checked the window, I met similar resistance. But I figured my getting stranded up here was a sign, one telling me I shouldn't leave until I'd accomplished *something*. I needed to find out if Blythe Donnelly was Megan's mother before I left the island and this seemed like my best chance.

I walked around to the other side of the house and found a frosted glass window too high up to peer into. Probably the bathroom. I wasn't tall enough to see if it was latched shut, nor was I sure I could fit through that opening if it happened to be unlocked. But I was damn sure going to try.

Breaking and entering in a foreign country is *not* a smart move, but I was willing to risk it. It just felt like the right thing to do, the PI thing to do. I'd heard no sounds of life in the vicinity aside from the distant barking of the dogs that seemed to own this city, that and the squawking of a macaw in the huge, gnarled mahogany tree at the edge of the property. I'd be in and out and no one would know the difference.

I walked over to the shed. Getting in there proved no problem. The door was open, probably because the small building held nothing of value. There were trash cans, a box filled with house paint, some garden tools, an old metal bucket, and a plastic milk crate. I'd been hoping for a stepladder, but no such luck.

I had no choice except to use the bucket and milk crate. I carried them over to the window and stacked them underneath. Not the most secure stepping stones to my target, but it would work. My purse was a problem, so I pocketed the phone as well as the small flashlight from my key ring, then stashed my leather bag behind an aloe vera plant alongside the house.

Now for the window. Tottering on my makeshift ladder, I fit my fingers under the sash and pushed up. I heard a little cracking sound, like paint loosening. I kept working away until a small space appeared at the bottom. One last shove with the now sore heels of my hands and the old window gave up the fight. I raised the glass completely. The opening proved not as small as I'd anticipated, and I managed to pull myself half-way through before the bucket toppled off the crate. Getting out wouldn't be as easy as getting in.

On my descent into the bathroom, I hit my knee on a faucet and cursed under my breath before getting my footing in the tub. Now that the sun had finally set, the room was dark and I had to let my eyes adjust for a second. I then climbed out of the tub, my heart going ninety to nothing. Even though no one seemed to be home, I'd never climbed into a stranger's house through a window before. But the adrenaline surge came more from excitement than fear. I was kinda liking this little adventure.

The bathroom door was open and I peered out. The light I'd noted after looking through the window shed a muted glow down a narrow hall straight ahead. I went in that direction and came to a living room lit by one table lamp beside a burgundy loveseat. A telephone table by the front door was piled with unopened mail so I went over and searched for a recent letter and checked the postmark. The mail had started piling up about a week ago. Then I noticed a hand-written note on the floor. Seems someone with the first initial K was caring for the house. That someone could drop by at any time. Better get busy.

I decided the writing desk would yield the most information, and after several minutes spent examining the contents of every drawer and cubbyhole, I discovered Blythe Donnelly worked as an accountant for a real estate firm. But that was about all I learned. Either she shredded her bank statements and other bills, or she didn't keep them in this desk. I moved on to the bedroom.

Thanks to closed wood shades I had to turn on my flashlight to find the lamp on a small bedside table. I switched it on. A white matelassé coverlet and two plump pillows graced the high queen-sized bed. An embroidered footstool, the Shaker-style bed tables, and a matching dresser were the only furniture. But on the bureau, a photograph of a woman standing beside an island native who had the hugest teeth I'd ever seen caught my attention. She had her arm around the man and they were both holding fishing poles. I walked over and picked up the framed picture for closer examination, then whispered, "Uh-oh."

I had found the mystery woman from the wedding, the woman Mason Dryer had captured in his composite. The same woman Quinn Fielder wanted to question. The woman who might well be Megan's mother.

10

As I set down the photograph, Blythe Donnelly's house suddenly seemed smaller. And since I had neglected to close the bathroom window, mosquitoes had joined me, buzzing around my head like little vultures. Before I went to shut the window, I took out my phone and clicked off a couple shots of the photograph, using my flashlight to enhance the meager light.

I retraced my steps to the bathroom, thoughts zinging through my head like the bugs surrounding me. How had Donnelly ended up at Megan's wedding? Had the inquiries I made prior to last Saturday reached her somehow? Or had someone else informed her that her daughter was about to get married?

But when I slid the window shut, I decided I was jumping to conclusions. I had no hard proof Megan was Blythe Donnelly's child, just a pile of circumstantial evidence. I needed DNA to be positive—and I was standing in a houseful of the stuff. Being no expert on evidence collection, I wasn't sure what would be the best thing to take with me. On TV all you needed was a damn coffee cup. I glanced around the bathroom, but nothing jumped out at me. I started to open the medicine cabinet above the pedestal sink but then spotted a toothbrush. Did toothpaste ruin DNA? I had no idea, but I took it anyway, wrapped it in some toilet tissue, and put it in my pocket.

I then returned to the bedroom to see what else I

could find to connect Blythe Donnelly to Megan. After opening the closet I immediately surmised the woman lived alone. The beige, chocolate, tan, ecru, and white clothing all seemed to be the same petite size. No men's suits, shirts, or trousers.

I dragged over the footstool so I could get a look at the top shelf of the closet, all the while wondering why I didn't feel an ounce of guilt for rifling through a stranger's house. But Daddy always said the truly guilty run even when no one is chasing them, so maybe my sense of purpose made guilt no more than a second thought.

I spied a taped-up box in a far corner advertising Myer's Rum in bold letters. When I slid the box toward me, I knew it didn't hold bottles. Too light. I took the box down from the shelf and set it on the floor. It was bound with old, yellowed tape, and I guessed it had been stashed up there for some time. I peeled off the tape and did a damn poor job. Next time Donnelly looked at this box, she would know it had been opened.

The box was only half full and on top of the meager stack of papers I found the deed to the house and an attached real estate contract. Donnelly had paid cash twenty years ago. If that's when she came to Jamaica, the timing was right.

Next I found a Grand Cayman bank account statement with a six-figure balance dated about the same time, but the account had been closed several months later. Since these were the only financial records I'd found, I figured she kept everything else locked away somewhere, probably in a bank or a concealed safe. She obviously had a source of income because she'd purchased five cars during her time in Kingston—and those were all bought with cash, according to the receipts I found.

Then I came to a stack of pictures, all poor-quality snapshots. The first was Donnelly with another fishing pole, only she was much younger in this photo. The others showed her trekking through mountains, riding a bicycle, or fishing the turquoise waters of the Caribbean. Aside from whoever took the pictures, she was alone.

Near the bottom of the box I found an old passport—had to be old because it was olive green. I opened to the first page, but nothing had been written in the spots for name and address or whom to notify in an emergency. I turned to the photo page and Blythe Donnelly stared at me, her hair dyed black, her face unsmiling and haggard. The passport had been issued the year Megan was born, and if Dryer's composite had shown a likeness, this unflattering photo of the younger Donnelly revealed a stressed and troubled woman who did not favor Megan as much as the composite, though the resemblance was still there. I photographed every page of the passport, noting Donnelly had been born in Dallas in 1961.

Finally I picked up an unsealed envelope as aged around the edges as the tape that had secured the box. Inside was a folded document and a plastic hospital ID bracelet—a tiny band with a pink sticker attached and the words *Donnelly female* written in blue ink. I opened the paper and read, but I didn't comprehend what I was seeing.

The document bore an official seal, was signed by a Dr. Johnson and cosigned by Elizabeth Benson, midwife. It was a death certificate for an eight-pound baby girl born the same day and year as Megan, with the baby's death from "birth complications" occurring a day later.

"This doesn't make sense," I whispered.

About then I realized that I had been so focused on what I'd found that I had pushed all other noise to the background. But the sound of my voice must have brought me back to reality.

The dogs I had heard in the distance when I first arrived now seemed to be in the near vicinity. Like right outside the house.

I quickly clicked off shots of the death certificate

and bracelet until my phone battery bleeped a warning. Damn. Any power left would be needed to call Jug, praying he answered this time. Then I remembered his number was in my purse, the one stashed outside the bathroom window. *Brilliant move, Abby.*

I replaced the box's contents in roughly the same order, then returned box and footstool to their original spots. I shut off the bedroom light and went back down the hallway to the kitchen. The dogs sounded like they were at the back door and I peeked out the window. I couldn't see them, but they were close. And from all the snarling and yapping I was hearing, I feared I was about to have a less than pleasant encounter with them.

I started opening cupboards and looking through drawers for a key that might get me through the deadbolted front door, but the only thing I accomplished was to make enough noise to draw the dogs closer. I flicked a switch by the back door—also dead-bolted— and an outside light came on. I had hoped this would scare them away and maybe it did, because it got real quiet.

I peered out the window again.

There they were, staring at the door, stone still, heads cocked. Four of them. Skinny, mangy, toothy animals—all mutts about the size of German shepherds. Four against one. I didn't like the numbers. And then another one came prancing around the corner of the house.

And the little bastard was clutching my purse in a very strong-looking jaw.

Christ on a cracker! I needed a dead bolt key and about a pound of steak to distract them. But then I noticed a glass cookie jar on the counter filled with dog biscuits.

Now I understood the canine interest in this house. Donnelly must like these critters. Either that, or throwing food at them was the only way she could escape.

I grabbed a handful of biscuits, went to the bathroom, and climbed into the tub. I'm a good whistler, thank God, and sure enough the dog pack started barking and I soon heard them whining and yapping outside the window. I balanced on the edge of the tub and tossed several biscuits out the window as far as I could. The four hungry ones raced after them, but the one with my purse didn't budge. The animal sat down and stared at me.

"Nice puppy," I whispered, using a sweet, gentle tone. I began to wiggle out the window, head first, still muttering, "Good doggie, nice doggie." When I was almost out, I tossed a biscuit at the dog's feet.

She didn't even glance at it—had to be female what with this strange attachment to my bag. But the other dogs must have caught on because they turned and started back toward me. I threw the rest of the food at them, but being half in and half out of the house limited my skill as a pitcher. The biscuits didn't go as far as I'd hoped, so I had to move fast. I ducked under the sash, tumbled out through the window, and rolled onto the grass.

"Hello, baby," I said to my purse thief.

We were practically nose to nose.

She sat—definitely a girl—and her tail swept back and forth on the lawn. Deciding this was just a big baby with a prize to show off, I offered my hand.

But the others must have had noses on their tails because they turned again and came running after the biscuit she still hadn't touched. She moved closer to me as they pounced for the food.

One treat and four dogs fighting for it raises plenty of dust and fur. But above their yelps and growls, I heard the unmistakable sound of a car engine. Then tires grinding up the gravel road. I could be staring down the barrel of a real dilemma if the person who'd been collecting the mail, or even Blythe Donnelly herself was coming home.

I had to get my purse back. Now.

"Can I have that, baby?" I said softly.

More tail wagging. No growling.

I placed a tentative hand on the dog's broad, golden skull and stroked.

She dropped my bag and I let out the breath I'd been holding. But my relief was short-lived because the others had gotten over their tiff now that the last biscuit was gone and they were creeping toward me, snarling all the way.

I picked up the purse, stood and stepped back, reaching in the bag for Jug's card.

Four sets of canine teeth were bared, but then something unexpected happened. Purse Dog came to my rescue. She faced my aggressors, putting herself between them and me. Meanwhile I found Jug's number, took my phone from my pocket, poised my flashlight over it, and dialed as fast as my shaking fingers would allow.

He answered on the first ring.

"I need you in a hurry," I said and gave him the address. He said okay. The battery warning sounded again right after he hung up. Too much picture taking.

The teeth-baring standoff between the dogs grew louder and then I saw a light sweeping the ground on the other side of the house, a light headed in my direction.

I was scanning the landscape for a hiding place when I heard a loud *pop*.

One of the dogs yipped and took off running, tail between its legs. The others followed—all except for my friend. She stood her ground.

The pop had come from a rifle—seems the owner of the flashlight happened to have a weapon. And a uniform. And when he came up to me with that rifle pointed at my chest, I also noticed he had *Dog Police* embroidered above his pocket.

Then he changed his focus and targeted my partner, pumping his rifle several times.

The idiot planned to shoot her.

"Hey! This is my dog and if you hurt her, I'll have you arrested," I said.

He looked at me and grinned. "Is that so, mon?"

"Yes. She and I are locked out of my house and—"

"You don't live here and neither does she." He gestured at my friend with his gun. "I chase that bitch two, three times a week."

Okay. Lie number one failed. Try another. "I do live here and I want to adopt this wonderful—"

"Miss Donnelly live here long time, so unless she die and give you this place, you don't belong here. The cops pay me nice for burglars. You a burglar?"

If he was asking, I still had hope of getting myself out of this mess. "Of course I'm not a burglar. Blythe and I go back a long way and—"

"Miss Donnelly keep to herself and I never seen you round here."

Lie number three also seemed doomed to failure. Maybe I could salvage it. "We haven't seen each other in years, but—"

"First time she leaves the island you comes round here opening her windows." He nodded up at my escape hatch. "She no like that stuff. Now you and me, we gonna visit the jail."

He stepped toward me, but the dog and I had definitely bonded. She growled.

The guy raised his rifle and aimed.

"No! Please don't!" I raised my hands in surrender. "What can I do to make you listen?" I was thinking of money and at the same moment remembering I had very little to offer.

He lowered the muzzle slightly. Then I heard another car approaching. The cop turned his head, and we both saw Jug's cab pull up to the shed.

"I think my ride is here," I said.

Jug got out of the cab and called, "Hey, beast! What you do with my lady?"

"This bobo your lady?" the cop said.

"Yeah and she be some bobo, mon. Give me plenty agony, though."

Both of them laughed and if I read their tone correctly, I'd say lecherous was the operative adjective.

But if trash talk worked, I'd play along. "Hey, honey, this is the dog I was telling you about." I placed a protective hand on my rescuer's head.

"You no want that flea bag," Jug said.

The cop smiled. "Hey, lady says she wants to take the dog home, you take the dog. But you know I need something from the both of you, mon. See, your lady's story been changin' every five seconds. She don't know when to shut up."

I started to answer his insult with one of my own but realized he was right. I bit my lip.

Jug reached in his pocket and pulled out a wad of Jamaican bills. "This is all I got, mon."

The dog catcher took the money and counted it, shaking his head. "Cops pay me way better if I bring them a burglar."

I pulled out my wallet. Travelers checks do not make great bribes. He didn't want them. And what little Jamaican money I had left didn't please him either. But he liked my watch, my sapphire ring and my tiny gold bead earrings. He also liked my phone, but when I balked, Jug offered a heavy gold chain from around his neck and that was enough to buy my freedom. Once he'd cleaned us out he went away.

While Jug closed the bathroom window and returned the crate and pail to the shed, I tried to interest the dog in the only thing I had left—my Altoids. She liked chasing them, but kept bringing them back and dropping them at my feet.

When Jug was finished covering up my crime, he and I walked to the cab, the dog panting happily after us. I tried to say good-bye, but she looked so pitiful and I was so worried she had an air rifle attack in her imminent future, I pleaded with Jug to take her along with us. He looked unhappy, but didn't really argue all that much as he pushed the dog into the backseat. Then Jug and me and the dog drove off together.

11

Knowing the Plaza Hotel would shun a canine addition to my room, Jug drove us to his place. He lived in a shack on the mountainside that actually looked in far better shape than the other dilapidated houses in his neighborhood.

"My wife gonna kill me when she see this dog, miss. You gotta help me explain." Jug had taken a piece of rope from his trunk and tied it around the dog's neck to use as a leash.

Between the fleas she'd shared with me on the ride over and the mosquitoes that had attacked me at Donnelly's house, I felt ready to crawl out of my skin.

"I owe you big-time," I said, scratching my ankle, "so whatever I can do, I will."

The three of us made our way up the dirt path to a front porch strung with brightly colored bulbs. Maybe it was always Christmas in Jamaica. Jug tied the dog to a rickety railing surrounding the porch and opened the front door.

"Where you been, mon?" called a feminine voice after the door opened.

The smell of curried something filled the small room we entered. Sitting on a rustic-looking bench were three smiling black-skinned children. The two boys and a toddler girl switched their attention from a thirteen-inch combination TV and VCR playing cartoons and grinned at Jug. They all shared his same wide smile.

"Hi," I said. "I'm Abby."

They just stared back at me, and the girl put four fingers in her mouth.

Then Jug's wife appeared in the entry to what I assumed was the kitchen. She wore a red and yellow striped strapless dress and was beautiful in that unique Jamaican way—long necked, dark and tall, her hair in beaded dreadlocks. She was also very pregnant.

Wiping her hands on a thin white towel stretched like an apron over her firm round belly, she nodded at me, then turned questioning eyes on Jug.

"This be the lady I been working for," he said. He gestured at me. "Miss Rose, this is my Martha."

"Call me Abby," I said.

Martha smiled tentatively, but the smile immediately disappeared when the dog barked.

"You didn't bring no dog round here, Jug," she said, sounding more than a little pissed off.

Jug elbowed me. "You tell her."

"Actually, *I* brought the dog," I said. "It's kind of a long story, and—"

But before I could finish speaking, Jug's two oldest—the boys wearing torn T-shirts and shorts—leaped off the bench and streaked past us through the screen door.

I looked out after them and saw the dog kissing both of them with an enthusiasm dogs only heap on children.

"How many times I tell you we can't afford no dog, Jug? We got too many mouths to feed already," Martha said.

"I plan to fix that," I said quickly, hoping to curb her obvious anger. "I'm hiring your husband for an important job."

Jug looked at me with surprise, an expression that clued Martha in at once.

"We don't take no charity here, miss," she said coldly.

Just then the girl, who had been watching us with

wide dark eyes, began to whimper. Jug walked over, swooped her up in his arms, and kissed her. She buried her head in his neck.

"This won't be charity," I said. "I have to get back home but I haven't finished my work here and I'm hoping Jug can help me."

"What kind of work?" she said warily.

"Before I explain, do you have any cortisone cream?" I had been resisting the urge to rake my nails up and down my arms until they bled.

Martha came over, lifted one arm, and examined the red welts that had risen there. I looked like I had the chicken pox.

She made a tisking sound, shaking her head at what she saw. "I got no cortisone, but I got something else." She pulled me toward the kitchen, saying, "Jug, go make sure that dog don't send any fleas onto my boys."

After my arms had been treated with pulverized aloe vera leaves mixed with some other plant Martha ground up with, and after we'd all eaten bowls of curried rice and jerk chicken, Martha gave each child a sugarcane stalk to suck on and sent them back to the little TV.

"You really got a job for Jug?" Martha asked.

We were sitting around a cotton blanket on the tile floor near a stone hearth in the kitchen. Martha had stacked our wooden bowls to one side and gave Jug and I small glasses of amber rum.

"I do have a job, if he's willing. First, though, let me tell you why I'm here." I sipped my drink, and though I always add Diet Coke to my rum, this needed no additions. It was delicious and warm, and if I drank enough, I figured my still stinging arms and legs wouldn't be bothering me. I'd be passed out.

Jug had heard some of my story on the way over here, but Martha listened intently, and gently rubbed her belly when I mentioned the tiny pink bracelet and death certificate I'd found in Donnelly's house.

"The death certificate is making me wonder if I'm on the wrong track," I said. "I'm hoping Jug can do a little research on the island while I go back home and try to find out more about Blythe Donnelly. I have the name of the midwife who attended the birth and—"

"What's her name?" Martha and Jug said almost in unison.

"Elizabeth Benson," I replied.

They both nodded knowingly.

"You know her?" I said.

"Just the name," said Jug. "Jamaica is not a big place, miss, and we got plenty experience with midwives."

Martha rolled her eyes. "Too much experience, you ask me." But she smiled at Jug, who reached over and took her hand.

"I'd like you to find this woman, see what she remembers about Donnelly and her baby."

"What if he can't find her?" Martha said.

"Then he can't find her, but he still gets paid for looking. His time is valuable."

She laughed. "That be news to me."

Jug slapped her knee playfully. "I can find anyone. Cost you a hundred dollars U.S. Special deal for you."

"Let me decide the price, okay? I guarantee you it will be more than a hundred."

Martha grinned widely. "Oh, he can do it okay, now that you gonna give us enough for the dog. Gonna take lots of trouble to get rid of those fleas."

Jug looked at her, eyes bright with what I could have sworn were tears. I think he wanted that dog as much as the kids did.

"We call her Bobo, like the cop called missy here," he said with a smile.

He and Martha laughed loudly, so of course I had to ask. "And just what does bobo mean?"

Martha said, "Bobo means fool, mon."

12

I sat in the quietest corner of the Kingston airport—
a spot more at din level than the chaos level fifty yards
away. My plane to Houston would board in about
fifteen minutes, so I took out my freshly charged cell
phone. I had plenty of voice messages.

I'd thought about listening to them when I woke
up, but I'd slept longer than I should have after last
night's activity and had enough time before coming
here only to have Jug drive me to a bank. We set up
an account for him and I deposited two hundred dollars. Once I got back home, another ten grand would
appear by electronic transfer—something I hadn't told
him. I wanted it to be a nice surprise. He'd saved my
butt, and God knows he needed money for his family.
Meanwhile, I'd provided him with a printout of the
birth book record and death certificate. He seemed
eager to hunt down the midwife and ask her what she
remembered, if anything. When he'd dropped me off
at Norman Manley Airport, we'd said our good-byes
and hugged like the good friends we'd become. I
would miss that guy.

I accessed my voice mail, bending over and plugging
one ear so I could hear. The first message was from
Jeff asking me how I liked Jamaica and telling me
he'd be gone for a few days to pick up a murder
suspect who had fled to Seattle. The next was from

Kate asking when I'd be home and telling me that Diva was pouting. Gee. What a surprise.

The last voice message was from Graham Beadford, and I immediately wondered how he'd gotten my cell number, but then I recalled I'd given it to Roxanne, so she'd probably given it to him. He said he wanted to meet with me about a matter "of interest to us both" and provided his suite number at the resort where he was staying.

This has money written all over it, I thought. But I wasn't about to invest time or money in someone suffering from Anheuser's disease. My ex had cured me of getting involved with alcoholics for a lifetime.

I erased the messages, then called Angel's cell number. He answered on the second ring.

"Hi, Angel. I was wondering if you could do a little research for me on my case."

"Sure. I got nothing going right now except watching this dentist lady cheat on her husband. Galleria tryst. A little window shopping for jewelry, a little wine drinking, a little stayover in a fancy hotel. Like watching an old episode of *Lives of the Rich and Famous.*"

I told him about the progress I'd made on Megan's behalf and asked him to check out Blythe Donnelly, born in Dallas in 1961. He told me that as soon as he snapped a few pictures of the lovebirds exiting the hotel, he'd head back to the office and get busy. I thanked him and clicked the phone off.

I had just enough time before I boarded to visit the duty-free shop. Jamaican rum makes for good sleep, mon. Martha had taught me that much.

True to Kate's report, Diva was aloof when I arrived home that evening. But she warmed up as soon as I sat down in the living room with my Diet Coke. I gave her some much-needed attention, then called Kate to tell her I was home. I filled her in on my trip, not sharing exactly how I'd learned the things I was telling her. She must have been tired because she didn't ask too many questions. I had just hung up when my doorbell rang.

I went to the foyer, saw Angel through the peep-hole, and quickly opened the door.

"Did a drive-by to see if you were home yet and saw your car," he said after I let him in.

"Want a drink?" I asked. "Got some nice rum."

"No, thanks." He was holding a large brown enve-lope and as usual looked like he came right off the dry cleaner's rack—pressed white shirt, creased kha-kis, and a silver belt buckle, this one so huge it must have weighed five pounds.

"Come on in and sit awhile," I said, leading him through the foyer.

He glanced around as we entered the living room. "Nice place. Nice neighborhood. You like this better than River Oaks?"

"A million times better. So were you able to find out anything on Blythe Donnelly?" I asked, eager to get my hands on that envelope.

"What there is to know." He sat on one end of the sofa and crossed his legs, which showed off his worn but well-cared for alligator boots.

"Because she's lived in Jamaica so long?" I sat, too.

"There's not much to know because she didn't live all that long." He opened the envelope.

"What are you talking about?" I said.

"She's dead, Abby. She died in 1974." He removed a sheet of paper and handed it to me.

It was a copy of a small newspaper article from the *Dallas Morning News,* the death notice for Blythe Donnelly, who had passed on from "complications of cancer" at the age of thirteen. The notice was very detailed, probably a last tribute written by a devas-tated family who had lost someone they loved far too soon.

I said, "Okay, so maybe the woman in Jamaica is a different Blythe Donnelly. Maybe—"

"That's possible, but not likely. I don't think two Blythe Donnellys were born on the same day in the same year in Dallas, Texas, do you?"

"You're right," I said. "And considering what I found in Donnelly's house—cash transactions, a large bank account disappearing, the lack of friends—I'm betting there's an explanation."

"I won't ask how you gained access to that information," he said.

"I seem to have forgotten myself," I said with a grin.

"Just so you understand that this person you're tracking is using a stolen identity and could be in big trouble."

"I understand. So now what?" I said.

"This could be tough," he answered. "We're not dealing with someone stealing personal information to rob a person blind. This sounds more like a woman who needed to disappear. And there could be a hundred reasons why."

"Criminal reasons?" I asked.

"Or personal," he said. "A way out of a tough life."

"So what's my next step?" I asked.

"There are several ways to go at this, but I'd begin by checking missing person reports around the time this woman showed up in Jamaica."

"That's probably a humongous number of people," I said.

"Not necessarily. You have a location—Dallas—and that narrows the field. Not likely someone in Maine would hunt up death certificates in Dallas trying to find a good candidate for their identity theft. We weren't exactly a nation of computer users back then."

"You've got a point," I said. "So I'll definitely start with missing persons."

"If you need any help with your research, let me know. I've got connections in Dallas, a few friends who used to be cops up that way." He stood and I followed suit. "And now I better get home. Becky's cooking venison stew and I'm not about to miss out." He patted his starched, flat belly.

After Angel left, I headed straight for my office, but once I sat down behind my desk, I paused. Angel had mentioned death certificates. If Donnelly wasn't really Donnelly, maybe the *baby's* death certificate wasn't real either. Maybe Donnelly had been trying to hide the child as well as herself. And maybe the records copied to my phone computer could offer additional information. So I transferred all the birth and death files from the e-mail message onto my desktop PC.

It took me only fifteen minutes to discover that the baby's death certificate had not been scanned or even manually keyed into this particular database, though loads of other information from that year had been compiled. The infant's records could have been lost in the hurricane . . . and then there was the other possibility. The baby's death had been faked.

But though I wanted to get busy on this angle, the doorbell rang again and this time the visitor was not nearly as welcome as Angel.

"What can I do for you, Aunt Caroline?" I asked when I opened the door. "Because I'm busy working on—"

"A murder case in Seacliff?" she asked sweetly.

Damn. That's all I needed was her dipping her pen in my ink. Kate must have let something slip. "Listen, I'd love to visit, but—"

"Do you know a police person named Fielder?" she asked.

Double damn. Better find where this leak had come from and shut off that faucet as soon as I could. "Come on in," I said.

I offered her a drink, and once we were seated on the sofa, her with a glass of white wine and me with the rum and Coke, she said, "So tell me what you've been up to, Abigail."

"Why don't you go first? Obviously you've been snooping around in my business."

"Why would you think that?" She offered her best shocked and dismayed expression. "And I really don't appreciate your tone, considering I came here to offer you valuable information."

I needed this woman in my life like an armadillo needs an interstate. But knowing her, I'd better play nice or she'd clam up. "Sorry if I sounded rude, but I've had a long day. What information are you talking about and what's this about Fielder?"

She smiled and sipped her wine, leaving bright pink lip marks on the rim. "You know how much I care about you, Abigail. And I'm concerned for your welfare. So before I tell you, why don't you explain how you got mixed up in all this?"

I knew why she wanted to know and it had nothing to do with my well-being. The next time she played a foursome at the country club, she hoped for center stage with her society friends. And she would get exactly that if she could reveal unpublished details about James Beadford's death. The quickest way to find out what she knew and get rid of her was to give her just enough information to satisfy her.

I summarized what had happened at the wedding reception, focusing more on the response of the guests than on anything substantive. I mentioned the scream, the ensuing chaos, how long we all had to stay in the house. She then asked who did the catering, what the bride wore, and did I think the wedding gown was totally ruined? It seemed clear she didn't give a rat's ass how this tragedy affected Megan and her family.

"Now tell me about Fielder," I said. "How did you connect her name with mine? Did you read it in the newspaper?"

"She called me," Aunt Caroline said, looking as proud as a cat with a mouthful of feathers.

I blinked. "Wait a minute. She called you? Not the other way around?"

Aunt Caroline picked a piece of lint off her camel wool slacks. "She had a lot of questions about you, Abigail. And she certainly knew plenty about your past."

I took a hefty swallow of my drink. What the hell was Fielder doing?

"And the gist of these questions?" I asked.

"She wanted to know if you had a personal relationship with the Beadford family and if so for how long. Of course I couldn't answer that question."

"What do you mean you couldn't answer? I told you the last time you were here that Megan hired me a few months ago."

"Have you forgotten how you cut me out of your life since last summer?" she said. "What makes you think I would know who your friends are or—"

"This has nothing to do with my friends. What else did she want to know?" I was pissed off and she knew it.

Her smug smile disappeared. "I came here to inform you about the call from Fielder, so don't get irritable, Abigail. Because you've been out of town, which I had to hear from this police woman, too, I was unable to offer this information sooner."

"Fielder knew about my trip?"

"She said you went to Jamaica. Whatever were you doing there? The Bahamas or Grand Cayman are a far more preferable—"

"So she's been following me? Bugging my phone? What?"

"I have no idea. When we spoke, she seemed very interested in the unpleasantness at your house last summer. The murder, the subsequent—"

"She could have read about all that in archived newspapers or HPD reports, so why contact you?"

"She told me she's gathering background on those who attended the wedding and she certainly couldn't call that austere Detective Kline for information considering how the two of you are . . . *involved*."

"It's *Sergeant* Kline," I said tersely, wishing this idiot woman would get to the point.

"You have an intimate relationship with him, I assume, and I'm sure in the law enforcement world that makes for communication difficulties between police people, *n'est-ce-pas*?"

Apparently having Jeff followed to locate me hadn't provided Aunt Caroline with enough dirt about the two of us to satisfy her curiosity. She was fishing for more.

"Quit the games and tell me what Fielder said."

Her mouth tightened into a pucker and she averted her gaze, obviously miffed I wasn't about to discuss my private life with her. "She wanted to know if you'd planned this vacation to Jamaica and when you were coming back. And I'm being totally forthcoming when I say that she *did* ask me how you handled that messy situation last summer. I told her you nearly got yourself killed and—"

"Is that all?" I cut in.

She fiddled with her three-karat diamond ring. "I came here with the best of intentions. If someone were investigating me, I would certainly want to know the details."

"And you've told me next to nothing. Is there more?" I said.

"No."

I stood. "Then thank you and good night. I had a long flight and I'm tired. You remember the way out?"

She took her time leaving, all the while trying to pretend none of her probing into my life and talking about me to Fielder was of any consequence. But it was. It bothered the hell out of me. Fielder had been digging through my past and was keeping track of my whereabouts. So who had told her I'd gone to Jamaica? Surely not Kate. She would have mentioned it the minute I called her earlier today. That left Jeff. Maybe it was a small thing, maybe he didn't think his discussing me with his old girlfriend Quinn mattered, but it did. It mattered too much.

So without thinking, I picked up my phone and called his cell.

He answered on the second ring, saying, "Hey, Abby. Are you at home?"

"Oh, I'm home all right. And I just found out you've been talking to Fielder about me. I don't like that, Jeff. I stay out of your cases and you can just stay out of mine."

Silence followed. A sickening silence, the kind that washes over you like dirty water. I'd made a mistake. A bad one.

His voice was as cold as liquid nitrogen when he finally answered. "We'll talk some other time, okay?"

Click.

I squeezed the receiver and shut my eyes. This foot in mouth disease of mine was gonna kill me yet.

13

Though I was dead tired, sleep did not come easily. I'd been such an idiot to call when I was still hot from my encounter with Aunt Caroline. I tossed and turned and finally at three A.M. I called Jeff again and got his voice mail. I apologized several times in a rambling sleep-deprived monologue that probably made me sound like an even bigger jerk than before. At least I was able to get some rest afterward, but I wondered about Jeff. How much had I pissed him off? How much sleep had *he* gotten? Hopefully I could ask him soon.

The next morning I showered and ran a few errands, cat food and coffee being the priorities. Around noon I arrived home with three bags of groceries. Or should I say three bags of comfort food along with the cat chow and coffee—chips, jalapeños, salsa, ice cream, and regular Coke—and all in quantities far greater than one female should consume in a year's time. So what? I would drown my troubles in saturated fat and sugar.

But when I'd polished all this off, I had a bellyache so bad it felt like my bloated gut had broken one of my ribs. And this self-indulgence did not make my phone ring or cure my guilt at being such a bitch to a guy who deserved so much better. So I left another message on Jeff's cell—this one short and sweet, offering another apology.

This personal drama had knocked me off track and I knew it. Time to get to work. After I took some Alka-Seltzer, Diva and I headed for the office.

I got on-line and typed "missing persons" into the search feature in the *Dallas Morning News* archives. I then chose the dates to narrow my search, typing in 1985–1986. I got eighty-three hits. Wow. Eighty-three people disappeared or were found dead without identification in that one year alone. Apparently nameless victims were dumped at least once a week in Dallas. Scary. But right now I was more interested in missing persons who might not be dead, so when I came across an article about B&B Stainless Supply while searching for missing persons—the company the Beadford brothers once ran in Dallas—my already unhappy tummy tightened. *What the hell?*

I was riveted to the article with unblinking attention. This connection was no coincidence. It couldn't be. I printed out the article and reread it, then sat back in my chair, rubbing between my brow with thumb and index finger. A woman named Laura Montgomery, who had worked for B&B as an accountant, was indicted for fraud, and it was this fraud that led to the company's descent into bankruptcy. But that wasn't what made my heart pound and my mouth go dry. Two days before trial, Laura Montgomery disappeared. And not long after that a woman named Blythe Donnelly buys a house with cash in Jamaica—a woman who happened to be an accountant with a six-figure Grand Cayman bank account. That woman then shows up at Megan's wedding twenty years later, wearing winter clothes right off the rack—clothes she would not need in Jamaica. Surely she came to see her daughter get married—a daughter who had grown up in the house of the same man Laura Montgomery betrayed. How the hell did that happen? This was crazy and complicated and made me feel like someone had just piled rocks on my shoulders.

My stomach was churning by now, the nausea an

irritating distraction. I had to find out more. Trying to
ignore the gurgling in my gut, I got back to work,
this time plugging Laura Montgomery's name into the
newspaper's archive search engine. Plenty of hits
turned up. She'd been twenty-four when she skipped
bail, and one article speculated that her embezzlement
of close to half a million dollars in B&B funds had
been the work of a very intelligent woman and that
her escape to the unknown had been part of the plan
all along. The last article mentioning her name appeared in 1988 and detailed the reemergence of James
Beadford in Houston as an oil company supplier of
stainless steel—the newly created Beadford Oil Suppliers. The headline read, "Businessman Bounces
Back After Employee Runs Off with Everything." According to the piece written three years after Montgomery left Dallas, no trace of her had yet been
found.

But I still couldn't be positive Montgomery and
Donnelly were the same person since photographs
were not archived on the site. Surely pictures existed.
And there had to be a mug shot of Montgomery, too.
Angel mentioned some friends in Dallas who might
help and I called him, leaving a message when he
didn't answer his cell phone or his office number.

Now what?

And then I remembered the phone call from Graham Beadford and that got me to thinking. Laura
Montgomery worked for B&B, so Graham would have
known her. Was that why he called me? Because he'd
recognized her at the reception? So why wait until
now to tell me? And why call me rather than Fielder?
Those questions needed answering pronto.

Since I had no idea when Angel would get back to
me on the pictures of Montgomery, I decided to call
Graham and set up the meeting he'd requested. He
didn't answer in his hotel room, and I got no response
at the Beadford house, either—and that was probably
a lucky break. If Roxanne answered, she'd surely ask

what I wanted with him. Nobody was home anywhere, probably because James Beadford's funeral had been scheduled by now. Perhaps everyone was at the visitation. The obit would have provided those hours.

But before I could log on to the *Galveston County Daily News,* my stomach cramped so bad I doubled over. And then I was racing to the bathroom all the while reminding myself to never eat an entire jar of salsa in one sitting again.

An hour later, with half a bottle of Pepto swimming in my stomach, I entered the Forest Rest Funeral Home located off the interstate on the way to Galveston. The visitation was tonight and tomorrow as I'd guessed.

Nothing like the faint odor of embalming fluid mixed with the scent of lilies to up your nausea level. But maybe it was the hushed organ music that made me feel sick all over again. I hate organ music almost as much as I hate rap.

A woman dressed in a navy suit and wearing white gloves stood guard in the dimly lit lobby. Those gloves struck me as weird and creepy, like something out of that movie *Whatever Happened to Baby Jane?* Not that I recall any gloves on Bette or Joan, but I got the same feeling from this woman as I had from sitting through that flick.

"Welcome to Forest Rest," she said. "Are you here to pay your respects?"

No, I'm here with my mariachi band to liven things up, I thought. But I politely said, "The Beadford visitation?"

"Ah yes. This way."

I followed her down a wide corridor and couldn't help but notice they were doing a damn fine business at Forest Rest. Caskets and mourners in every room. But the Beadfords' spot was far more crowded than the others I'd seen. An album-sized book sat on a table outside the entrance.

"Please sign before you go in," she said, before she slipped away.

Sign-in books had brought me to this point, I thought, adding my signature to the page. Glad I wasn't in charge of this one. Not here, thank you very much.

I scanned the room from the doorway looking for Graham, but my gaze was drawn to a stone-faced Megan in one corner. She was clinging to Travis and nodding at a steady parade of people offering their condolences. Probably the same people who had been celebrating her wedding not long ago.

Sylvia stood nearby, looking sad but composed and wearing a different black dress than the one she'd had on the other day. Her beauty-shop hair made her about six inches taller.

I'd thrown on a wrinkled brown linen dress from my suitcase—everything else the least bit funereal needed laundering—and since the temperature in this room had to be colder than the sixty degrees outside, goose bumps as big as hills rose on my arms. I started in Megan's direction, but then Roxanne attacked from my flank.

She grabbed my sleeve and said, "Thank God you're here. You have to stop her." She pulled me by the elbow in the direction I'd just come from and I saw why. Courtney was on her way out.

Not wanting to cause a ruckus in this somber venue, I went along with Roxanne, whispering, "Why do I need to stop her?" I was hoping my quiet tone would offer her a clue as to the negative impact of acting like a crazy woman in a funeral home.

No such luck. Roxanne spoke loud enough for God and everybody to hear, saying, "She announced this is the most boring place she's ever been and that she 'wants some action.' You understand her intent, don't you?"

I was afraid I did, but though I wanted to tell Roxanne I was not a shrink or a drug counselor or a preacher, this girl was so determined to involve me in the family's private business I knew she wouldn't care how much I protested. I could vomit on Roxanne to get her to leave me alone, but since I'd already puked my guts out once tonight, there probably wasn't enough left in me to make an impression.

So I went with her, and we caught up with Courtney in the lobby where the white-gloved woman was just opening one of the huge double doors to let her out.

"Hey, Courtney!" I called. "Could I talk to you for a minute before you go?"

"I'm out of here," she yelled over her shoulder and left.

Roxanne gave me a shove in the middle of my back. "You cannot allow her to destroy her life."

The greeter raised her eyebrows expectantly and looked at me as if to say, "Yes, do something."

Why was I such a sucker for the needs of the wackos of the world? I had no good answer as I hurried after Courtney, Roxanne on my heels.

Courtney was hoofing it through the parking lot and I shouted, "I only want a minute of your time; then you can split."

"Don't tell her that. You'll be enabling her," Roxanne said.

Living with you is probably more enabling than anything I could ever do, I wanted to say. But since Courtney had halted, I hurried over to her rather than respond to Roxanne.

Courtney's outfit, a blue jeans skirt and a baggy sweater, had me looking like I might get nominated for "Best Funeral Attire of the Year."

Lips pursed, one hand on her hip, Courtney said, "What do you want?"

I tried for a sincere smile. "Must be a tough night cooped up with a bunch of strangers and a dead man."

"What do you know about it?" When she swiped at her bangs—her hair was streaked with what looked like red and green food coloring since I'd last seen her—I noted that her hand was trembling. I didn't think it was from the cool evening air.

"My daddy died last year," I said, "and this was the part I hated the most. Shaking hands with people I hardly knew when all I wanted to do was get away from everyone. Even the word visitation makes me kind of sick."

"Yeah. You don't look so hot. So why don't you go home and take care of your own self?"

"Hey, if you want to get wasted I can't stop you," I answered.

"Shrink your own head, lady." She pulled a cigarette from her small shoulder bag and put it between her lips, then smirked at Roxanne, who had joined us. "Got a light, sis?"

"What demons possess you?" Roxanne said. "What—"

"Cut the drama," Courtney said to her sister. "And Abby should get on down the road because she couldn't care less about anything but her own agenda."

"Nothing says an agenda can't involve others," I said quietly.

"The others being my cousin Megan?" she said.

"Why do you have to alienate everyone, Courtney? Abby has offered to help you," Roxanne said.

I offered? Must have missed that part of the conversation.

Roxanne continued with her lecture. "Dad will be very disconcerted if he discovers you vacated the funeral home without offering Aunt Sylvia an explanation. And he will consider that a perfect excuse to continue this latest binge. I understand your behavior has been triggered by the horrendous events at the wedding. But if you keep on this path and upset Dad, we'll be forced to contact those zealots in his AA group and—"

Courtney gave a short sarcastic laugh. "What in hell makes you think his plunge into another vat of whiskey would be triggered by anything but pure selfish need? Have you seen him offer one bit of support to anyone? Have you seen him show his face even for one second tonight?"

"I know you are not as malicious as you sound," Roxanne said, blinking back tears. She turned to me. "She really isn't like this all the time. It's the drugs talking."

Courtney made a disgusted face and said, "No, it's *me* talking."

"Um, I came here to speak to Graham," I cut in. "Did you say he isn't here?"

"Good listener," Courtney said, rummaging in her purse. "Glad someone's paying attention. Where are the fucking matches when you need one?"

"Do you know where I could find him?" I asked. "He called me and—"

"Check the resort bar. And if he's not there, try the other watering holes in that cutesy little town, all two of them." Courtney found the matches and lit her cigarette with shaky hands, then blew smoke in her sister's face.

Roxanne went into a fit of coughing so obviously fake I almost laughed.

Courtney, though rude and tense from what was most likely the beginning of withdrawal, didn't seem to need any intervention from me.

"Thanks," I said. "I'll head to the hotel and find him."

Roxanne's forced coughing abruptly ceased. "But you mustn't leave. You have to assist her."

"She has to help herself," I said.

I turned and walked to my car, leaving a distraught Roxanne still sputtering at her sister.

The drive to the resort and conference center on the bay took about fifteen minutes. On the way, I considered all the questions swirling in my head. Did Graham know why Sylvia and James adopted Megan?

Was that the information he hoped to sell me? If so, I might just be willing to pay him for the truth.

Once I entered the lobby, I followed the signs to the bar. A curved wall of windows overlooked the water and hundreds of lights glittered on the dock and marina. But though the lady bartender knew Graham by name and said he'd been in earlier, she told me he left at least an hour ago. I made my way to the elevator and rode up to the twelfth floor to look for 1234, the room number he'd mentioned in his call to me while I was in Jamaica.

The long hallway was deserted and so quiet I swore I could have heard someone drop their pajamas behind one of the dozens of doors lining the corridor. The hall eased right as I closed in on Graham's room. Since his was next to the vending machines, I picked up on the hums of the refrigerated soda machine and the ice maker.

And then I heard a voice coming from behind Graham's door, shouting, "No! God, no!"

I ran the last few feet to his room just in time to hear an awful, strangled scream. I pounded on the door with my fist. "Graham! Are you okay?"

I gripped the door lever out of pure instinct even though I knew hotel doors were always locked. But right after my fingers wrapped around the handle, the door opened violently. I was yanked forward.

And then just as ferociously that door came flying back at me, the edge hitting my left cheek with the force of a baseball bat. I fell to the floor, white light shattering my vision. I made a futile grab for a black-trousered leg as someone stepped over me, but I was too stunned by the blow to even think or move. I blinked hard and looked into the room, trying to focus. The blue sheer liner drapes that covered the glass doors to a balcony blew toward me in the ocean breeze.

Then numbness and confusion gave way to unbelievable pain. I tried to get up, knowing I needed

help. Mistake. The room went all cockeyed, then bile
and the awful taste of Pepto rose in my throat. I could
only slump against the wall and close my eyes.

14

"Señorita? You okay?" a woman asked.

I opened my eyes and saw a blurry brown face close to mine. Pretty face. "I'll be fine, but what's that noise? Because it's damn annoying."

"Sirens outside. You don't look so good. Your husband hit you and leave you here like this?"

"Husband? Last time I checked, I didn't have one of those. Listen, would you mind helping me up?"

She was squatting in front of me, and I saw she was wearing a gray cotton maid's uniform. She took my upper arm, and with her support, I stood. I had to lean against the wall once I was upright since I felt dizzy and as sick as ever. And my face. Yikes, could anything hurt more than this?

"I could use some air," I said.

She helped me across the room, saying, "I gotta call my manager. You need a doctor."

Those sirens, a persistent whine before, were now much louder and when we got out on the balcony, I understood why.

A man was lying below on the well-lit stone walkway, his body surrounded by a small crowd. One leg was bent at a sickening angle and blood was pooled around his head. A rescue truck came speeding up, and two paramedics jumped out and pushed the gawkers aside so they could get to the man. Being this far up I couldn't tell if it was Graham, but I remembered the anguished shout I'd heard right before I got smacked in the face. I had definitely recognized his voice.

"Oh no," I whispered.

"You and the man have some trouble?" the woman said.

I didn't answer her. I was watching a police car arrive. It lurched to a halt, lights flashing so brilliantly in the dark I had to squint. Two cops got out simultaneously. A second later, a woman in the crowd was standing next to the policeman and pointing up to our balcony. Pointing at us.

It had taken the cops only about three minutes to reach Graham's room. By that time, I was sitting on the floor in the hallway with an ice bag pressed to my face, thanks to Maria—the woman who had come to my aid. One cop asked me my name while the other went into Graham's empty room. He asked if I needed a paramedic and I told him no, I was fine. Then he said, "You and the jumper have a fight?"

"Are you crazy?" I said.

That didn't go over too well.

"Why don't you think about what happened and we'll talk in a minute," he replied sternly. He stood outside Graham's room, his hand on the billy club hanging from his waist, his posture saying he'd give me a swat on the other side of my face if I made any more references to his mental health.

The responding officers were from the county, but since this was Seacliff, I figured my favorite chief of police would be here soon. So when he asked me again what happened, I told him I'd prefer to wait and talk to Fielder.

Sure enough, she came up to the twelfth floor several minutes later. She had Maria open one of the unoccupied rooms, and I stayed there while Fielder talked to the maid.

I sat in a gold velvet armchair by the window, my

ice pack dripping down my arm, my face was blessedly numb now. Fielder entered a few minutes later, shutting the door after her. Her red blouse and straight, short black skirt complemented her thin, long-legged figure.

She sat across from me, the standard hotel issue round table between us. From her expression, I guessed she was plenty pissed off. "What the hell happened in that room, Miss Rose?"

"I have no idea," I said.

"Oh? So you've got amnesia?" she said. "Because Graham Beadford is dead, and I need you to recover your memory damn quick."

So it *was* Graham who fell. "I do not have amnesia," I said. "But I don't—"

"Then what's the problem?"

Would you let me talk? I almost shouted, but instead came back with, "I think the monkey pox has affected my memory." I held up my free arm to show off a few of my thousand mosquito bites. I said this with a smile, but the pain had now been replaced by a white-hot anger—anger at myself for not being quick enough to keep Graham from dying, along with anger at Fielder for being surly with me for no good reason.

She took a deep breath and leaned back. "Let's start over. Did you and Graham argue? Did he hit you? Because self-defense in Texas can get anyone off."

I looked at her dumbfounded. Jeff always said that cops who jump to conclusions destroy cases, miss evidence and to quote him directly, "are royal fuckups. The worst kind of cop."

"You're making a mistake," I said calmly. She was pathetic. Not worth getting mad at if she was making assumptions like this.

"Am I? The maid said she found you in his room, and it couldn't have been more than a minute after Beadford went off that balcony."

"I need more ice," I said, meeting her gaze. "And

after that, maybe a lawyer." I dropped the leaky ice pack on the middle of the table. It fell with a splat, and water spilled out around the broken plastic. Thanks to the gravity gods, a stream of icy water headed in her direction.

She pushed away from the table to avoid getting wet, then stood. "I'll send one of the paramedics to check out your injuries. But I'm not done with you."

She strode out, and once she was gone, I went to the mirror that hung over the long Spanish-style dresser against one wall.

"Oh my God," I whispered. It was a miracle I still had any enamel left on my teeth. A purple line extended from cheekbone to chin on the left side of my face, the door mark surrounded by a deep blue swelling on either side. I touched a finger to the bruise and winced. Just then a paramedic arrived, and without so much as a second glance at my injury, he got on his walkie-talkie and told whoever was on the other end that they needed a stretcher in room 1240.

"I walked in here and I can walk out," I protested, but when he told me my face could be fractured, I decided a trip to the emergency room might not be such a bad idea. I was feeling sick to my stomach again and knew I might have a hard time driving. Besides, this was the best way I could think of to get away from Fielder.

The most ridiculous thing about my ride in an ambulance to the same hospital where I'd met with Sister Nell only a short time ago was how they strapped me like a mummy, neck brace and all, to what felt like a frozen surfboard. Turns out the backboard hadn't been refrigerated, though. I was simply freezing. And even after I was x-rayed, scanned, and shot full of medicine for the nausea that just wouldn't quit, I still shivered and shook like it was ten below zero in the hospital.

"You're a little shocky from the trauma," the nurse who gave me the injection told me. She then wrapped a warm cotton blanket around my shoulders, placed another on my lap, and said she'd be back.

The medicine had burned like the dickens when it went in, but now my stomach was finally feeling better. Better, that is, until Kate showed up looking all panicked and upset. I hadn't called her, so how had she found me?

She stood in the doorway to my emergency room cubicle for a second, swallowed hard, and forced a smile. But knowing her, she didn't like what she was seeing.

I quickly held the ice pack up to my face to hide the enormous bruise. "It's really not as awful as you think," I said.

"The doctor said you've got a hairline fracture in your maxillary bone. I'd say that's awful enough." She walked over next to me and started to touch my face, then thought better of it. Instead she took my hand and squeezed. "So what were you doing at the hotel, Abby?"

"I went to see Graham and was about five seconds too late. But how did you know?"

"An Officer Henderson called me. Did you see what happened to Mr. Beadford?"

"Nope. I didn't even see the door hit me, it happened so fast."

"Jeff is on his way, and he is going to be so upset to see you like this."

"On his way from Seattle?"

"No, he came home and called me when he didn't find you at your place, asked if you were with me. Then Henderson called on the other line while we were talking and said you'd been hurt, so I picked Jeff up and we drove down here together."

"Wait a minute," I said, holding up a hand. "Maybe getting whacked upside the head has—"

Just then Jeff appeared in the door. He looked tired and worried, but if there was any leftover anger in his eyes over my stupid, impulsive remarks, I couldn't tell.

"Are you okay?" he said quietly.

"Yes," I said. "And now that this stomach thing is better, I'm about ready to leave this place."

"Stomach thing?" Kate said. "What are you talking about? Did you get punched there, too?"

I removed the ice pack. "I was never punched. Can't you see the imprint of a door on my face?"

Jeff nodded. "Oh yeah. Think we'll be seeing that for a while. Did they give you something for pain?"

"A nurse shot me up with some medicine for this little stomach problem, but as for pain, my face is numb right now."

"Do you have a stomach virus, then? Or is it from being hit so hard?" Kate asked.

Uh-oh. I could see her homeopathic wheels turning. Yup, she was wearing that "I have just the thing to fix a stomach problem" look.

"My stomach's been upset all day, but now it's almost gone. I did drown myself in salsa, and combined with all that wonderful Jamaican food, I think I did this to myself. I do know why they call it jerk chicken now. It's because you feel like a jerk when you puke all over the place."

Jeff smiled. "If you're cracking jokes, you're feeling better. Maybe even well enough to tell me what went on tonight." He came over to my gurney and picked up the ice pack I'd set down. He gently rested it against my cheek.

"It's kind of hard to think right now." I looked at Kate. "Would you mind getting me a Coke? I feel better since I had that medicine, and I could use something to drink."

"Sure. Diet?" she asked.

"Regular," I said.

"You?" Kate looked at Jeff.

"Coffee." He rubbed the stubble on his chin with a knuckle. "Haven't slept since I don't know when."

After she left, I said, "Did you get my messages? Because I'm so sorry—"

He leaned over and kissed me lightly on the lips, then said, "Shut up. It's over." He dragged a chair beside me, sat down, and gripped my hand.

I felt every muscle in my body relax. We were gonna be fine. "Did you get to talk to Fielder?"

"Only for a minute. Kate dropped me off at the hotel so I could pick up your car, and Quinn was wrapping up the scene. Graham Beadford most likely got some help off his hotel balcony—a witness saw a shadow of someone else behind him right before he fell—so she's got two homicides now."

"I feel so awful, Jeff. I was right outside his room when it happened."

He gripped my hand tighter. "Looks like you dodged one, Abby. You sure you want to be a PI?"

"I have to do this," I said. "Just like you have to do your job."

"Yeah, I know, but . . . if anything happened to you—"

"Hey, just because someone tried to knock me senseless doesn't mean I'm quitting." I punched his arm playfully. "I'm as tough as you are."

"Probably tougher," he said with a grin. "You're gonna have a shiner to go with the rest of your blue and purple face tomorrow."

"You think so?"

"I know so."

"What upsets me is that I didn't see the guy."

"It was a guy?" he said.

"Honestly, I'm not sure."

"So your memory hasn't returned yet?" came a new voice from the doorway. *Fielder. Great.*

Jeff stood and nodded. "Quinn," he said politely.

I swear she blushed, but I wasn't sure why.

"Hello, Jeff," she said. "I'd like to ask Ms. Rose a few questions now that she's been treated for her injuries."

"Give her until tomorrow," he said. "She needs a good night's sleep and some time to recover." He reached into his pocket for his Big Red and offered Fielder the pack.

She refused by shaking her head and said, "I'm working a homicide, and you know better than anyone that I need answers. Now."

"Abby's been through a lot. She'll know just as much tomorrow as she does now."

"It's okay, Jeff," I said. "Ask your questions, Chief." I had something she wanted, and I liked being in that position. And I also had knowledge of other things, things I'd learned in Jamaica and things I'd learned since coming home. Things that might help her solve her case if she'd quit acting like she'd had a major power failure in her brain.

"You don't have to say anything, Abby—and those are words I never thought I'd hear myself say." Jeff opened two sticks of gum and folded them in his mouth.

Fielder wasn't about to give me time to reconsider my generosity, though. "What went on inside Graham Beadford's hotel room? Did he attack you first?"

"Attack me? I didn't even talk to the man. If you think I killed him, you're nuts."

"You were there when a man died. I need to know why," she said coldly.

"You're fucking up big-time, Quinn." Jeff's eyes had darkened. I couldn't remember seeing him look so angry.

She glared at him. "You don't supervise me anymore, Sergeant. And maybe you should open your eyes. Your girlfriend pretends to cooperate on the first murder, but when I try to find her, I learn she's left the country. And the minute she comes back, I've got another dead Beadford and no apparent motive. She's been at the scene of two homicides and—"

"Get out," Jeff said, his voice as hard as Superman's kneecap. "She'll talk when she's got a suit sitting next to her."

"Fine," Fielder said, but then pointed a finger at me. "You go anywhere, you tell me."

But before I could even nod, she whirled and left.

"I could have handled her, Jeff," I said quietly. This wasn't my rational, calm cop. Not that a little fire in support of me wasn't very much appreciated.

Jeff let out a huge sigh. "Jeez, I'm such a fool. See what you do to me?"

"The word for fool is bobo in Jamaican," I said. "And being a bobo isn't all bad. Now would you find Kate and please get me out of here?"

He grinned, chomping away on his gum. "Good idea." He turned and started out the door, but stopped and looked back at me. "Bobo, huh?"

"Yeah, mon. You be some bobo."

15

The next morning, while I was still trying to wake up, Jeff brought me a fresh ice pack. He was on his way to work and kissed me good-bye after telling me he'd written down the name of the man he considered the only decent criminal defense attorney in Houston. Then he pounded down the stairs, leaving me wondering if I really needed a lawyer. Surely Fielder would screw her head back on this morning and figure out I had no reason to kill the Beadford brothers.

Jeff's footsteps reached the front door, but after I heard the door open, the word "shit" echoed up the stairs.

Okay. Something was wrong. I swung my legs over the side of the bed and got up to see what was the matter. The room spun for a second, and I had to keep myself from toppling over by clutching the corner of the nightstand.

Jeff strode back into the bedroom and came over to help me. "When you get your sea legs, the press is waiting for you, Abby."

"The press? Why are *they* here?"

"Because there've been two homicides, and somehow they've learned you're involved. Get with the lawyer and tell Quinn Fielder exactly what happened last night so those buzzards will leave you alone."

"And what about the rest of it? Should I tell her

everything I learned in Jamaica?" The wood floor was cold on my bare feet and I shivered.

He picked up my bathrobe off the chair and draped it around my shoulders. "What do you mean by *the rest of it*?" But before I could speak, he held up a hand. "No. Should have known better than to ask that question. I'm still a cop and—"

"Why does that make a difference?" I lowered myself with his help and sat on the edge of the bed. I'd set a bottle of Motrin and a glass of water on the nightstand last night just in case and now spilled three pills into my hand and gulped them down.

"This is Fielder's case, and it involves your client. The less I know about it, the less I can say if she asks me."

"She'd ask you?" I realized how naive that sounded as soon as the words left my lips. "Yeah, she would. So I shouldn't tell you anything?"

"Not now. To Quinn, you're a suspect, and she seems bent on proving you have something to do with these murders. I know her pretty well, and considering she didn't leave HPD willingly—"

"Hold on. Maybe it's my messed up head, but I don't know what you're talking about," I said.

He sat next to me. "I told you she and I had a history. What I didn't tell you is that after our relationship ended, Quinn got a little weird, made some pretty bad calls in the field. A few of her collars fell through even though the perps were guilty. She didn't do the groundwork and paperwork to make them stick. Made a lot of bad assumptions and, well, the department suggested she get a fresh start somewhere else."

"So she got fired. Happens all the time."

"But she blamed me. She said I *distracted* her. Now I'm wondering if she's venting her old anger toward me on you."

"She blames you for her incompetence, and to get

even she wants to make me look guilty even if I'm not?" I said.

"I wouldn't go that far, but my guess is she wouldn't mind making your life miserable."

"And one way to do that is leak to the press that I was right there when Graham got pushed off that balcony?"

His face tight with anger, he nodded slowly. "I can see her doing that. Especially since there are some extenuating circumstances." I read worry in his eyes.

"How extenuating?" I said.

"She called me about that sketch artist and—"

"I know that."

He reached for his gum. "What you don't know is that she also asked me to meet her for dinner."

I felt my neck and shoulders tighten and that made my face throb. "And did you?"

"Yeah. She said she needed to talk through the case."

This was a three-sticks-of-gum confession, and I wasn't sure I wanted the details—but I was going to get them anyway. "So what happened?"

"She was feeling vulnerable, overwhelmed by the biggest case of her career. She drank too much wine . . . started getting a little personal under the table and—"

"One thing led to another?" I said quietly.

He grinned. "Now who's jumping to conclusions? Her hand on my crotch led me to walk out on her— for the second time in her life."

I smiled even though it hurt. "So she's the one with the green-eyed monster on her back now?"

He nodded. "The less I know about the case, the less she can involve me. And that's better for you."

"She's no problem for me."

"Tell her the truth, okay? Just make sure the lawyer is there."

"I'll be happy to tell her the truth," I said. "If she'll listen."

*   *   *

When Jeff left the house, he must have said something persuasive to the reporters because when I came downstairs, I saw only one car parked down the street and a lone van from a local independent network. Someone sat in the driver's seat of the white car. A stubborn reporter, maybe?

I needed coffee, preferably strong enough to walk into the cup, so I headed for the kitchen. But before I could grind a single bean, the phone rang. Maybe the press thought a telephone call might work better than hanging around the neighborhood. I let it ring while I took a bag of French roast from the freezer. But when Megan's voice came on the answering machine I rushed over and picked up.

"Hey, I'm here. What's up?"

"Will you be home for a while?" she said. "Because I'm almost to your place. I need your help."

"Is this about your uncle Graham?"

"In a way, yes. I'll be there in a few minutes." She disconnected.

Before she arrived, I debated whether to tell her what I'd learned, that her parents must have surely known the identity of the child they adopted. But when Megan showed up looking as pale and sick as I'd felt yesterday, I knew now was not the time.

I was carrying my mug when I let her in and offered her coffee as we came into the living room. She refused.

"You look pretty spent," I said, sitting down.

I gestured for her to join me, but she started pacing by the fireplace. "Courtney's missing. She's probably passed out in a crack house somewhere. I don't think she knows Uncle Graham is dead."

"I talked to her last night outside the funeral home, and though she didn't seem all that wasted, she might have been before the night ended. I could tell she had plans."

Megan chewed on her lower lip. "Roxanne was trying to call the *America's Most Wanted* producers this morning to see if they could find her, if you can believe that. I stopped her. And then I thought of you. I know you've done so much already, but—"

"I'll do whatever I can," I said.

Megan, already no more than a hundred pounds soaking wet, looked like she'd lost weight. And the fire in her eyes that I remembered so well from our first meeting was dying little by little. Too many bad things had happened too fast.

I stood and blocked Megan's path when she turned in my direction. "Let's slow down," I said. "Make a plan."

She blinked, then stared at my face. "Abby, my God. What happened to you?"

"Just a little argument with a door."

"I was so wrapped up in my own problems I didn't even notice. Is this my fault? Did this happen in Jamaica? Did you get—"

I gripped both her shoulders and looked into her tired eyes. "When's the last time you ate?"

"I can't think about food now. We have to do something about Courtney. She needs me. They all need me. Even if they're weird and crazy, they're still my family and—"

"And you can't help them if you don't take care of yourself."

Her eyes welled. "I probably can't help them anyway, but you can. Find out who killed my father and my uncle, Abby."

"I don't know, Megan. I haven't been doing this PI thing all that long. I'm not sure I have the skills to investigate murder. Maybe Angel can get more involved in your case. He's had loads of experience."

"I'd rather have you. You certainly couldn't do any worse than that policewoman. She doesn't tell us anything, and she was so abrupt with my mother and me last night. Almost cruel."

"She's trying," I said, not believing I was actually defending Quinn Fielder.

"I don't trust her, but I absolutely trust you," she said.

"So you want me to find Courtney or the murderer-slash-murderers or all of the above?"

"All of the above," she said, nodding decisively. "I'll pay you whatever you want."

"We'll figure that out later, but first off, the two of us are going to sit down in my kitchen and have some Frosted Flakes. I need some brain fuel even if you don't."

A half hour later, after Megan joined me in a bowl of cereal, a big glass of orange juice, and coffee, she seemed a little more like the young woman who'd walked down the aisle such a short time ago. I felt better, too. My face still hurt, but my insect bites were almost a memory and my stomach felt normal for the first time in twenty-four hours.

I'd decided Jeff might be a good resource to help us locate Courtney, but before I could phone him, Megan's cell rang.

She flipped it open and answered, then mouthed, "It's her."

Gee, I thought, *easiest detective job I'll ever have.*

Megan listened for a second, then said, "It's not your fault, Courtney. Someone pushed him. You couldn't have stopped that from happening."

I heard Courtney's voice—her loud, slurred voice—saying, "It's all my fault. I want to die, Meg. I want to die!"

"Don't say that," Megan said. "No one else needs to die."

"Ask her where she is," I whispered.

"Tell me where you are," Megan said firmly. "I'll come to you. I'll pick you up."

Megan listened intently for what seemed a long

time. Then her face relaxed. "Okay. I'm coming. Don't leave."

She closed the phone and looked at me. "She's at the Starfish Motel near Galveston."

"I'll Mapquest it and we're on our way," I said.

On the drive south, Megan asked me about the Jamaica trip. I hedged, told her I had a few leads but nothing solid to report yet. Thank goodness she was consumed by the current situation and thus didn't press me. She needn't know her birth mother might be an embezzler and a fugitive or that other giant secrets had been kept from her. At least not until the DNA sample I'd sent off came back in a few weeks. I changed the subject by offering my version of what happened at the hotel last night and how guilty I felt about arriving too late to help Graham.

"Oh my God, Abby," she said after I finished explaining. "I didn't even know you were there."

"If I'd arrived a minute earlier, I may have prevented Graham's death."

"Or gotten yourself killed. I mean, look at you."

"I prefer *not* to look at me. By the way, your uncle phoned me when I was in Jamaica and said he wanted to talk about something that would interest me. I'm worried that whatever he wanted to discuss had something to do with his death."

"Why would he call you rather than the police? He hardly knew you." She began twisting her wedding ring.

"My point exactly. But that call will probably show up on some phone record and make Fielder even more suspicious of me."

"Suspicious of *you*? What reason could you possibly have to hurt my uncle or my father? You didn't even know them before the rehearsal dinner."

"Ah. A voice of reason in the wilderness. Refreshing, Megan. So what about Roxanne and Courtney? Would they have any motive to want Graham or James dead?"

Megan hesitated, probably realizing for the first time that "finding the killer" meant looking close to home. "I—I don't know. Both of them seem to have more personal problems than the last time I saw them. But murder? I can't even think about them like that."

"I got a taste of some genuine animosity toward their dad last night when I talked to them at the visitation." I glanced down at the map I'd printed off the computer. We were getting close to the exit.

"From what my dad told me, Uncle Graham and Roxanne did have a blowup about six months ago."

"A blowup?" I merged right and exited the freeway a few miles before the Galveston causeway.

"My cousins lost their mom to cancer about ten years ago," she said.

"Sylvia told me."

"Anyway, Roxanne reacted by pulling closer to Uncle Graham, becoming more like a mother than a daughter. And Courtney totally rebelled. So Roxanne became the favorite, until she got that odd boyfriend who played in the Dallas symphony."

"Violin, by chance?" I asked, remembering Roxanne clinging to one of the musicians the day of the wedding.

"How did you know?" said Megan.

"She was stuck like a cocklebur to the violinist at your reception. Anyway, what happened with the boyfriend?"

"I think it was the only time since they dissolved their business that Dad and Uncle Graham joined forces on anything. Apparently the boyfriend had been treated for bipolar disorder and would call up in the middle of the night or come over and play his violin outside Roxanne's window. When he got Roxanne to max out one of her credit cards, Uncle Graham called Dad for help. A few weeks later the guy ended up with a new position in Boston."

"So Roxanne figured they had a hand in this and was pissed off with both her father and her uncle?" I asked.

"Knowing Roxanne, she'd never admit to that. She wanted to blame everything on Courtney."

"On Courtney? How does that logic work?"

"She thought Courtney told Uncle Graham about the boyfriend's health problems."

I nodded. "Okay, so Roxanne had reason to be pissed off at all three of them." I wanted to ask about Courtney's substance abuse history, how long she'd been abusing, but we had come to the turnoff for the Starfish Motel. Seconds later we pulled into the parking lot.

We were greeted with peeling paint, a few broken windows patched with duct tape, doors marred by grime and mold and brown bottles and empty beer cans littering the area. The place oozed sleaze.

I parked not far from the room Megan pointed out, number twenty-one. We both got out of the car, but before we could take two steps, a door swung open and Courtney staggered out into the sunshine.

She shaded her eyes and shrieked, "Yee-ha! It's Megan!"

She wore the same clothes she'd had on when I saw her last night, only the blue jeans skirt was now on backward and she wore no shoes. Arms above her head, she shouted, "It's my birthday, Megan! Did you know that?"

"It is *not* her birthday," Megan whispered out of the side of her mouth.

"She's sure celebrating something," I said.

"I don't get it. On the phone she was crying and saying she wanted to die," Megan said. "Now look at her."

"Probably been snorting coke since you two talked."

Courtney swayed in our direction, bridging the gap between herself and Megan and then falling into her arms.

"I'm here to take you back home," Megan said.

Courtney pulled away and laughed. "Home? Didn't you know?"

"Know what?" Megan said quietly. She was putting on her usual strong front, but her breath was coming fast and she was twisting the ring around and around.

"Our house in Dallas was repossessed. Let's celebrate that!"

Megan turned Courtney back toward the room, saying, "You have a home with us. Now, let's get your stuff and get out of here."

I followed, but before I entered the motel room, I heard a car engine. I looked around and saw a white Taurus slow to a crawl as it passed the motel. *White Taurus.* Wasn't it a white Taurus parked on my street this morning? Had the reporter followed me all the way down here?

But then I recognized the driver. She was wearing that cloche hat. The woman and I locked eyes for an instant, and then she put the pedal to the metal and sped away.

What the hell was she doing? Following her daughter? But I didn't have time to consider other possible explanations because a guy tore past me out of number twenty-one. At least he didn't slam a door into my face, something I was mighty grateful for. I had to smile as I watched him run to a rusted blue pickup, though. He was naked as a worm aside from a straw cowboy hat.

I then stepped into the dimly lit room. It smelled like a mix of semen, urine, and sweat, the stench so strong it nearly knocked me back out the door. Courtney was sitting cross-legged on the queen-sized bed, an unlit cigarette hanging from dry lips. Megan had her hand over her mouth and nose, and I was tempted to do the same.

"I've got a pint of Jack Daniel's somewhere for the party," Courtney said, her words all running together. She then looked at me and said, "Who invited you, bitch? Oops, I *can* call you bitch, can't I?"

Megan started to say something, but I cut her off by raising a hand. "Call me whatever you want. Just be nice to Megan, because she cares a lot about you."

"Yeah, she came here for my birthday."

"No, she came here because you asked for her help," I said.

Courtney looked at me, her heavy-lidded eyes dark and empty. "Yeah, but why'd she have to bring *you*?"

"I volunteered. But this isn't about how much you dislike me. This is about how both of you have lost your fathers in a week's time and how you need each other. Roxanne needs both of you, too."

"My father?" Courtney said, looking confused. The cigarette fell from her lips onto her lap, but she didn't seem to notice.

"You told me you'd heard about him on the news," Megan said.

"Oh," Courtney said, swiping a hand through her hair. "That's right. He jumped off the roof. But you know something? I always told him he wasn't allowed to die until they found a safe place to bury his liver." She raised her head to the ceiling and started to laugh, but seconds later her shoulders started to shake and she began to sob. And seconds after that, Megan was beside her, holding her, stroking her cousin's messy hair and trying to comfort her.

I stepped outside for some fresh air and to make a call. This girl would need more help than Megan could offer. I'd seen used syringes on the nightstand, and the white stuff on the carpet by the bed probably wasn't talcum powder.

Kate was with a client when I reached her office, but I had her receptionist interrupt. After I told her the situation, Kate said she'd contact either a drug counselor or someone from Narcotics Anonymous and get them over to the motel as soon as possible. With any luck, they'd get Courtney into a detox unit pronto.

* * *

Courtney had thrown a minor fit but did not protest as much as I thought she might when the drug counselor arrived at the motel room. She seemed to connect with the guy—maybe it was their similar cobra tattoos. Anyway, he happened to be one of Kate's success stories when she was working under a supervising psychologist. The guy was a recovered addict now certified as a drug counselor. With his support, Courtney was admitted to a mental health facility in Galveston, the whole process taking about two hours. Then a relieved Megan drove Courtney's car back home while I decided to get my interview with Fielder over with.

The acne-scarred Henderson was again working the desk at the Seacliff Police Station. But there was a whole lot more action than the last time I'd been here. The place was crawling with cops in khaki, blue, and green uniforms from every jurisdiction.

"Man, who threw you against the wall?" Henderson asked with a grin when I'd entered.

"I had a little accident," I said. "Is the chief in?"

"She hasn't left. Found her asleep in the chair this morning. I'm worried about her. This case is eating her lunch. She even had you on the short list of suspects."

"Yeah, she hinted at that."

"The chief doesn't hint, Ms. Rose." Henderson grinned, then stood and gestured for me to follow him down to Fielder's office. "Yesterday she was swearing like a sailor about you and how you were the next Lizzie Borden, but she's got her sights set on someone else today."

"And who's this latest suspect?" I asked.

My timing was off because Henderson opened Fielder's door just as I asked the question.

The woman might be over her head with two murders in a week's time but that didn't mean she'd gone deaf. "Don't be pumping my officers for information, Ms. Rose. Henderson, leave us alone."

"Yes, ma'am," he answered, his cheeks as red as a baboon's butt. He knew he'd been the cause of her irritation with me and probably felt guilty.

"And you can go home, Henderson. You've been here long enough today." She didn't look at him, just snatched up a folder and shoved some papers inside.

"I'll leave when you do, ma'am," he said, bowing out of the room.

Wish I could go home. From her wrinkled clothes, her eyes shadowed beneath by the darkness of fatigue and her surly attitude, this conversation promised to be unpleasant.

"Where's your lawyer?" she said. "Because I don't have time to wait around for whoever you've hired."

"I don't need a lawyer," I said quietly.

"Oh, but won't that upset your *boyfriend*?" She still hadn't looked at me, focusing instead on the task of rearranging things on her desk—and there was plenty to rearrange. Folders, papers, pictures, Styrofoam containers from takeout, two Dr Pepper cans.

"Too bad if it upsets him. I make my own decisions, Chief. I'll bet you do, too."

She met my gaze, a rare moment of eye contact. "So you're ready to tell me what happened?"

"I would have told you last night, but—"

"But I was a bitch. Is that what Jeff told you? That I was an incompetent bitch?"

"You know, I think you'd interrupt me even if I were talking in my sleep," I said.

"So sorry," she said sarcastically. "Sit down."

I took one of the chairs facing her. "Graham Beadford called me while I was in Jamaica. He wanted to talk to me—what were his words?—about a matter of mutual interest or something similarly vague."

"Really?" That piece of news perked her up.

"Don't get excited. I have no clue why. When I couldn't reach him, I asked Courtney where to find him. She directed me to the hotel last night. I was too late."

"What time did you arrive?" She picked up a red rubber band and began stretching it one way and then another.

"Maybe eight o'clock? I'm not really sure."

"Cops just *love* unsure witnesses." She had the rubber band on her wrist now and took to snapping it against her skin. "Take me through what happened from when you arrived until you were struck."

I detailed the events starting with seeing Courtney and Roxanne at the visitation.

Snap snap snap went the band against her flesh. "So you didn't see who hit you with the door?"

"I saw a black pant leg. Can't even remember the shoes. But whoever did this crime had to be strong enough to push Mr. Beadford over that railing."

"Not if Beadford was drunk," she said.

"Yeah, you're probably right," I replied.

She smiled a little. Seemed she liked being right. "And you have no idea what Graham Beadford might have wanted to talk to you about?"

"Wish I knew." Though I had developed a few theories, I wasn't willing to part with them until I sat Megan down and explained them to her first.

"Could Beadford have wanted money?" More rubber band snapping.

"Seems logical. At the reception he practically asked me for a job at a computer company I used to manage."

"Is that so?" she said.

"And I've just found out his house was repossessed. He needed money," I said.

"He wanted to work for you?"

"I don't know. From the way he phrased it when he called me in Jamaica, I didn't get the impression he was looking for employment." *More likely he was hoping to sell information,* I thought.

"Okay, why else would he call you? Did he come on to you at the reception? Did he want a date or something?"

I wanted to laugh. "Definitely no come-ons involved."

She stretched the elastic hard and twisted it, letting out a frustrated sigh. "What's your best guess on what he *did* want?"

"The only thing he could have provided that would interest me was information on Megan's adoption—and that means he had to have known I was working for her."

"So maybe he did know."

"Who told him?" I asked.

"Whoever knew about your little assignment."

"My *little assignment*?" I said.

"Okay, your *job*," she conceded. "Who knew besides Megan?"

"My sister . . . and Jeff . . . and—" I stopped myself, not wanting to offer up the other name. Travis knew. And had lied to me about his part in getting Megan to hire me.

"And who?" She leaned toward me, her tired eyes now bright with interest, the elastic forgotten and dangling from her thin wrist.

"Travis," I said. "Travis knew."

She sat back in her chair and folded her arms across her chest. "Now we're getting somewhere."

"But why would Travis tell Graham about Megan's adoption search? And how would that information lead to Graham's death?"

"Maybe Travis didn't intentionally tell him anything," she said, squinting in thought.

I could see where she was headed, because if Travis let it slip to Graham about what I was doing, and Graham threatened to tell Sylvia about Megan's hunt for her birth mother, that would make a tragic situation at the Beadford house all the more difficult. Travis would have eagerly played the white knight to protect Megan from more stress. And I could see myself doing the same thing.

"So you're thinking Graham may have hit up Travis for money when he couldn't reach me?" I asked.

"You, Travis and Megan did not want Sylvia to know about this birth mother search, right?" she said.

"Yes, but an unemployed college student wouldn't have much to pay a blackmailer," I said.

"That's why Graham tried to hit you up first," she said with a smug smile.

"And when Travis didn't have the cash to shut Graham up, he pushed him off the balcony? That's the puniest motive for murder I've ever heard. It's not like Sylvia wouldn't find out what I've been doing some other way—a possibility I've mentioned to Megan myself."

She twisted the rubber band on her wrist so hard her hand started to darken. Her mind was working on something—something that made her drop any interest in me because she said, "I'm finished with you for now, Ms. Rose."

"Thanks. Best news I've had all day." I rose and walked out. I'd been prepared to tell her about Jamaica, about the woman at the wedding and what her presence might mean, but I was tired of Fielder's attitude. Besides, she'd be calling me again once she grew a few new brain cells.

16

I left through the back entrance of the police station and managed to get to my car before any reporters noticed me. I checked around for a white Taurus, but if Blythe Donnelly had followed me here, I didn't spot her. My guess was, she was probably shadowing Megan anyway.

I sat behind the wheel feeling guilty about inadvertently casting suspicion on my client's husband. I needed to fix this. So how? By casting suspicion on the birth mother Megan so wanted to find? It was a lesser of two evils dilemma, and I decided Donnelly was a mystery I needed to solve now more than ever. And if I intended to find the killer or killers, I also needed to learn more about James Beadford and his brother. Jeff always says the victims have all the answers if you look hard enough.

It dawned on me as I pulled away from the police station that despite their denials, James and Sylvia probably recognized the so-called stranger at the reception. They had her child, after all. Many years may have passed, but Laura Montgomery—Donnelly *had* to be Montgomery—had been important to them in more ways than one. Had been important to Graham, too. Surely they'd remember her face. And if they had recognized her, any one of them may have spoken to her that afternoon.

Had Graham somehow contacted Montgomery after

the wedding? Was that why he'd called me? Or was he trying to get money out of *her*? She certainly had good reason to pay up if Graham knew her real identity. And with Graham probably as drunk as a waltzing pissant, even a small person like Montgomery could have pushed him over the balcony. Hell, I probably could have pushed him off.

I pulled onto the main highway not liking Laura/Blythe as the killer any more than I liked Travis as a suspect—probably because I didn't want this case to be about one piece of bad news after another for Megan. So what about Sylvia? How much did she know? I'd been assuming she was aware of who Megan's birth mother was, but maybe she didn't. Still, if Blythe and Laura were one and the same, wouldn't Sylvia have recognized her as the person who brought B&B Stainless Supply down. And if so, why had neither she nor Graham said anything to Fielder when they were shown photographs and the composite?

I had no answers, but there might be a good place to start—Beadford Oil Suppliers. The bankruptcy story might be common knowledge to the current employees. What better place to find out about feuding brothers than at the business they once shared?

I grabbed my phone, called information, and got a number. A minute later I had the address and was heading north to Clear Lake City to visit the Beadfords' place of business.

Their office was on the third floor of a shiny black building on El Camino Real not far from the Space Center. Beadford Oil Suppliers consisted of a large partitioned room with one small front desk where a dark-haired young woman sat keying on a computer.

"Can I help you?" she asked, not looking up.

"I'd like to speak to the person who's worked here the longest," I said.

My odd request got her attention, but once she got a load of me and my ugly puss, she couldn't stop staring. Finally she said, "Um . . . are you sure you're in the right place? This is a big building and it's easy to get confused."

Guess she decided my bruise somehow affected my ability to navigate through the world. "Sorry, I should have introduced myself. My name is Abby Rose and I'm a friend of the Beadford family. I'm here on Megan Beadford's behalf."

"On her behalf? For what?"

"Do you even *know* who's worked here the longest?" I said, leaning an arm on the counter separating us. Daddy always said if you want to beat around the bush, answer a question with a question.

This tactic seemed to work because she said, "I think that would be Mr. Reilly."

"Mr. Reilly. Good. I'll speak to him."

"Um . . . sure." She glanced over her shoulder, but I got the feeling she might be looking for a security guard rather than Mr. Reilly. I never realized a messed-up face could become such a social barrier.

"Which cubicle is his?" I asked, not willing to be escorted out without getting what I came for. "I'll just introduce myself."

"He—he doesn't have a cubicle, so—"

"Don't get up. I'll go find him." I marched around her desk and passed about six spots occupied by men and women making what sounded like sales calls. None of them looked older than thirty-five. They would be no help concerning the distant past, but one of them did point out Reilly's office. Guy must be a bigwig if he rated privacy.

Meanwhile the receptionist had come after me, but I beat her to Reilly's door and knocked. A male voice called for me to enter and I opened the door.

The young woman had caught up to me and spoke to the man I assumed was Reilly. "This is Miss Rose. She says she's a friend of the Beadfords."

"Then by all means come in," he said.

The woman shrugged and walked away.

Reilly rose from the chair behind his desk. A thin, bald man wearing a wide-lapel jacket, he had huge glasses covering nearly a third of his narrow fifty-ish face. But his purple and yellow tie? Wow. If it were a piece of art I'd call it "Nerd Rebellion."

"What can I do for you, Miss Rose?" he asked, checking out my face with what seemed to be genuine curiosity rather than pity.

"Call me Abby." I smiled and pointed at my cheek. "Ran into a door in the dark."

"That was one nasty door," he said, shaking his head sympathetically. "Do you have a headache? Because I'm getting one just looking at you."

"No, I'm fine." I noticed boxes stacked against one wall and another group on the floor next to me by the door. "Are you moving out?"

"Moving in. I've been assigned to this office now that . . . now that Mr. Beadford is no longer with us. Needs a good fumigation, wouldn't you say?"

"It is a little musty. So this was Mr. Beadford's office?"

"No, not his. Belonged to the young man who's taking over for Mr. Beadford." He sniffed several times. "Musty. Yes. That's it. Better get someone on this. Might be mold growing in the walls." He picked up a Palm Pilot pen and bent to tap on the electronic organizer sitting on his desk.

"So who *is* taking over?" I asked.

"One of the salesmen—though in my opinion the boy's not ready to run a multimillion dollar business." Reilly placed a hand on the back of his chair. "So how can I help you?"

"I'm a private investigator and Megan Beadford hired me to look into the matter of her father's death."

"They haven't arrested anyone yet?"

"No, and I'm sure you can understand she wants to know what happened as soon as possible so she can put this matter to rest. Would you mind answering a few questions?"

"You don't wear perfume, do you?" he said.

"Uh, no," I said, taken aback by the non sequitur.

"I didn't think so. Good for you. Because we'd have to make this a very short conversation if you did. I blame my divorce on perfume. My ex-wife never understood what effect her drenching herself in that stuff had on me. The sneezing, the headaches, the—"

"That must have been tough," I cut in. "Now, to continue with our discussion."

"How long will this take?" He glanced back at the computer monitor. The screen was filled by an Excel spreadsheet. "Because Mr. McNabb has me on a deadline and—"

"Holt McNabb?"

"Yes," he said tersely. "You know him?"

By the look on Reilly's face, I figured I wasn't taking any risks when I said, "Unfortunately, yes."

"He doesn't understand people. No matter what faults Mr. Beadford had, he understood people. You need that trait when you're in charge."

"You sure do."

He sighed. "It's very stressful working for someone new."

"I can see that." I sat in a chair facing his desk.

He followed my lead and eased into his chair.

Before he could go off in another direction, I said, "Do you have any idea why someone might have it in for Mr. Beadford?"

"He did have a . . . *haughtiness* about him, and I suppose that put some people off. But that's no excuse to take his life."

"Are you saying he wasn't well liked?" I certainly hadn't liked him much when I met him.

"Mr. Beadford was indeed well liked. Tough, but fair. And he paid well. Supplying stainless parts to the manufacturing and petroleum plants around here is a very competitive business and he knew the value of keeping his good salespeople."

"And are you a salesman?"

"Oh no. I'm the accountant."

The accountant. Had he been around when Laura Montgomery did her dirty deed?

I was ready to ask Reilly a few questions about the past, but apparently he wasn't ready.

He said, "When we started up Beadford Oil Suppliers after the move from Dallas to downtown Houston we had a small space in a building where you could actually open the windows. These days you can't find a place where you can open windows. Do you have any idea how detrimental it is to your health to be constantly breathing recirculated air?"

"Indeed I do. And how did Dallas compare? You said you worked there first?"

"You know, I hardly remember Dallas except for all the stress surrounding Mr. Beadford's need for my expertise."

"Stress related to the bankruptcy?"

"So you've heard about that. It was a very difficult time for everyone. I had to make sense of the mess that woman made and show Mr. Beadford how she did what she did so no one could steal from him again. And I succeeded." He smiled, and I swear his cheeks touched the rims of those giant glasses. "I must say he never forgot. My Christmas bonus has always been generous."

"You said *that woman.* Tell me about her."

"His first accountant?"

"Yes, the one who embezzled from him."

He nodded. "Laura Montgomery. A bright woman. She had two sets of books. Took the Beadfords for just about everything."

"That's what I've heard."

"Does she have something to do with his murder?" Reilly said. "Because she disappeared and—"

"I'm not sure. That's for the police to figure out. I'm just gathering information. Do you know Sylvia Beadford?"

"Of course," he said. "Nice lady. But perfume? She is worse than my ex-wife."

"Does she come here often?" I was thinking if she did, she might have done the same back in Dallas and could have known Laura Montgomery.

"My ex-wife? Thank the lord, no." He laughed.

"I meant Mrs. Beadford."

"Oh. No, not often, but she did drop by on occasion. She'd bring Mr. Beadford shrimp po'boys from some little restaurant near their house or sometimes they'd go out to lunch together. The smell of shrimp, unfortunately, lingers long after it's consumed."

"Did you meet Sylvia in Dallas or when the business moved here?" I asked.

"I met her in Dallas. She was more devastated than Mr. Beadford when they had to file for bankruptcy. Most of that money belonged to her."

"Really?"

"Oh yes. They were co-owners."

Co-owners, huh? Then she probably had met Montgomery. "And what about Graham Beadford? Did you know him?"

"Never met him. From what Mr. Beadford told me, his brother had some emotional problems after the business went under—which is perfectly understandable. And now I hear he's . . . he's gone, too."

"Yes. It's an awful time for the family. I have another question. When you joined the company to help straighten out the bookkeeping mess, what was the word about Montgomery? I mean, I'm sure people talked."

"Not to me. I was an outsider brought in to fix things. No one said anything to me about her—no one except for Georgia."

"Georgia?"

"Georgia Jackson. She'd been Ms. Montgomery's secretary. Georgia and I worked closely for a time, and being black, she used some kind of oil on her hair. She always smelled like coconuts."

"And what did *she* say about Montgomery?"

"I don't remember specifics. But it was probably of

a sympathetic nature. She was such a nonjudgmental person."

"Do you know what happened to Georgia after the business moved?"

"Do I know? Of course. Mr. Beadford tried to hire back most of his people, but only three of us were willing to relocate. Myself, Georgia, and Robert."

"And is Robert still here?"

"He died more than ten years ago. Smoker." He shook his head in disgust. "Now there's an odor that—"

"And what about Georgia? Does she still work here?"

"She retired."

"And when was that?"

"Last year. She drops by, though. Takes care of her grandchildren while her daughter works, but when she has time off, she'll bring cookies or pecans from her trees. League City has hundreds of pecan trees. But I never eat anything she brings. Children are not the cleanest creatures on God's earth and who knows if those grandchildren helped make those cookies or bag those nuts."

I was about to ask for the woman's address, but I noticed Reilly's gaze had moved to beyond my left shoulder and he had stiffened. "Mr. McNabb," he said, nodding.

I turned.

Holt stood in the doorway looking like a different man than the one I'd encountered at the rehearsal and wedding. He wore an expensive-looking suit and his blue eyes were cold and clear and boring into me.

"Why are you here?" he asked.

"I'm . . . doing a favor for Megan. She wanted me to personally thank all the people at the office for their kindness during this difficult time." Weak cover story, but it might fly. The less Holt knew about me and my reasons for being here, the better I felt.

"Am I included in those thank-yous?" he said.

Before I could answer, Reilly said, "Miss Rose was just telling me Megan was especially grateful for those lilies you sent."

Thanks, Reilly, I thought. *You may be goofy, but you're okay.*

"I'm glad she liked them," Holt said. But he still looked more than a little suspicious. "So you came here as some sort of ambassador for Megan?"

"I guess you could say that," I said.

He looked at Reilly. "I need those numbers on the new account."

"I'm almost done," he answered.

"Good." He turned and walked away.

I got up, thanked Reilly, and followed Holt.

"Wait up," I called to his retreating back.

Holt stopped and faced me.

"Congratulations on the promotion," I said, doing my best to sound sincere.

"Someone had to step in. Sylvia was in no shape to make decisions, and we had orders piling up."

"I see. And she appointed you to take over?"

"That's what James would have wanted. Someone who knew the company inside and out."

He was obviously avoiding my question, so I pushed a little more. "And this is a permanent position?"

"Why do you care?" he asked.

"No need to get defensive. I'm just trying to be friendly . . . make conversation." I was guessing Megan knew nothing about the takeover.

"Are you saying you want to be friends?" He smiled.

Did he have a little "charm switch" in his brain that he flicked on when needed? Because he'd definitely moved into charisma mode.

Guess he didn't want Megan or Sylvia to receive a bad report about him from the likes of me. I decided to play him while I had the advantage. "How do you like the new job?"

The switch must have had a short circuit because his

handsome features tensed—not an attractive change in demeanor, either. "What are you fishing for? Did Travis send you?"

I didn't answer immediately, mainly because I was trying to figure out where he'd come up with *that* idea. Before I could reply, Holt took my arm and started toward a hallway that led to the restrooms. "I want to hear what he said about me, but away from my staff. They don't need the distraction."

"I can walk without your help," I said, pulling free.

"I'll bet you can," he mumbled.

"Isn't Travis your best friend?"

"He *is*. But he's not a businessman. He could never handle this job, even though I think Megan wants him to step in here. And why does this matter to you, anyway?"

"It doesn't," I said. "I'm here because Megan is my friend and she asked me to come." *Sort of,* I added to myself.

"So she's checking on me?"

What's with the paranoia? Is he into drugs, too? But then I remembered something my daddy used to say— that a paranoid is a person with all the facts. Holt no doubt possessed a few facts that I didn't.

"Guilty conscience, Holt?" I. said. "Did you and Travis have a falling out?"

"No way," he said. "But when the police questioned me, I had to tell them the truth. Had to tell what I knew."

"And what do you know?"

"I told Chief Fielder what I'd overheard between Travis and James at the reception. And now Megan's probably gotten wind of what I'd said and wants to fire me. That's what you get for telling the truth. Now if you don't mind, I've got work to do."

He strode away, and I left the office knowing that whatever he'd told Fielder, it wasn't good news for Travis or Megan.

17

By the time I arrived home, I was hungry, tired, and depressed. I needed to talk to Travis and find out why he'd lied to me about when he'd learned Megan had hired me. And then there was that argument I'd witnessed between him and James Beadford at the reception—the argument Holt may have overheard, too. Yup, the boy had some explaining to do.

While Diva and I were finishing off microwave pizza, Kate arrived with arnica gel for my bruises, which I accepted without argument. I'd learned long ago not to complain about her homeopathic interventions. While she was plastering my face with goo, Angel dropped off Laura Montgomery's mug shots. He had to run off for a case he was working, and as soon as he left, Kate and I spread the pictures out on the kitchen table and agreed there was no doubt this was the woman we'd seen at the wedding.

"What does this mean, Abby?" Kate asked. "Did she come there to kill Megan's father?"

"I don't know. I can only say I have a lot to tell you about this woman," I said. "A whole lot."

Kate leaned back in her chair and folded her arms. "Go for it."

After I filled her in on Jamaica and the bankruptcy and Blythe Donnelly, she said, "And you haven't told Megan that her birth mother gave her up to the very people she'd embezzled money from? Why not?"

"First off, Megan needs more bad news about as much as a mermaid needs a bicycle. And second, I don't have all the facts. I want to be able to answer every question."

"I understand, Abby, but this is a murder investigation. Have you told Chief Fielder?"

"I haven't told anyone but you."

She screwed the lid back on the jar of arnica gel. "If the Beadfords adopted Megan from Jamaica, that means they knew where Laura Montgomery or Blythe or whatever you want to call her was and they didn't tell the authorities. Isn't that a crime?"

"Since she was already indicted and awaiting trial, I would think so."

"Why didn't the Beadfords just drop the charges rather than help her get away?" Kate asked.

"I don't know. Maybe they wanted those charges hanging over her head as insurance that Montgomery could never come back and claim the baby."

"Makes sense. So any way you look at it, Montgomery sold her child to buy her freedom," Kate said, shaking her head sadly. "I see your point about not laying this on Megan yet. You do need to find out more."

I rubbed a glob of gel that was oozing toward my ear. "Maybe the baby's death certificate was forged to facilitate getting infant Megan out of Jamaica or maybe there's plenty more I don't know. I need to get the full story."

"This is so complicated, Abby. Are you sure—"

"I'm on this like a rattler on a roadrunner. I *will* find the truth."

She leaned toward me and pushed aside a strand of hair that had stuck to my cheek. "If anyone can, you will."

Kate left a few minutes later and I was ready to soak in a hot tub. But I hadn't even made it to the stairs when the phone rang. I sighed and took the call in my office.

"Abby?" said Sylvia Beadford.

Amazing how one small word can convey panic.

"What's wrong?" I asked.

"They've . . . arrested . . . Travis," she managed.

Damn that Fielder. She hadn't wasted any time. "When?"

"Two deputies took him away a few minutes ago. Megan followed them to the police station. But she told me to call you. She said you could help."

Sylvia wouldn't say that if she knew how much I'd helped so far. "I'll do what I can, but are you okay?" I swear she was hyperventilating.

"It's j-just that I'm alone here and I don't know what's going on and—"

"Where's Roxanne?"

"She's gone—she went to visit Courtney at the hospital—and . . . what should I do? Should I be with Megan?"

"No. Sit tight. I'm on my way to the police station."

Before I left, however, I found the number of the lawyer Jeff had recommended. I grabbed the scrap of paper and took it with me.

The attorney's name was Whitley, and I had him on the line before I even hit the freeway. I explained the situation with Travis and he said he'd meet me at the Seacliff station. Next I called Megan's cell, and when she answered she sounded almost as desperate as her mother had.

"I heard they've arrested Travis," I said.

"Mother told you?"

"Yes," I answered.

"I don't know what's going on, but Travis did *not* kill my father, Abby. He could never kill anyone."

"I called a defense attorney. He'll be there within the hour."

"Don't tell me you think Travis *will* be charged with murder," Megan said.

Okay, I won't tell you that. "Hopefully Chief Fielder is only conducting a formal interview, but no matter why he's been brought in, I sincerely hope Travis keeps his mouth shut until Mr. Whitley arrives."

"Travis has nothing to hide," Megan said, sounding more pissed off by the minute. At least she still had some spunk.

But obviously Travis did have something to hide or he wouldn't have lied to me about what he knew and when. Megan, however, would be in no mood to hear about that, so I changed the subject. "Your mother sounded pretty upset."

"She's been in meltdown mode since my father died," Megan said. "That's why I told her to stay home. She couldn't do much here except get in the way. I'm in the way myself, but I'm not leaving. Not without Travis."

"I'll be there in about forty-five minutes," I said, "and if you do see Travis in the meantime, tell him not to say anything. And the same goes for you if Fielder pulls you in."

She sighed heavily. "Okay."

I hung up and made my best time yet to Seacliff. When a Porsche pulled into a parking slot right next to mine, I guessed correctly that the lawyer had also arrived.

He was a mid-thirties Armani man, just who you'd expect to climb out of a red Porsche, but that's where the stereotype stopped. He was soft-spoken, dark haired, and all-intense eye contact—the sort of guy who could definitely distract Quinn Fielder. *Nice choice, Jeff,* I thought as I filled him in on the case.

We walked into the police station together, and Megan leaped from a plastic chair and ran over to us.

"This is Mark Whitley, Megan. I've told him about the case, and he's willing to take over from here if you have a dollar for a retainer."

"Uh, sure." She reached into her purse and produced a crumpled five. "This is all I've got."

Mark flashed his whiter-than-Aspen-smile. "That will do," he said gently.

He turned to my friend Henderson. In a firm, cool tone Whitley said, "I understand my client is being interrogated. Please interrupt that interview immediately, as Mr. Crane is now represented by counsel."

Henderson smiled over at me. "Ask Miss Rose here. The chief has quite a temper and I don't think she'd appreciate—"

Whitley's fist came down on the desk with enough force to rattle the plastic organizers in front of Henderson. "Do it now, Officer."

"Yes, sir." Henderson jumped up and ran down the hall as fast as a six-legged jackrabbit. A few seconds later he returned and gestured for Whitley to follow him.

I could see visible relief in Megan's tired, drawn face.

"Let's sit down. I need to tell you something," I said.

I explained about my talk with Fielder earlier and how Travis had lied to me the day after the murder about when he'd learned Megan had hired me.

Megan said, "He's being arrested because of some stupid little lie that I insisted he tell everyone?"

"Hiding that information from others makes sense, but why lie to me?"

"Maybe he thought someone would overhear you two talking and mention it to my mother."

"Okay," I answered, "but there's more. I saw something else on the day of your father's murder—which I didn't mention to the police. But Holt McNabb saw it, too. And I think he told Fielder."

Megan's lips paled to near white. "Told her what?"

"Your father and Travis got into a heated argument at the reception—out by the pool."

She twisted her ring. "So? It's not like they hadn't argued before."

"I could tell they were both spitting spite, Megan."

"I don't care what you saw. Travis would never harm my father. It's Holt who's got the problem, tat-

tling to the police about his best friend like some kin-
dergartener. How did you find out, by the way?"

"Because I paid a visit to Beadford Oil Suppliers.
Did you know Holt took over?"

"That's ridiculous," Megan said. "He may have
been a good—"

"Did you say Holt is doing James's job?" came a
voice behind us. We both turned to see Sylvia Beadford standing there.

Megan rose. "I told you to stay home, Mother."

"I couldn't. You and Travis need me," Sylvia said.

"Abby's taking care of things. She found us a lawyer and—"

"A lawyer?" She slowly sat on the nearest molded
chair, her coat opening to reveal dark slacks. But even
sensible winter clothing couldn't stop her from choosing yet another pair of awful high-heeled shoes. These
were black leather with rhinestone buckles. "Are you
saying Travis killed James?"

Megan strode across the room and pointed a finger
at Sylvia. "Don't you *ever* call Travis a murderer."

Sylvia leaned away from Megan's trembling finger,
her daughter's aggressive reaction obviously scaring
her. It scared me a little, too. Megan was beginning
to crumble.

I put a hand on Megan's shoulder and said, "Why
don't you get some air? I'll find you the minute I hear
anything from the lawyer or from Travis."

Megan closed her eyes and took a deep breath. But
her voice was still ripe with anger when she said,
"Good idea." She marched outside.

I sat next to Sylvia, who had begun to cry. Her ton
of mascara wasn't waterproof, and the tears made a
wide inroad on her thick layer of makeup.

"You actually believe Travis killed your husband?"
I asked.

"I don't want to, but he and James . . . well, they
never got along." She bit her bottom lip.

"But he'd need a pretty big reason to commit murder with a hundred people in the next room," I said. "Do you know what that reason might be?"

"All I know is my husband didn't trust Travis."

"Trust him with what?"

"With Megan's future. Did you know Travis was once a rodeo cowboy? And now he's in graduate school for some silly something—wants to be a graphic artist—whatever they do."

Whoa. Aunt Caroline must have taken over Sylvia Beadford's body. Politely as I could, I said, "So Travis isn't interested in becoming a businessman?"

"James always dreamed Megan would marry someone who would manage the business, and frankly so did I."

"So maybe Holt was a better choice for a son-in-law?" I asked.

"Holt? Of course not," she scoffed.

"From your earlier reaction I'm guessing you didn't know he'd taken the reins at Beadford Oil Suppliers," I said.

"I didn't. How did you find out?"

"I stopped by your husband's office and saw for myself. And you didn't ask him to do this?"

"No . . . but I suppose someone had to step in. I haven't even thought about . . . about anything since James died."

"And that's understandable," I said. *So Holt lied to me today.*

"Holt's capable enough, though," Sylvia said thoughtfully.

"So you don't mind?"

"James thought Holt showed promise, said once he finished sewing his wild oats, he'd be a success at whatever he chose to do with his life. But still, he should have consulted with me first." She shook her head. "But I can't blame him for stepping in. I should have gone to the office right after James died. Yes, I should have . . . I mean, I haven't had t-time to—" More tears fell.

I reverted back to my original question. Maybe she could get ahold of herself with sufficient distraction. "Do you know of any specific problems between Travis and your husband other than the trust issue?"

She pulled a wad of tissues from her coat pocket and used one to blow her nose. "Not really. James only wanted Megan's happiness and told her that if she insisted on marrying Travis, he wouldn't stand in the way."

"Not exactly a ringing endorsement," I said.

"James was an opinionated man. He never shied from speaking his mind."

"And how did Megan react to him *speaking his mind*?" I asked.

"They went a few rounds on her choosing Travis, but in the end, as I said, James said that if Travis was the one, then so be it."

"And how about you? Do *you* like Travis?"

Before she could answer, the desk phone started to ring and Henderson came running down the hall to answer. I wondered where he'd been. Listening at Fielder's door?

I would have asked him because he probably would have told me everything, but Travis and his new attorney appeared almost on his heels. Neither of them were smiling, but then this was ugly business.

"Where's Megan?" Travis said to Sylvia, sounding exactly as I would have expected someone to sound after an hour with Quinn Fielder—mad as eight acres of snakes.

"She went for a walk," I said quickly. "It was kind of warm in here. What's going on?"

Whitley offered a tight smile. "Chief Fielder has agreed that before she picks up Mr. Crane in a squad car again, she'll need evidence rather than hearsay."

Man, I wish I could have been in the room when that little confrontation went down. Jeff would be getting a great big thank-you from me tonight for sending Mark Whitley to rescue Travis.

18

When I arrived home, Jeff was busy in the kitchen. A batch of redfish was defrosting in the sink, ones he'd caught and frozen the last time he'd had a real weekend off. I never refuse when someone besides Kate offers to cook me a meal. Besides, Jeff handles a skillet far better than I do. My job is usually the salad, a task I attended to while he pan-grilled the fish and fixed up a mess of home fries. Gosh, didn't they smell like heaven while they cooked?

"Wine?" I asked once our food was on the kitchen table.

"Not for me. I have a stakeout tonight. Got a lead on a gang member wanted in a drive-by. Killed a ten-year-old kid."

"Now I definitely need wine." I pulled a bottle of chardonnay from the fridge and poured myself a large glass before sitting across from him.

"Did you call that lawyer?" he asked, digging into his potatoes.

"Yes, but not for me."

He put down his fork. "Abby, I wish you'd—"

"I'm not a suspect anymore." I took a sip of wine.

"How did that happen?"

"Fielder found someone more interesting."

"And so now you're saving this person's ass. Must be either the bride or the new husband."

"How did you guess?" I said.

"I'm a detective, remember? And I happen to be familiar with your modus operandi. You'd help a shark catch his breakfast." He resumed eating, heaping both fish and potatoes onto his fork at once.

"It's Travis, but I want to know how you guessed."

"I was there when Quinn first interviewed him after the murder. I figured he was hiding something."

I set down my fork and rested my chin on my hand. This was the kind of stuff I needed to know if I wanted to be a decent PI. "How could you tell?"

"First off, liars always answer your questions, but rarely ask any of their own—mainly because they're focused on keeping their story straight. But you would have expected this guy to ask questions, especially since he had been separated from Megan for more than an hour. He didn't."

"You mean he cared more about protecting himself than asking how she was?"

"No, more like he was protecting her and didn't want the interrogation to head in Megan's direction."

"Okay. What else made you think he was hiding things?"

"He used phrases like *To tell you the truth* and *To be perfectly honest* about ten times. And most often, *To tell you the truth* was followed by *I don't know.* That's the kind of stuff you hear from people with secrets."

"And why would Megan be a suspect, too?"

"She was found with the body and knew the victim well. She loved him."

"Right. She *loved* him. How does that translate to murder?"

"Read any Shakespeare lately?" He had finished eating and pushed his plate away.

"You're right. Dumb question. But I didn't know you liked Shakespeare."

"There's a lot you don't know about me." He reached over, took my hand, and pressed the palm to his lips.

"When do you have to leave?" I asked.

"Eleven."

I checked my watch. "I could learn a lot in three hours."

He rose and started to clear the table, but I stopped him and led him upstairs. The next few hours in Jeff's arms were exactly what I needed. By the time he left for his stakeout, all the tension of the last week was gone. I was relaxed, focused, and eager to visit Georgia Jackson tomorrow. Maybe she could tell me things about Laura Montgomery and her relationship to the Beadfords. And perhaps even why Montgomery would risk returning to the States for her daughter's wedding.

When I reached Mrs. Jackson by phone the next morning, she said she'd be happy to meet with me if I didn't mind coming to her house in the afternoon. She had grandchildren to care for. Glad to have the chance to talk with her, I made the trip south to League City, a sprawling, busy town about twenty miles down the interstate. Her small brick house was surrounded by pecan trees—Reilly had mentioned pecans—and Mrs. Jackson answered the door immediately.

She was a tall, lean woman wearing a denim jumper and a navy cardigan. Her home smelled like a cookie factory. Before I could even sit in the living room chair, Mrs. Jackson gestured to a brown, smiling girl with a head full of bouncing braids, who ran to me carrying a paper plate loaded with chocolate chip cookies. On her heels came a younger boy carefully holding a glass of milk with both hands.

"Good job, children," said Mrs. Jackson. "You go play now."

"But—" started the boy.

"Cedric, Granny says go play. Understand?" She leveled a stern but loving look in the children's direction.

"Yes, ma'am," the kids said in unison. They turned and disappeared into a hallway off the living room.

"Excuse them, please. They're a work in progress," she said. "And the milk was Cedric's idea. Feel free to pass on their hospitality."

"Are you kidding? This is the best welcome I've had in a long time." I sat and bit into one of those heavenly cookies and washed it down with cold milk.

"You said this was about Laura when you phoned. Please tell me she's been found." Her expressive face—a beautiful cinnamon color spotted with freckles over her cheeks—showed concern mixed with sadness.

"She is definitely alive." I finished off the cookie, set the glass on the table next to me, and settled deeper into the overstuffed chair.

"Praise God," said Mrs. Jackson, clasping her hands and raising her eyes to the ceiling.

"You thought she might be dead?"

"I didn't want to think Mr. Beadford was capable of hurting her, but the notion was always there in the back of my mind. And you have lifted that burden. I do thank you, Miss Rose."

"It's Abby."

"And I'm Georgia," she said with a nod.

"So you're saying you thought Mr. Beadford might have harmed Laura after she stole from him?"

"Seems you know Laura's story, but what do you know about James Beadford?"

I proceeded to tell her what I knew and how I had come to know it.

"So the brothers are dead. What a crying shame," she said when I'd finished telling her about the murders. "But are you thinking Laura killed Mr. Beadford and his brother?"

"I don't know. I'm simply trying to find the truth."

"She would *not* do such a thing. Never in a million years." Georgia sat back in the ladder-back chair she had pulled from the connecting dining room and folded her arms.

"So tell me about her."

"She had a temper, yes. But what I was trying to

say is that maybe you need to know more about *him* to understand why he was killed. A stubborn man with a huge ego is capable of making many enemies," she said.

"I understand you relocated to work for him again. Why do that if you didn't like him?"

"Who said I didn't like him? God, I loved the man like a son. But he was a sinner, and sinners always pay. Laura, too. A beautiful, willful girl. But no one ever taught her about the evil power of vengeance."

"Vengeance?" I said.

But before she could answer, a screech sounded from the hallway and Cedric came running to his grandmother, a pair of scissors in hand.

"I didn't do it, Granny. I didn't do it," he wailed.

The girl followed him, her hand to her forehead, blood seeping between her fingers. Fat tears slid down her cheeks.

Mrs. Jackson grabbed the scissors, stood, and took Cedric by the arm, whipping him into her chair in one swift motion. "Stay put, son." She turned to me and said evenly, "Please excuse us for a moment, Abby."

She led the girl to the back of the house. Cedric looked at me and said, "I'm telling the truth. I didn't do it."

If Jeff's theory held any water, Cedric did indeed do it. "What happened?" I asked.

"She was going to cut her hair and I stopped her. That's the God's truth."

"Is it?" I tried to mimic that laser stare his granny had offered earlier.

His lower lip quivered and he didn't answer. He didn't need to.

When Georgia and the girl returned a few moments later—a Band-Aid covered the wound on the child's forehead—Cedric said, "I'm sorry, Granny. I didn't mean to cut her."

"I still owe you a licking for lying. And Aisha is

owed one for letting you near those scissors. Separate rooms." She pointed toward the hall and both children scurried off.

She eased down in her chair, pulling her sweater tighter around her bony shoulders. "Tell me how they'd handle that little episode in some day care? Probably wouldn't even notice. And we wonder why our children have strayed so far from what's right. No discipline, I say. Now, what were we discussing?"

"Vengeance," I said.

"Ah yes. Did you ever read *Jane Eyre*?"

"Yes, but—"

"Guilty pleasure of mine, reading about little white girls with silly problems. Anyway, that author made a few decent points, and since I was reading that book when Laura went astray, I remember what Brontë said about vengeance because it seemed to fit at the time."

"Sorry, but my memory isn't as good as yours." I needed to trust that Georgia would get to the point sooner or later. I was fast learning to allow people to tell me what they knew at their own pace.

"Brontë said vengeance is as tempting as wine, smells wonderful, but when you drink of it, it makes you feel like you've been poisoned. Pretty smart woman, huh?"

"Very smart."

"I think Laura was poisoned by her own need for vengeance."

"Vengeance and not greed?" I asked. "She did steal a lot of money."

"She didn't have a greedy bone in her body. But Laura knew money was Mr. Beadford's soft underbelly. And the love of that money was his downfall. Laura took advantage of his weakness."

"Are you saying she embezzled his money to get even with him for something?"

"That's what I'm guessing."

"For what?" But I was beginning to understand.

"I think I've guessed enough. I have no direct knowledge of anything except Laura's character. Of her weakness. Of his weakness."

I wanted to scream *So guess anyway!* But I knew this woman had such a strong sense of fair play it wouldn't help. I said, "His weakness was his love of money. What about Laura's?"

"Poor judgment. Impulsiveness. I suppose youth is a built-in weakness, isn't it?" She smiled, and in that smile I saw what she'd been implying, what *I* had to say rather than have the words come from her lips.

"They were having an affair, right?"

Georgia said nothing. Didn't even blink.

"Yes. That's it. He dumped her, and she got even by stealing his money."

Georgia shut her eyes and came close to a nod. "As I said, I had no direct knowledge. No proof."

"But you are an insightful woman. I think that's enough proof for me. Is there anything else about Laura you could tell me?"

"Nothing except she was smart. Misguided, yes. Foolish, yes, but intelligent and caring. Of course not as smart as Miss Charlotte Brontë or she would have known better than to do what she did."

A few minutes later I left Georgia Jackson's home with a Ziploc full of cookies and walked to my car in a chilly drizzle. That drizzle turned to a steady rain by the time I reached home, the afternoon now as dark as night.

Diva was sitting on the kitchen counter by the answering machine when I came in, which meant I probably had messages. She's conditioned for plenty of petting while I listen, and I stroked her as I pushed the play button.

Jug's cheerful voice filled the kitchen. "Miss, this be Jug here. Got plenty of news, so call me quick as you get in." He hadn't left his number and it hadn't shown up on the caller ID so I'd have to hunt up his card.

The other message was from Megan and I called her back first.

"Hi, Abby," she said once I had her on the line. "Travis and I wondered if we could drop by this evening."

"Sure, but why?" I asked.

She lowered her voice. "My mother is right around the corner. We're just finishing up with the funeral director after setting up Uncle Graham's services. Is seven okay?"

"Fine, but—"

"Great." She hung up.

That was strange. Did she want an update on the mother hunt? If she did, was I ready to tell her all I knew, even the latest? That apparently her birth mother had had an affair with her father and—

"Holy shit!" I slapped my forehead with the heel of my hand. "Now I get it."

19

I took Diva's face between my hands and put my nose an inch from hers. "James Beadford adopted his own daughter, cat!"

She was not impressed by my lightbulb moment. She struggled free and ran off, leaving me with a handful of calico hair.

I should have considered this possibility sooner. Why else would James Beadford have brought the child of the woman who'd nearly ruined him into his home?

I had to tell Megan, but was tonight the right time to load her up with a heavy dose of family and company history, none of it too pretty? No, I wanted the DNA report in hand and Kate sitting beside us when that conversation took place. Kate's the expert on dealing with emotions.

I unzipped the cookie bag—I definitely needed a chocolate fix—and ate while I dumped the contents of my purse onto the kitchen table to look for Jug's card. Three cookies later I had him on the line and he sounded as cheerful as when we'd last seen each other.

"Sorry I don't call sooner, miss. But Martha, she be having so much trouble."

"Oh no. Her pregnancy?" I asked.

"Yes, but everything irie now."

"Irie?"

"Means everything fine. We got us a new daughter yesterday. We call her Rose."

A tiny lump formed in my throat. "Thank you, Jug."

"Me the one be thanking you. Where you get so much money to be giving it to your taxi man?"

"Doesn't matter. I want to hear about the baby. How big is she?"

"Let me figure in American." He paused. "Ten pounds. So hard on Martha. She say no more babies, mon."

I laughed. "I don't blame her."

"But I got more news, miss. Found your midwife. The one who delivered that baby you been asking about."

"You're kidding!"

"She be some booguyaga. I'd never trust no birthing to her. Gravelicious woman, though, so your money talked loud and clear. She told me everything."

I wasn't sure what those odd words meant, but I got the gist. "And what's everything?" I asked.

"That she was paid to drug your lady after she gave birth—kept her drugged about a week, if she remembers right. She gave the little girl to a lawyer from the U.S. and told the mother the baby died."

"This lawyer's name didn't happen to be Caleb Moore?" Moore—the man who'd handled the Beadford adoption.

"Ya, mon! That's the one. You know him?"

"Not personally, but I know who hired him."

"I see you been working hard on this, miss. Me, too. I found out who made the fake death certificate. Man be dead now, but you be needing that, too?"

"Not now, but maybe later. You've done a great job, Jug. Kiss that new girl for me."

We said our good-byes, and I'd no sooner hung up when Jeff called. By the time we finished talking, the cookie bag was empty. He told me his stakeout had been productive last night, but now he had a mountain of paperwork and would probably crash at the station tonight. *Boo-hiss,* I thought after I hung up.

After my nonstop cookie fest, I skipped dinner and instead managed to get a few more boxes unpacked before Travis and Megan arrived. I made a pot of coffee for Travis and me. Megan said she was too jittery for coffee. She did seem fidgety, and with each passing day she was looking more washed out, her porcelain skin now blotched and her eyes heavy with fatigue and worry. How I wished what I had learned about her past could bring her some relief, but that didn't seem remotely possible.

Travis helped me move several boxes blocking one chair in the living room, and once we were seated, Megan spoke.

"I think Travis wants to explain why he lied to you." She squeezed his hand and nodded. "Go ahead, honey."

Travis looked like a dog after a neutering—pained, pissed off, and sad. "Truth be told, I had to keep my story straight. It's what I told Fielder so I thought I'd better stick with it when you asked."

"Why lie about knowing Megan had hired me, even to Fielder?" I asked. *And why* keep *lying,* I said to myself, Jeff's impression of Travis still fresh in my mind.

"I wasn't about to talk about Megan's private business. Not with Fielder. It wasn't right."

"So you were protecting Megan?" I sipped my coffee and leaned back against the sofa cushions.

"Who said she needed protecting?" he shot back.

Megan switched her grip to his knee. "It's okay, Travis. Abby's helping us, remember?"

He released a long breath. "Yeah. I know. But I've never seen you hurting like this, Meg."

"I can help you," I said, "but you need to come clean, Travis. What did you argue about with Megan's father because I saw it. Holt must have heard it and Fielder now knows it."

His stare went from Megan to me, and all the tension and then some returned. "That's no one's business."

"You don't believe that and neither do I," I said. "What's the big secret? At least tell your lawyer if you won't tell me."

"What happened between James and me that day will stay between him and me. Just know I would never hurt Megan by killing her father."

"But if you have nothing to hide, I don't see—"

The sound of breaking glass made me start, and coffee spilled onto my jeans. Good thing it wasn't hot enough to do any damage.

"What was that?" said a wide-eyed Megan.

Diva provided a clue when she flashed past us and raced up the stairs.

"She probably knocked something over in the kitchen," I said. "Let me make sure she didn't hurt herself."

I found her cowering under my bed. She hadn't left any bloody footprints on the stairs or in the bedroom and was probably just spooked, so I offered a few soothing words and left her where she was.

"Sorry about the interruption," I said when I returned to my guests. "Now, Travis. I—"

"They argued about money," Megan said. "Travis was too embarrassed to tell you."

Travis's earlobes were red, his eyes downcast. Had they concocted this story while I was distracted? And if so, why? "Money?" I said, my tone infused with all the skepticism I felt.

"My father had agreed to pay for Travis's last year at graduate school, but he took the offer back the day of the wedding," Megan said.

"What a nice gift for his newest relative. And that's the story worth lying about to the police? I don't think so, guys."

The sound of Megan's cell phone prevented a response.

By the look on her face after she answered, the call was not welcome. "Slow down, Roxanne. I can't understand you."

Megan listened for a second, then said, "I'm at Abby's house. Why do you need to know?"

More silence, then Megan said, "You're scaring me, Roxy. What's wrong with you?"

I held out my hand for the phone. "Let me talk to her." God knows I'd had plenty of practice trying to interpret Roxanne's peculiar communications.

When I had the phone, I said, "What's up?"

"Like I told Megan, this is fate, Abby. They're with you, just as they should be."

"I'm not sure I understand."

"Please protect them from the vicious publicity that will certainly be generated by my confession. I am on my way now to turn myself in. Please let them both know I love them very much."

"Wait a minute. What are you confessing to?"

"I killed them."

A shiver shot up my spine. Roxanne's calm, cold manner gave me the heebie-jeebies. "Who did you kill?"

"Uncle James and Dad. They interfered in my very private affairs, something they had no business doing."

"Are you talking about your violinist friend? The one they sent to Boston?"

"I see you have been informed about the tragedy that has become my existence. And now I must say good-bye. Chief Fielder is waiting for me."

The line went dead, and I stared at the phone for several seconds. The rumble of thunder above seemed fitting accompaniment to this strange development.

Megan broke the silence. "Did she say what I thought she said?"

"Yup."

"And what was that?" said Travis.

"She confessed to killing her father and her uncle," I answered.

Megan closed her eyes and shook her head. "That's why she didn't show up at the funeral home today. She was probably busy thinking up this latest drama. What is wrong with Uncle Graham's girls?"

"Maybe she's hungry for attention," I offered. "I can't see her killing her own father."

"Sorry, but she's a nutcase as far as I can tell," said Travis. "I say either one of those cousins is capable of just about anything."

"But they've had such a rough time, Travis," said Megan.

"Lots of folks have a rough time and don't end up acting psycho," he answered.

Megan's gaze fell to her lap, and she twisted her ring. "I know you're right, but I still care about them both."

"I understand. They're family," I said. "And if it helps, the night Graham died, I left Roxanne in the funeral home parking lot and went straight to see her father. I don't think she had time to get to the hotel before me."

"You don't know for sure, though," Travis said.

"Okay, maybe there's an outside chance she made a dash to her father in travel speed worthy of NASCAR. But even though the girl's not working with a full string of lights, I'm with Megan. She's not a killer."

"So what do we do?" Megan asked.

"Let Chief Fielder handle her," I answered. This was a solution I liked. Oh yes. I liked it very much indeed.

"After the way the chief treated Travis, shouldn't we go there or get her a lawyer, too?" Megan said.

"Why not wait and see what happens? If Roxanne is making this up, the chief will figure it out," I said.

Travis reached over and took Megan's hand. "Abby's right."

"I hope so," Megan replied. But she didn't sound convinced.

They left a few minutes later, the rain again reduced to drizzle. But the temperature had dropped a wicked twenty degrees in the last hour. I hurried upstairs and put on a sweatshirt, then adjusted the thermostat. But a chill lingered, one that seemed to come not from the change in weather but rather from my own discomfort.

Megan and Travis's visit had unsettled me. These were two people I had come to care for, but they were both unraveling under the stress and revealing parts of themselves I wasn't sure I liked. The once soft, sweet Megan seemed as nervous as a horse on a high wire. And Travis? The guy was a seething pot of emotion. Understandable? Sure. But still troubling.

Diva had followed me downstairs, and recalling the breaking glass, I decided I'd better see what she'd destroyed this week. Another sugar bowl? A glass she just had to stick her snout in?

Nothing seemed amiss in the kitchen, so I checked the laundry room—no problems there—and then decided she must have done her damage in the small glassed-in terrace. I flipped on the light switch by the entry, and sure enough, a Mason jar filled with clothespins that had been sitting on the picnic table now lay in pieces on the tile. I took one step into the room and stopped.

I wasn't alone.

20

"I like your cat," said an unfamiliar female voice. "Very friendly, but a little clumsy."

I took a step back, wondering how quickly I could get to the phone.

"I have a gun, so don't think about calling for help," the woman said. She'd been sitting in one of the wicker chairs in the shadowed corner, but now stood. I saw a flash of silver in her hand.

As Daddy used to say, there is nothing more convincing than the business end of gun. I didn't move.

She walked to the center of the room until she was under the ceiling fan light—and I was suddenly glad I hadn't made that call.

"I've been dying to meet you," I said, "but please don't take that literally."

Laura Montgomery smiled with all the self-assurance holding a weapon can provide. She wore a green sweater, the shoulders soaked with rain. Not exactly warm enough clothing for tonight's weather, but you don't need many warm clothes in Jamaica, so her wardrobe was probably limited. She'd skipped the hat, and curved tendrils of damp hair clung to both cheeks. Her gun hand was mottled by the cold—a small-caliber gun, similar to the .22 Daddy bought me for my sixteenth birthday, the one I wished was in my pocket rather than in my office.

"Now that the newlyweds are gone, I hope you'll take a little friendly advice," she said.

"Friendly? With a weapon in your hand?"

"I wasn't sure what kind of welcome I'd receive. After all, I did break into your house. Damn easy by the way."

"Turnabout is fair play," I said.

Her eyes widened in surprise.

"Nice little place you've got in Jamaica," I said, adding a tad of my own arrogance.

Her voice edged with anger, she said, "You are a very busy young woman. That's why we need to talk."

"You don't need a gun for that. I'm happy to sit down and—"

"No, thank you. We'll talk right here, right now."

"Okay. You're the boss."

"Tell me what your relationship is to my daughter."

"Simple. She hired me to find you."

That cracked her "I'm tough-as-nails" demeanor. *"What?"*

"You heard me. I've been looking for you for months. She wanted her mother at her wedding. Apparently she got her wish."

"S-she knew about me?" I'd apparently pressed her panic button because her face had paled.

But I was a little confused. "That's why you came out of hiding, right? To attend your daughter's wedding?"

"Yes, but not because—are you saying she knows *everything* about me? Knew I was there that day?"

Ah. Now I understood. "No. She doesn't know much of anything yet—how you're a fugitive, how you've been following her. That kind of information has to wait for just the right moment, and with her father murdered and her uncle dead, now is not the time."

"I'm truly sorry about all that's happened," she said, but I sensed she was distracted, was trying to figure something out.

"You're sorry?" I said. "Sorry you killed them?"

She flinched, stared at me. "From what I overheard between the three of you here tonight, someone else wants to take responsibility for those deaths. And that's the best news I've had since I arrived in Texas. I can go home now."

"Go home?" I offered a sarcastic laugh. "I don't think the police will let that happen."

Renewed fear flickered in her eyes. "So you've told them about me?"

"I sure tried to tell them, but that's a long story. Maybe we can make a little deal here. You tell me what I want to know, and maybe I'll delay reporting your reappearance to the police."

"A deal? If you think I killed two men, what's to stop me from killing you?" She raised the gun a few inches to emphasize the point.

What *would* stop her? I was reading desperation in her tense face and scared eyes, and desperate people do crazy things. The only defense I had was what I had learned in the last few weeks, so I kept talking. "You care way too much about your daughter to kill one of her friends—and I am her friend."

That got her. Her shoulders sagged. "I didn't even know she was alive until a few weeks ago."

"You thought she died at birth."

"And I suppose you also know that bastard stole my daughter? She was the only reason I ran before my court date. I wasn't about to have a baby while I was in prison, have my child end up in foster care. And it turns out, she was the only thing that could bring me back here. I swear, if James had been in the room when I learned how he'd taken my child, I would have killed him with my bare hands."

And I believed her. Revisiting her anger had her tensing up, and her grip on the gun seemed viselike now. Did she even know how to use it? An untrained person holding a gun is about the scariest thing on earth. "Listen, I don't plan on running for the phone or screaming for the neighbors, so could you put the gun down?"

But she was so wound up she started waving the weapon instead, riding her emotions like some freaked-out kid on a roller coaster. "Can you believe what he did to me? How could anyone be that cruel? I lost my daughter and thought it was somehow my fault she died. I believed I deserved what happened, thought I had to be punished for the crime I'd committed."

Adrenaline spilled into my blood and made my skin prickle with the tension. Keeping my eyes on the .22, I said, "I realize Megan was raised by your worst enemy, but—"

"Her name was *Claire*."

"Right," I said softly. "Claire. But she's very much alive. A beautiful young woman. Kind and loving. And I know she wants to meet you in the worst way."

Obviously not the right words. She pointed the gun at my chest. "That will never happen. You will not tell her about me."

"Okay. Sure. But—"

"Liar," she spat. "You'll tell her the first chance you get if I let you live."

"So kill me, then," I said, sounding braver than I felt. "But one way or another, she'll find out. She's determined to learn the truth about you, and if I'm dead, she'll find someone else to help her."

We stared at each other for what seemed an hour, but it had to be only a few seconds. Then she relaxed the gun hand, letting it drop to her side. "He made me pay for what I did to him. For twenty long years."

"But he's gone now and maybe you and Megan can—"

"No. My daughter couldn't possibly forgive me for what I did. I'm a common criminal." Her eyes had misted, and she blinked several times until they cleared.

"And couldn't possibly forgive your affair with her

father?" I asked, wanting to add, *And couldn't forgive you for killing him?* But that question might rile her up enough to make her point that gun my way again.

She nodded. "Believe it or not, I used to love that asshole."

"And he was Megan's biological father, right?"

She nodded.

"Listen, I promise to help you work things out with your daughter, but I need all the facts. How did you know about the wedding? How—"

"Abby?" came a muffled voice from the vicinity of the kitchen. Aunt Caroline's voice. Damn her to hell!

My aunt started pounding on the back door, saying, "I know you're home."

As far as Laura Montgomery was concerned, Aunt Caroline might as well have been the FBI. She whirled and rushed out the terrace door into the darkness, shattered glass crunching underfoot, clothespins spinning on the tile after her retreat.

A part of me wanted to run after her, tackle her, make her tell me more, but a loud voice in my head overruled this idea. "Let her go for now," it said.

So I closed the terrace door and went to let my stupid aunt in. She was the last person I wanted to talk to, especially since she'd just screwed up my chance of finishing the job I was hired for.

"Abby, what's wrong?" she asked as soon as I let her in.

"Nothing. So glad you dropped by." No hiding the sarcasm. I was too pissed off. I headed for the coffeepot to refill the mug I'd emptied on my jeans earlier, not trusting myself even to be civil.

"No coffee for me, thank you. I can't stay."

Now, there's the best news I've had all day.

"I see you're upset," she said. "You've got those little furrows between your eyebrows. Do you know how expensive it is to cosmetically repair damage that could be avoided if you'd pay attention to your emotions, Abigail?"

"No, but I'm sure you do," I said wearily. "Listen. I've had a long day. Why are you here?"

"I found you some work, just as I promised." She smiled like she'd just invented Coca-Cola.

"I told you not to do that," I said.

"But Libby needs your help. You remember my friend Libby?"

I nodded, stirring sugar into my coffee. Libby had a fake British accent and carted an Irish wolfhound around in her Mercedes.

"She adopted a new puppy from the shelter—got a schnoodle if you can believe it. Schnoodles are very in. Anyway, this dog has seizures, and Libby feels it's her responsibility to find the original owner and see if there are more puppies who might be afflicted. She hopes to then find them homes with owners who have the resources to—"

"You want me to work a *dog* adoption case?" I said through tight lips.

"Why yes. You fancy yourself an investigator and—"

"I don't investigate dogs . . . or cats or birds," I said, my voice rising. "And if she adopts an elephant with hives, I won't do that case, either!"

Aunt Caroline stepped back, looking indignant. "How ungracious of you, Abigail. I taught you to be—"

"Save it," I said.

She pulled her fur collar up around her chin. "I came here with the best intentions, hoping to show you that I'm willing to embrace the new *working girl* Abby. Obviously you don't appreciate my efforts, and so I will bid you good night."

She, too, departed into the night, leaving me frustrated and angry.

And then there was the guilt. How did she manage to be such an idiot and still make me feel like everything wrong between us was my own doing?

21

The next morning, after I'd rethought the events of
last night, I knew I had to report that Laura Montgomery had returned to the States. Since she had been
arrested, though not tried for the embezzlement, that
meant the statute of limitations didn't apply. She was
still wanted by the authorities. If I had any intention
of moving beyond provisional PI status in the future,
I had to play by the rules. I called Angel for advice,
and he told me that since Montgomery had fled from
a Dallas jurisdiction, I could report my "sighting" on-
line. And, since the case was cold, Angel figured it
would probably take the Dallas cops at least a week
to put someone on it, pull the files, and get back to
me. In other words, this approach would buy some
time.

Next I called Kate at her office. With Megan's
mother making an appearance, it was time to tell my
client what I had learned. That DNA results I'd been
so eager to get didn't even matter anymore, but Kate's
presence when I spoke to Megan did. The receptionist
said Kate would be free for lunch at eleven thirty,
which gave me an hour to get my act together and
make it to the Medical Center. I also needed to find
out what had become of Roxanne the Confessor, and
once I was on the road, I called Megan to find out.

But she didn't answer. Travis did.

"Hi, Travis. So what happened with Roxanne's confession last night?"

"When we got home and told Sylvia what Roxanne had done, all three of us went down to the police station. Roxanne refused to see us. Fielder told us Roxanne is not under arrest, but she decided to keep her overnight as a material witness."

"No arrest. Obviously Fielder wasn't convinced by this confession—at least not yet."

"Yeah. Not yet."

"Fielder's probably being careful this time after what happened when she hauled you in. Does Roxanne have a lawyer?"

"Apparently she refused legal help, too. Megan's hoping Fielder will let her out in time for Graham's visitation tonight. Sylvia's decided he should be buried next to his brother—which I don't get since they weren't exactly best buddies—but I'm not making those decisions."

"How's Megan today? I'm concerned about her. She looked so tired and pale last night."

"I'm pretty concerned myself. I wanted to talk to you about—" He paused. "Hang on. I hear her coming down the stairs." A second later Travis said, "Hey, Meg. It's Abby."

Megan got on the line. "Did Travis tell you they kept Roxanne overnight?"

"He did, but maybe Fielder wanted to give Roxanne some time to rethink her confession." I'd reached the Medical Center and had to pay attention to traffic or get myself killed. "If it would make you feel better, I'll swing by the Seacliff Police Station later and see if I can find out anything."

"Abby, you've helped so much already and—"

"Consider it done. I'll see you at the funeral home this evening and give you a full report." Megan gave me the time and location—the same as her father's services—and I clicked off the phone and plugged it into the recharger.

Maybe tonight I could get Travis alone. Get his

opinion on when I should tell Megan everything I'd learned. Would she be happy to know she'd been adopted by her biological father or angry he hadn't told her the truth? And would she be happy to know her birth mother was alive or disgusted the woman was a fugitive? I had no way of knowing.

Finding a spot in the parking garage of Kate's building proved as challenging as always, and after my fifth trip around winding narrow lanes and concrete pillars, I slipped into a spot meant for a "compact" car. Absurd. Ninety-nine percent of the vehicles in Houston are SUVs or trucks.

Kate was waiting in the reception room when I arrived in her tenth floor office. She wore blue today, a pale cashmere sweater and navy wool slacks. The colors complemented her creamy skin and dark hair, and I decided it felt good to see a rested, happy female for once. Rather than go out for lunch, she suggested we order Chinese, and we went to the family therapy room after she called King Food.

I love the therapy room. It's the most comfortable, homey place imaginable. The lighting casts a pink glow over the spacious area—according to Kate pink is the most calming color. Two sofas and four armchairs surrounded an oval coffee table, and classical music played in the background today rather than Kate's usual favorite, Jazz. Me? I would have opted for Dave Matthews if I came for a head shrinking. His music is about as real as it gets.

We sat in the "big chairs" as I call them, two huge overstuffed cranberry chairs you could get lost in. I removed my shoes and tucked my feet up.

Kate said, "I see you've been using the arnica gel. Your face looks so much better."

"You were right about that stuff. Worked like a charm. Wish I had a magic fix for this case. Yesterday was chock-full of surprises."

I brought her up to snuff and had just finished when the receptionist brought in the food.

After she was gone, I said, "Kate, I could use your support when I sit Megan down and tell her all this."

"I planned on being there." She pushed her rice around with her chopsticks. "But I have another concern for now. This confession of Roxanne's. That girl is unstable, Abby."

"My guess is she's not guilty of anything besides being as nutty as a bag of ballpark peanuts."

"You think she's protecting Travis with this confession?" Kate asked.

"I don't know what's going on in her mind, but she did confess right after she found out Travis had been brought in for questioning."

"So maybe she *is* protecting him?"

"One thing I know for sure about Roxanne is how much she cares for Megan and Courtney. If that means protecting Megan's relationship with Travis by going to jail, I think she'd be more than willing to take the fall."

"If she does get arrested, I'm worried how Courtney will handle it. Emotionally, she's very fragile right now," said Kate.

"Fragile? That's an adjective I never would have chosen for Courtney." I was eating with a good old fork, a far more sensible utensil than chopsticks. I speared a piece of sweet-and-sour pork and loaded it up with the yummy pink sauce before putting it in my mouth.

"I talked to Courtney late last night, and believe me, she's not the same girl you met. I'm visiting her this afternoon, by the way."

"She's lucid?" I said.

"Lucid and depressed. But that's what I expected at this point."

I planted my fork in my untasted glob of white rice and left it there. "You know what? Roxanne's confession came on the heels of Travis's episode with Fielder, but it also came soon after she visited her sister yesterday. Maybe it's not Travis she's protecting."

Kate offered an "I don't think so" look. "What could Courtney have said that would send Roxanne off to martyr herself?"

"I don't know. But I'm fresh out of ways to find out who killed James and Graham. If she's got any ideas. I'd love to hear them. Mind if I tag along?"

Kate frowned, seeming none too thrilled with this request. She finally said, "Courtney would have to agree to see you. And if she starts to decompensate—she'll be experiencing plenty of ups and downs in the next few days—you'll have to leave the room right away."

"Yes, ma'am, Dr. Rose. You have my promise."

We drove in separate cars since the private psychiatric facility was about halfway to Seacliff. I planned on visiting the funeral home this evening and I wouldn't have time to make two trips back and forth to Houston.

The psych hospital was a sprawling redbrick building surrounded by live oaks and plenty of shrubbery. And the obligatory ten-foot-high chain-link fence. The only thing missing was razor wire.

"Who's paying for this? Sylvia?" I asked as we walked a concrete path toward a set of double glass doors.

"Believe it or not, Courtney has medical insurance," Kate said.

"She has a job?" I said, surprised.

"No, she told me her father paid for her coverage."

"I know for certain *he* didn't have a job. Wonder how he afforded it."

"Maybe you can ask Courtney," Kate said, reaching for the door.

My sister was greeted by the staff with smiles and hugs, and there were introductions all around. I was provided with one of those stick-on visitor badges and then we walked down a long corridor to Courtney's room.

Stopping outside number 120, Kate said, "Let me ask her if she wants to see you . . . and at some point I will need time alone with her."

"Why don't you do that now? I see some chairs down the hall where I can park it until you two are done talking."

"You sure?" Kate looked amused.

"You think I can't handle a few crazy people?"

Kate glanced around and whispered, "Keep your voice down. I'll come and get you if Courtney okays a visit."

"Gotcha," I answered.

She knocked on Courtney's door, cracked it an inch, then slipped inside.

I headed for the chairs stacked outside what turned out to be a game room. The place was empty, so I went to a card table and sat down in front of a deck of cards. I started shuffling, but before I could lay out a round of solitaire, a heavy woman with red cheeks and a serious wheeze sat across from me.

"You new?" she asked.

"Oh, I'm not a patient," I said.

Her hair was thinning, and she wore a purple and gold LSU T-shirt. "Then I'm not, either." Her thick drawl wasn't Texan—more like the deep south.

"Really, I'm not a patient. I'm waiting to visit someone."

"Who? Bill?"

"No." I dealt my hand, hoping she'd leave. Her scent reminded me of a perfumed poodle and her heavy breathing made me nervous. I sure hoped they had medical doctors here, too, if she wheezed herself unconscious.

"Bill has wife issues, and I thought you might be the girlfriend. I'm Amelia, by the way." She extended a plump hand.

"Nice to meet you. I'm Abby." We shook hands, and it was all I could do to not pull back too quickly. Her flesh was, well . . . squishy.

"*The* Abby. Courtney's Abby?" Her eyes bulged with interest.

I wasn't sure it was a good idea to admit I was *the* Abby, but she had my attention. "You know Courtney?"

"Honey, we all know each other in this place. She was hoppin' mad at you when she was admitted the other day. Screaming and hollerin' to beat the band once the drugs started to clear her system. You put her in here, right?"

"I think she put herself in," I answered.

"She has father issues," Amelia said, nodding.

"What does that mean?" I flipped three cards to start my game.

"Her father got murdered and that poor girl is thinking it's all her fault. I don't usually feel sorry for the druggies, but I do for her. Puny thing, too. Needs a big pot of red beans and some boudain."

"She said her father's death was her fault?" I asked.

Amelia coughed a few times, then pulled a tissue from her sleeve and spit into it. "Damn asthma. Anyway, Courtney is sorta like Owen—he was here last time I was in. Owen was a druggie with father issues just like Courtney. But I didn't feel the least bit sorry for *him*. Especially not after he punched me."

The last time? And he *punched* her? Maybe this wasn't the right person to be talking to.

I was considering wandering back toward Courtney's room, but Amelia reached across the table and poked me in the chest. "I can tell what you're thinkin', and you can just quit passin' judgment, girl. I have a lithium regulation problem. That's why I have to be admitted here more than most other folks."

I stood. "Sure. I understand. And now I think I'll go see about Courtney."

"Guilt issues?" she said.

"You mean Courtney?" I said.

"No. You." She raised her nearly nonexistent eyebrows knowingly.

Now how in hell did she peg me as the guilt-ridden type? I didn't want to know, so I started down the hall.

"I'll tell you about Courtney if you'll sit with me for a spell," she called.

I stopped.

"Please? I don't get many visitors."

I reluctantly returned to the table. Though she might not have reliable information, she obviously paid attention to the patients here. Maybe she knew something.

Amelia gathered up the cards and placed a protective hand over the deck. "Courtney talked plenty yesterday. Cried a lot too—but not that gulpin', outta-control kinda crying like most first timers. She just needed to talk. She was missing her father, wishing she could have prevented his death. Once the drugs wore off, it'd finally sunk in she'd never see him again."

"She probably hasn't been herself for months," I said, "and I imagine it was pretty tough when she woke up in the real world and had to deal with his murder."

Amelia smiled. "You ever consider becoming a therapist, girl?"

"No, ma'am. We already have one of those in our family. So tell me your other insights into Courtney." Her information might not be helpful, but it was sure interesting.

"Things changed when that oddball sister showed up. Courtney got all sad and stoic. You talk about cryin'? That sister was one big whiney, sniveling baby. Sometimes I wonder how I land in here time after time and someone like her gets to walk around like she's actually normal."

"She *did* just lose her father," I said, wondering why I felt the need to defend Roxanne.

"You're right. I was being insensitive. See, that's why people are put off by me. Anyway, I did hear Courtney tell her sister not to do it when the sister was leavin'."

"Not to do what?"

"I don't know. Courtney just said, 'We've caused enough trouble, so don't do it.'"

We've caused trouble? What did that refer to?

Just then I heard Kate call my name, and a second later she peeked around the corner of the game room. "Hi, Amelia," she said.

Amelia beamed. "Hi, Dr. Rose. You look so fine today, but then you look fine every time I see you."

Kate thanked her and then addressed me. "You can see her now. She's doing pretty well."

I stood. "Thanks for your help, Amelia."

She nodded and picked up the cards while I followed Kate.

All the blinds were pulled down in the room, and only one lamp provided light. Courtney sat on the edge of her twin bed, arms wrapped around herself, her gaunt face actually looking healthier than the last time I saw her. Her party-colored hair was clipped back. Gone were the earrings, dark eyeshadow, and heavy makeup. Gone, too, was the wild-eyed mania. She looked younger and sadder.

"Hey," she said when I entered. She wore blue jeans and a checkered shirt with a lace collar that had Roxanne's taste in clothing written all over it.

"Hey," I replied. "Tough couple days, huh?"

She nodded, her gaze focused on her lap.

"Kate said you wouldn't mind if I talked to you."

"I'll talk to you, but not about my sister. I don't want her to get in trouble."

"Seems she's done that all by herself," I said.

Kate had taken a seat on the empty bed across from Courtney, and I did the same.

"Okay, in any *more* trouble," Courtney replied, shades of her old contrary self surfacing.

"I only want to help you—you and your family. A little honesty is required first, though."

She lifted her head and looked at me for the first time. Her eyes were red rimmed and her nose was running. "You lied, so why I should I trust you?"

"I lied?"

"I know why you and Megan are tight, so you can quit acting like you're her best friend."

I looked over at Kate, eyebrows raised.

"Can you please explain, Courtney?" Kate said.

"Why should I? We're all fucked anyway." Courtney crossed her leg and her tennis-shoed foot began to bounce. She wiped her nose with one bony hand.

Kate said, "This might be the way out of the mess you've made. Abby is pretty good at what she does, and when she says she wants to help, she's being sincere."

Courtney stared at Kate for a second. "You mean she's a good PI?"

"That's exactly right," said Kate.

"Both of you are good at your jobs, aren't you?" Courtney said. "So fucking perfect. And then there's Roxanne and me. Weirdos. Misfits. That's who *we* are."

"We went over this earlier," Kate said softly. "No one is perfect. And even if you were, your being perfect will never change anyone else. It wouldn't have made your father love you any more than he was capable of, and it won't bring your parents back from their graves."

If Courtney didn't start crying I just might. This was heavy stuff. So I focused on what Courtney had said. She knew I was a PI. Had Kate told her? "Did my sister explain about my professional relationship with Megan?"

"No." A short, sullen no at that.

But I pressed on. "So how did you find out?"

"Roxanne."

"Okay. And how did she know?"

"When we came down for the wedding a couple weeks ago, she overheard Megan talking about you to Travis. About how she wanted to find her real mother."

"You both knew who I was the first time we met?"

"Yeah." More foot wagging. She looked at Kate. "When's the next medicine? Because I'm getting pretty shaky again."

"Dr. Wagner does your meds, but I'd guess you're on an every-four-hours schedule," Kate said.

"What time is it?" she asked.

"Three," I answered.

"Shit. Another hour. Are you about done? 'Cause I need to walk around or something."

"I'll walk with you," I said softly.

"Yeah, right. So you can pump me for more info and then get the hell out of here? Everyone takes what they want and leaves."

"You don't have to talk to me," I answered.

We locked eyes for an uncomfortably long time.

"You can do what the hell you want, but I've gotta move before I crawl out of my skin," she finally said.

"I need to make notes on Courtney's chart," said Kate. "You can meet me at the front, Abby."

"Write something that will get me out of here, okay?" Courtney asked, almost smiling.

"When you're ready," Kate replied. "And we both know that's not today."

Courtney seemed to accept this, and we left the room together. We traveled every wing in silence, passing a few other "pacers" on the way. When we started the same route over, Courtney finally spoke.

"My dad wasn't such a bad guy."

"I didn't know him very well, but he sure did step up to the plate the day his brother died. That showed character. So tell me what you liked about him."

"He was funny and smart. Yeah, he drank too much. But he would have been okay if my mother hadn't died."

"And maybe you would have been okay, too?" I asked.

She fell into silence again. We kept walking, with me matching her rapid strides past closed doors, kitchens, and therapy rooms. I shouldn't have mentioned her mother. She probably wasn't ready to deal with that right now.

About five minutes later she spoke again. "That shit the doc was saying about needing to be perfect? It must run in the family, because my dad was that way, too."

"Did he want to be perfect for you?" I asked.

"Nah. For Uncle James. He always looked up to him—the big brother and all that crap. But then Dad had to go and ask for his job back. Uncle James practically laughed in his face." Her tone had turned bitter.

"You were there?" I asked.

"Oh, I was there, all right. It happened the first night we arrived, and the family went out to dinner. Uncle James humiliated Dad in front of Megan, Aunt Sylvia—hell, everybody. And it got so quiet at that table I had to split. Made my first score in Houston that night. Another shining moment in Courtney's life."

"How did Roxanne handle that wonderful dinner moment?" I asked.

"She pretended it never happened. But Dad didn't. He got even. I was there for that, too. 'Course he didn't know I was just around the corner listening."

My heart sped up. Was she about to tell me she saw her father kill his brother? "You heard or saw something?"

She halted. Turned to me. "My father did *not* murder his brother, if that's what you think."

"I *was* thinking that, but obviously I'm wrong. Set me straight. Help me solve these murders, Courtney."

She cocked her head, her expression serious, the anger gone from her face. "You hardly ever hear *I'm wrong.* Everyone wants to be right. Hell, I want to be right. But I was wrong, too. I was so wrong to do what I did."

This time I made a conscious effort not to prejudge or assume. I just wanted her to keep talking. I touched her emaciated upper arm and gently squeezed. "We all make mistakes. God knows I've made plenty in my lifetime."

"I heard him make the phone call, Abby. I heard every word."

"What phone call?"

"He called Megan's birth mother. He knew her. He knew where she was, and he called and he told her that her daughter was getting married in a week."

So that's how Laura Montgomery found out about the wedding. "And you feel guilty for eavesdropping? That's not exactly a crime, Courtney. Did you tell the police?"

She started walking again, and I followed.

"No way. See, I was looking out for myself, and I could have gotten in big trouble. But now, without the big C, it's sunk in that I blackmailed my own father. Makes me feel like I drank Draño. What do you think of a person who blackmails her own father so she can buy cocaine? What kind of person does something that despicable?"

"A person who isn't thinking clearly," I said evenly. "Did you threaten your father, tell him you would talk to your uncle James about Megan's birth mother?"

She nodded. "Dad so wanted to make Uncle James pay for being an asshole. Wanted to see his face when this woman showed up at the wedding. So he gave me five grand to keep my mouth shut for a week. And every fucking penny went in my arm or up my nose."

She sounded so disgusted with herself it was almost scary. She obviously needed the protection this place offered. I said, "Kate is a wonderful therapist, and you're getting the help you need now."

"Too late. Way too late. And now Roxanne has—" She stopped herself.

"What about Roxanne? Is she feeling as guilty as you do?"

Courtney shook her head vehemently. "I can't talk about her. I can't hurt the only person left in the world who loves me."

"We need to get to the truth," I said firmly. "For everyone's sake. Does Roxanne feel as responsible as you do for your father's death?"

Courtney stopped walking and stared straight ahead, arms limp at her sides.

I came around and stood in front of her. "Do you think Roxanne killed them?"

Courtney closed her eyes and shook her head sadly. "She didn't know what to do with her anger. She wasn't like me. I picked the perfect way out. I medicated myself. But Roxy is so . . . *different*. She just pretends all the time. Lives in this big fantasy world. And when she found out Dad and Uncle James sent away the guy she loved—and that the jerk went willingly—she got all calm and syrupy. But she had to be pissed off. *So* pissed off."

"And you think that's why she killed them? Over something that happened months ago?"

"I don't want to believe it, but maybe she had no other way to deal with her anger."

"So why choose what was supposed to be the happiest day of Megan's life to settle the score? Don't you think she cared way too much for Megan to do something like that?"

"Maybe she was jealous of Megan's happiness?" But Courtney didn't sound so sure now.

"Then why not kill Megan, or better yet, Travis? Make Megan feel the same loss your sister had felt."

"That's ridiculous. She adores Megan."

"Exactly my point," I said. "I don't think she killed anyone. Have you considered the possibility that she was protecting you?"

Courtney's lids slowly closed and opened. Then I could tell by her eyes that she was putting something together. "She could have had another motive. If she killed them, then I'd have no money for drugs. And the way her mind works, she probably believed that would be a solution to my problem." She paused, stared into my eyes, then whispered, "Oh my God. What have I done?"

22

Kate stepped in after my talk with Courtney and took her to her room for another therapy session. Even though I had tried to reassure Courtney that no one knew for certain that Roxanne committed murder to protect her sister, Courtney wasn't convinced and had started talking about how worthless she was.

Meanwhile, I went out to my car and sat there thinking while Kate stayed behind with the once again agitated Courtney. I'd played my role of the concerned friend at the rehearsal and wedding while all the time Courtney and Roxanne knew I had another agenda. And Travis, the one person Megan wanted to protect the most, knew about me, too—and lied to the police. And what about Sylvia? Was she really in the dark when everyone else seemed to know Megan was searching for her mother?

I inserted the key in the ignition, but the questions kept coming. What about Graham? Had he researched my background because he knew why I was hanging around his niece? And who confronted James in the study that day with a Waterford vase in hand? Was it Laura Montgomery? And did she then get rid of Graham so he could never tell Megan the truth? From what I saw of her last night, she was certainly desperate enough to have committed murder.

So many possibilities, and as much as I hated the idea, I had to tell Fielder what I'd learned. I pulled out of the hospital parking lot wondering where I would begin with the story—and if she'd let me finish talking this time.

When I arrived at the Seacliff Police Station a half hour later, the place was back to normal. Guess the reporters got tired of being stonewalled. Henderson didn't even hear me come in. He wore a headset and was leaning back in his chair with his eyes closed. And I knew why.

A woman was crying, sounding like a calf calling his mama—a piercing, loud, insistent noise that would have had me wearing headphones, too.

I walked up to Henderson's desk and poked his shoulder.

He started and nearly fell backward, then hastily took off the headset and said, "What do you want?"

"I need to see her. *Now.*"

"You sure? Because she is in one foul mood." He nodded in the direction of the noise. "Ever since that Beadford girl got here last night we've been subjected to Roxanne's special brand of torture. You'd think she'd get tired."

"Roxanne is making all that racket?" I looked toward the hall where the noise was coming from.

"We're thinking about calling the county mental health officers to cart her off."

"All the more reason for me to talk to Fielder."

"She's pretty busy. Between rounds with Beadford, she keeps looking at pictures and video from the wedding. I told her she needs to leave it alone for a while, but ever since the preliminary autopsy and forensic reports came in this morning she's been working non-stop. She's majorly stressed out."

"Did you see those reports?" I asked.

"Are you kidding? She doesn't trust anyone with this case." Henderson stood. "Come on. Let me take you back there."

Once we reached Fielder's office, he rapped on the door. The crying was obviously coming from inside.

He called, "Miss Rose is here to see you, Chief."

"I'm busy," came the curt reply.

But then Roxanne spoke. "Abby's here? My Abby?"

Oh brother. Now I *belonged* to her.

Fielder said something indecipherable, and then Roxanne shrieked, "I need to talk to her!"

The click of shoes on the wood floor told me Roxanne might just get her wish.

Fielder yanked open the door and stepped aside for me to enter. "If you think you can make her quit crying, you are more than welcome to try."

Roxanne had been sitting in the chair opposite the desk, but when she saw me, she jumped to her feet and rushed over.

Hugging me so tightly I felt like I was dancing with a grizzly. Roxanne said, "Why doesn't she put me in jail where I belong? Why, Abby? Why?"

I gripped Roxanne's forearms, pushed her away, and held her at arm's length. "Can the three of us talk?"

"I *have* been talking, but she doesn't listen," cried Roxanne.

Sad, but true, I thought. I turned to Fielder, who looked run over, run down, and wrung out.

She said, "Can I release Miss Beadford to you? Otherwise, we might have to commit her. She refuses to leave the premises even though I have told her I have her statement and she's free to leave."

"I'll be glad to take her home if we can discuss her confession first." This was a bribe, pure and simple, but one I was betting Fielder might accept.

"And why should I do that?" she said wearily. But she turned, walked to her desk, and sat down. She was definitely ready to negotiate.

"I've learned a few things about this case in the last few days, things that might interest you," I said.

Roxanne and I had followed her, and we sat in the two chairs facing Fielder. Roxanne wore Dallas Cow-boys sweats and her stringy hair looked like she'd combed it with a dead fish.

"What have you told the chief?" I asked her.

She sniffed and her lower lip trembled. "The truth and nothing but the truth, so help me God. And now I'm going to rot in hell!" She let loose with one of those calf calls, and it was loud enough to rupture my eardrum.

Fielder looked like she might jump across the desk and strangle her.

I gripped Roxanne's knee and squeezed. "Shut up. No wonder she doesn't listen. Who could stand that noise?"

Roxanne stopped in midwail, snapped her mouth closed, and stared at me for a second. Then, in absolute control, she said, "I apologize for my inappropriate behavior, but this has been an extremely emotional time for myself and my family."

"Right. So what's with this confession? Did you kill them to protect your sister?"

Fielder offered one of those frustrated and disgusted sighs she was so good at. "Protecting Courtney? All I've heard is some cock-and-bull story about a fiddler boyfriend her uncle and her father sent out of town."

Roxanne jerked in Fielder's direction. *"Violinist.* And I loved him. Uncle James and Father conspired against us. Just like Romeo and Juliet, we were doomed. So I made them both pay with their lives."

"Okay," said Fielder. "And why don't you tell your beloved Abby how you killed your uncle."

"I hit him over the head with a vase."

"And what color was the vase?" Fielder said.

"You've asked me a dozen times. Why do I have to keep answering the same questions over and over?"

"Because you give me a different response every time," said Fielder.

"I was too overwrought to remember much about that afternoon. People in homicidal rages do not remember details. But Megan received several vases as wedding gifts and I know it was one of them. I think it was the blue and white Wedgwood."

"Right." Fielder looked my way. "You see what I'm dealing with here?"

I did. If you hit someone over the head hard enough to knock them senseless, wouldn't you remember what you used? Maybe Roxanne needed a good shock to refresh her memory. "I don't think Roxanne killed anyone, Chief. She's protecting Courtney because she knows her sister was blackmailing her father."

My words had an immediate effect. Roxanne leaped to her feet and stared down at me. "How dare you come here as my friend and then betray my sister and myself in this manner?"

"Courtney is willing to come clean," I said. "I suggest you follow her lead."

Roxanne slowly reclaimed her seat. Her frown reminded me of a kid whose gerbil had just died. I hoped she wouldn't start crying again.

"She admitted she killed them?" Roxanne said.

"Huh?" I said.

Fielder echoed my surprise with a "What?"

"It was most certainly the drugs," Roxanne said quickly, her eyes darting between Fielder and me. "She wasn't herself . . . but she's getting better. She wasn't responsible. You can't send her to jail for something she probably doesn't even remember doing."

"She didn't kill them, Courtney," said Fielder. "Despite what some people think"—I received a pointed stare—"I have been doing my job. Your sister is one of the few people with an alibi for both murders. The easiest part of this whole case was finding out who was selling her drugs and when. She met with her dealer outside the Beadford house during the reception and in the funeral home parking lot right about the time her father died."

Roxanne turned to me. "Is this some sort of ruse,

Abby? Because I am more than willing to go to the big house—that's vernacular for prison—because I *am* guilty."

"From what you've told me," Fielder said, "you're merely guilty of telling your father that Megan Beadford was looking for her birth mother. That's not a crime, Roxanne."

"It is to me," she said quietly. "Because that's what started everything."

I had to agree with her there, but I didn't say this out loud. I wanted no more calf calls in my immediate future.

Fielder said, "Could you *please* recant this confession now?"

She crossed her arms and looked downright defiant. "I'm not recanting if it means Courtney goes to jail for her drug problem."

Man, Roxanne had more grit in her craw than I ever gave her credit for.

Fielder pointed a finger at her. "You are wasting my time. Courtney is not going to jail—at least for now."

"See, Abby? She's lying. She *does* think Courtney is a cold-blooded murderer."

"Don't you get it?" I said. "Number one, your sister has an alibi. Number two, if Courtney killed your father and your uncle, how would she get money for drugs? After all, your uncle James *was* supporting your father. That's how the money flowed in your family, right? From Uncle James through your father and then to you." Yes indeed, combined with what Courtney had told me, it all made sense now.

"How did you know?" a wide-eyed Roxanne said.

"I put two and two together. After you told your father that Megan was looking for her mother, he wasted no time contacting the woman. He knew where to find her, which means he knew his brother's secret, and he figured Megan would learn that secret soon enough, too. James would have no reason to continue paying your father for his silence. Your dad wanted his revenge before the money stopped coming in, right?"

Roxanne hung her head. "Uncle James humiliated him so many times, and Dad thought he finally had a way to get even."

"So," I said, "with the money cow about to dry up, what better way to end their relationship than with a hefty dose of payback? I'll bet he loved seeing the look on James's face when Laura Montgomery showed up at the wedding."

Fielder said, "Wait a minute. Who's Laura Montgomery?"

"The woman in the composite. Megan's birth mother."

And I had to admit *I* loved the look on Fielder's face right now. Stunned and dismayed about covered it. And I was hoping she also felt like an idiot for having gone bucktooth and hangnail with me from the minute we met.

As it turned out, I was saved from having to take Roxanne home. Between Fielder and me, we convinced her that Courtney wouldn't be sent to jail. Courtney had an alibi, she was in rehab, and Fielder had no reason to go after her. So Roxanne called Sylvia, who agreed to pick her niece up.

While Fielder and I stood by, and Henderson smiled as wide as a game show host, Sylvia ushered Roxanne out of the police station like a mother duck, telling her she needed to bathe and rest up to be ready for the visitation tonight.

Once she was gone, Fielder said, "I never thought I'd be grateful to you for anything."

"So you *are* thanking me?"

"Yeah. You want to have dinner or something? Talk this case over?"

Henderson folded his arms and nodded, looking satisfied. "Very classy, Chief. I think you're getting the hang of this job."

"Would you shut up?" she said, but she was fighting a smile.

"You mean you want to talk over the case like two professionals?" I tried to keep the sarcasm out of my voice and think I succeeded.

She nodded. "I need to know what you've learned. I seem to have missed a few things."

"You had too much evidence and not enough manpower." I was suddenly feeling generous and forgiving in the face of her turnaround. "Like my daddy used to say, you couldn't see the pigs for the slop."

And I wasn't sure I could either, but I was enjoying this too much to make that admission out loud.

We ended up going to Quinn's surprisingly large house and ate leftover pizza right out of the fridge. At least the woman knew how to provide a decent meal. After we finished eating, we went to her living room, Dr Peppers in hand.

The place was organized and tidy like her office, the decor modern with sleek curvy tables and a leather sofa. One wall was filled with her father's framed awards. His badge was displayed in a glass box on a small table beneath the commendations, and I also noted a picture of him shaking hands with the first President Bush.

"You were very proud of him," I said.

"Be careful. Be careful," someone said from behind me.

I turned and saw a large freestanding birdcage. Inside, pacing on a thick dowel, was a snowy cockatoo.

"Meet Beefeater," said Fielder.

"Beefeater on the rocks, Beefeater on the rocks," said the bird, his head bobbing.

I walked over to the cage. "Male or female?" I asked.

"Male," said Fielder. "But be careful. He bites almost as hard as I do."

"Be careful, be careful," said Beefeater.

"He's beautiful," I said, stooping to get a closer look.

"He belonged to my dad."

"Hey, Dad, what do you think? What do you think?" said the bird.

"We both miss him a lot," she said quietly. She had kicked off her shoes and was sitting on the sofa. "He was the best damn cop in the world."

"My daddy's been gone a years," I said. "I miss him, too."

"Seems we have more in common than an interest in Jeff," she said with a wry grin.

I sat in the butter yellow chair next to the sofa. "Now, wait a minute. If we plan to be in the same room and—"

"Don't worry." She raised a hand. "Jeff is off-limits. That doesn't mean I don't think you're damn lucky, but I won't be making any moves on him."

"You mean any *more* moves."

"Damn lucky," spouted Beefeater.

"Shut up, Beefy." Fielder was blushing. "Jeff set me straight, so can we drop this?"

"Okay. Truce."

"You handled Roxanne when I couldn't, and I appreciate your help," Fielder said. "I've been too busy trying to prove how smart I am, how I can do this job despite the community's criticism. Seems I need to learn better interviewing techniques. I haven't had much practice other than with drunks, peeping toms, and adolescents who think playing with a can of spray paint is the most fun they've ever had."

"What kind of community criticism?" I asked.

"Snipes from city council members and people who like to write letters to the editor. They say my father handed me my job even though I had no experience and no idea how to handle crime in a small town."

"Is that true?"

A familiar anger flashed in her eyes. "Okay, it's

true. But not because I don't know how to be a good cop. It's because—"

"Good cop. Good cop, Quinn," said Beefeater.

She smiled and continued. "Handling my job has very little to do with policing and a whole lot to do with ass kissing. I'm no ass kisser."

"Really? I never would have thought." I grinned.

"I won't apologize for bringing a certain attitude to my job, and I think that's enough said. Let's get to work. You show me yours and I'll show you mine."

I went first, telling her all I had discovered in Jamaica, the scoop on Laura Montgomery, and I even confessed that the woman had come to my house. I was sure glad I'd reported this to the Dallas police because Fielder was a little miffed I hadn't called her last night. But she accepted some of the responsibility when I mentioned she hadn't exactly been too approachable.

"Now it's your turn," I said. "Henderson mentioned you received some reports today."

She nodded and took a sip of her Dr Pepper. "Interesting stuff. The autopsy report says the blow to the back of the head with the vase did not kill James Beadford but probably knocked him out."

"And he hit the corner of the fireplace when he fell. We knew that's what killed him."

"We *thought* we knew," she said. "But the blood evidence indicates he fell to the floor several feet from the fireplace."

I sat straighter. "Really? So did he wake up and fall again when he tried to walk?"

"Scuff marks on the wood floor made by the tips of his shoes indicate he was dragged to the fireplace."

Hair rose on the back of my neck. This was more ugly than I'd thought. "So the killer knew he wasn't dead and finished him off by ramming his head into the bricks?"

"Yup. And there goes my original theory that this was a crime of passion, an argument that went too far. Apparently that's not the whole story."

"Apparently not," I said half to myself.

"And the blood evidence also seems to clear Megan. The stains on her dress were consistent with her only cradling her father's head. There were no spatter marks, no traces of blood on her hem—things that would have been there if she'd dragged the body or struck him."

"You really considered her a suspect?" I asked, but then added, "Figures. You even thought I might have done it."

"I thought it was possible they had an argument and things got out of hand. Remember, I learned about the first-degree murder angle only this morning."

"I see your point. Jeff keeps reminding me that anyone is capable of murder given the right circumstances, so you couldn't eliminate Megan."

"We went to the same academy, so I'm with Jeff." She must have read my expression because she quickly added, "And that's a figure of speech, Abby. Can I call you Abby?"

"Sure." Did that mean I was supposed to call her by her first name? Because I wasn't sure I wanted to be that friendly. "Did you get any reports on Graham's murder?"

"Not yet. As I said before, he was full of booze, which made it easier to shove him off that balcony."

"Beefeater on the rocks," piped in the bird.

"Does he listen to everything you say?" I asked with a laugh.

"Yes, and I'm grateful someone pays attention. Anyway, there were no fingerprints in Graham Beadford's hotel room, so we have no convenient glasses with prints or the killer's DNA on the rim, and we didn't find footprints either. We always hope our murderers step in mud or paint right before they kill, but it just doesn't work out that way too often."

"Very funny," I said. "So there were no fibers on the balcony or skin under the victim's nails?"

"Like I said, we don't have the forensic reports

from that scene. Despite what people see on TV shows, I don't have instant access to the evidence, especially in a town where we have to rely on another county's crime scene people."

"And no one saw the killer but me?"

She shook her head, lips tight.

"This sucks," I said.

"This sucks," echoed Beefeater.

"You're both right," she said with a resigned smile. "I do have pictures and videos that show Travis and James in the background out on the deck. They appeared to be arguing and that's why I brought him in. But the rest of those thousand pictures I went through? Time-consuming, but worthless."

I told her what Travis and Megan had told me about the argument, how it was over money for grad school.

"So why couldn't he just say that when I questioned him?" The old fire was back in her voice.

"Don't have a walleyed fit. He didn't share this with me until yesterday." I didn't add that I wasn't sure I believed him. I didn't have anything but my gut reaction to his explanation, and I wasn't about to have her haul him in again because of me.

"With all the new information," she said, "I'm re-thinking motive. Could have been revenge. Could have been greed. Seems the only people with any money among the suspects are Sylvia Beadford and now her daughter. And Mrs. Beadford was rich before she even met her husband. Megan inherits half the estate, so that benefits Travis as well as the bride. The cousins and Graham Beadford weren't even mentioned in the will. The best man worked for James Beadford, and if Sylvia sells the company, he's shit out of luck."

"Holt's been busy making sure the company survives the setback of losing the CEO," I said. "So he's not SOL yet."

"Good thing, because he's in credit card debt up to his eyeballs like everyone else in their early twenties.

Graham Beadford had a steady income thanks to his brother, but what he didn't spend at a bar in Dallas called For Pete's Sake, he turned over to his daughters. They weren't making ends meet up in Dallas."

"Yeah, I found that out today. Could Graham have killed his brother hoping he'd inherit something from James?"

"It's possible, but then who killed him?" she asked.

"It keeps coming back to Laura Montgomery. She had the best motive to do away with both of them—and I hate to even think about that. Megan deserves better."

Fielder attended to a cuticle, her dark hair falling in front of her face. "In my experience, what we deserve and what we get don't often match up," she said quietly.

"Yeah," I said. "Sometimes."

"For Pete's sake, this sucks," said Beefeater.

And that about summed it up.

23

I had worn black chinos and a zip-up sweater for the visitation, but when I arrived at the funeral home the place was hot enough to pop corn in the shuck. I had to unzip the sweater. The fuchsia T-shirt I wore underneath was a little glaring, but if I didn't cool off I'd be sweating so badly no one would want to be within ten feet of me. The same greeter with those disturbing white gloves led me to the room where Graham's shiny closed casket was draped with a blanket of mums.

Megan came over to me when I walked in. She wore a gray sweaterdress and her hair was pulled back in a ponytail. Gray didn't suit her—it too closely resembled her skin tone. How much more could the poor kid take?

"Thank you so much for coming," she said, her voice surprisingly strong and in control. "Uncle Graham would have been proud of how many people showed up—even his friends from Dallas came." She lowered her voice. "But most of the men smell like they shared a keg on the way down here."

I smiled. "I think he would have liked that. Before it slips my mind, Kate said to tell you Courtney wasn't well enough to attend tonight, but she might issue her a day pass for the funeral."

"Did your sister say whether Courtney is accepting her treatment willingly?"

"I saw Courtney myself and I'd say yes."

Travis had just joined us, and he put his arm around Megan and squeezed her to him. "See? Finally some good news."

"I'm glad," Megan said. "Especially for Roxanne. She was so exhausted after her night in jail, she fell asleep the minute Mother brought her home this afternoon. I haven't had a chance to talk to her."

I took in the room for the first time—this one a mirror image of where James Beadford's casket had sat less than a week ago. Metal folding chairs were lined along the wall, and several old men sat together with clear plastic cups holding what appeared to be water—*appeared* being the key word.

Sylvia had come up with yet another black outfit, this one a pantsuit. She was talking with three men and a woman, none of whom I knew. Meanwhile, Holt spoke to a still fatigued-looking Roxanne. They stood in a corner next to a giant arrangement of white lilies and Holt had on his "I'm so sorry for your loss" face. She had adoring eyes fixed on him, and I considered warning her off before I left tonight. She didn't need another tragic romantic encounter.

An elderly couple came into the room then, and Megan turned her attention to them.

Travis took my arm and whispered, "Can we talk a minute?"

"Funny, I was about to ask you the same question."

While Megan walked the old man and woman over to the casket, Travis and I went into the hallway.

He rubbed at his mouth with a shaky hand. "You need to know something. Megan's father and I did not argue about money the day of the wedding."

So he'd finally decided to come clean. "I was pretty sure of that. Go on."

"But I'm afraid Megan knows what we argued about. I think her father told her right after he talked to me. And I think it upset her. A lot."

"You haven't asked her?"

"I don't *want* to ask her, Abby. Besides, that's not the reason I needed to talk to you. I want you to stop looking for her birth mother. You can pretend you're working on the case, but please, I'm begging you, just pretend."

"And why would I do that?"

"Just trust me. You don't want to find her," he said.

"I've *already* found her," I said. "And I know all about her."

He closed his eyes. "Damn. So you know she was at the wedding?"

"Yes."

"Then you realize she's not the person Megan hoped to find. This mother's not her dream come true, Abby."

"How did you find out?" I asked, wanting to add *And why the hell didn't you tell me?*

He hung his head. "The day of the wedding, I saw Megan's father talking to this woman after Sylvia sent me to find James. He and the woman were near the dock, and voices carry out there. I heard exactly what James was saying to her.

"And what was that?"

"He was saying Megan would have a jailbird for a mother and that he was going to the police first thing Monday morning. He kept asking her if it was fair to meet with Megan and then break her heart."

"Then what happened?"

"They saw me. The woman ran off around the house and James followed me up to the deck. I couldn't believe what I'd just heard. I knew how badly Megan wanted to meet her mother and James had the power to make that happen."

"So you two ended up arguing," I said.

"He planned to tell Megan everything before her birth mother got the chance to tell her side. Said it was his right because . . . because he was her biological father, Abby. Then he said Graham would pay through the nose for bringing the woman to the wedding. He didn't give a damn how all this would affect Megan on her wedding day. Then he told me to keep my mouth shut and stay out of his way."

"Why didn't you tell me?"

"Because . . . because . . . I wasn't sure. I had to protect her."

"You weren't sure about what?" But then I understood. "I get it. You weren't sure about *Megan*. You think she got so angry about the lies she'd been told all her life that she hit her father over the head and killed him?"

Travis blinked hard, his eyes reddening. "She'd never hurt him on purpose. But I know how upset she must have been."

"Listen, Travis. If she killed her father, accident or not, why would she ask me to investigate the murders? That doesn't make sense."

He looked at his boots. "I thought maybe she had to act as people expected her to—and that would be to do everything in her power to find the killer. Maybe she believed you wouldn't succeed."

"Maybe, maybe, maybe. You've been thinking up the wrong tree, Travis. She didn't kill him. And Fielder has proof she didn't."

His head snapped up and he stared at me, his eyes bright with hope. "Really?"

"Really. And there's more I need to tell you."

"Tell him what?" said Sylvia.

We both turned. She was standing in the hall just outside the entrance to the visitation room. How could she have snuck up on us with those shoes? They were ultra pointed with spike heels and had to have made noise. Yet neither of us had heard her.

"Tell him about my new job," I said quickly. It was the first lie that came to mind.

But Sylvia seemed to be paying little attention to me. She was staring at Travis. "Are you feeling sick?"

He swallowed. "I'm fine. Really."

"No, you're not. You're all flushed. Do you need some fresh air?"

Travis went over and took his mother-in-law's hands. "I'm finer than fine, but thanks for caring."

She smiled up at him, her eyes lost behind a quadruple coat of mascara.

Sylvia let go of Travis and held out a hand to me. "You must have just arrived. I'll come with you while you pay your respects. Megan mentioned how guilty you feel that you couldn't prevent Graham's accident."

"Um, yeah," I said. She knew damn well it was no accident, but who was I to present reality to her or Roxanne? As she led me toward the other side of the room, I turned and mouthed "later" to Travis.

The casket was a lacquered ebony with gold trim and a kneeling rail had been placed in front. Sylvia used the casket for support to kneel on the velvet cushion, and I followed suit.

She gripped my hand, her acrylic nails digging into my palm. "Lord, we pray for Graham's peace. He has found his home with You and all his worldly troubles have ended. Amen."

"Amen," I said and started to rise.

But when I let go of Sylvia's hand she seemed to go limp and had to catch herself to keep from falling.

I grasped her arm. "Are you all right?"

"I'll be okay. With all the preparations today, I forgot my blood pressure medicine. Guess that was a mistake. If you could just help me up?"

Supporting her by the elbow, I got her back on her feet.

"Do you need a drink of water? Or maybe I should tell Megan you're not feeling well?"

"No," she said adamantly, glancing over at her daughter, who was seated with Graham's drinking buddies. "You must not tell Megan anything. If you could take me home for my medicine, I'd also have an opportunity to talk to you in private."

Another secret conversation with one of the family? What would I find out from her that I didn't already know? "What's this about?" I asked.

She glanced around. "We'll talk at my house."

Holt and Roxanne must have noticed Sylvia's near fall because they came over to us with concern in their eyes.

"Are you all right, Aunt Sylvia? You look upset," Roxanne said.

"I forgot my medicine, but Abby has offered to take me home so I can get in a dose before I keel over. Can you handle the guests?"

"Certainly. I'm doing fine with Holt's support." Roxanne lifted her chin. "This is my father's visitation and therefore my responsibility."

"Of course, sweetheart. And you've been doing a stellar job. Tell Megan where I've gone if she asks."

Holt, looking a little uncomfortable, said, "Abby just arrived. Why don't I drive you home, Mrs. Beadford?"

I was guessing hosting a visitation with Roxanne was not his idea of fun.

He looked at me. "I need to talk shop with Sylvia anyway, Abby. She's got my nose to the grindstone at work these days, but she'll be a great boss. She's obviously learned a lot from James over the past twenty years."

So Sylvia had taken over at Beadford Oil Suppliers. That must have been a disappointment to poor Holt. And now he was reduced to kissing her butt, just as he'd probably done with James Beadford. But then, he needed the money, according to Quinn, so he'd better be on his best behavior.

I closed my eyes. *Oh my God, I'm calling her Quinn. This is too scary.*

Sylvia said, "Holt, I'd prefer you stay here in case any of our clients come by to pay their respects. I think that's what James would have wanted."

"You're probably right," Holt said. "But I'd be glad

to drive to your house while you stay here. If you tell me where the medicine is, I'll bring it here."

"No, no. That's not necessary. Abby doesn't mind, do you?" she said.

"Not at all," I answered.

We left then, and I tried a few prompts to get a hint what this was about on the short drive, but Sylvia changed the subject. We were going to do this her way; that much was obvious.

When we arrived, the house was icy cold, but I declined her offer of a drink, even though I would have loved a cup of coffee. I wanted her to get to the point.

She led me into the library, where her husband had died, and it definitely creeped me out returning to the murder scene—especially since I'd learned today how vicious a crime it had been.

After Daddy passed, I couldn't set foot in the room where he'd died for months afterward, but Sylvia didn't seem bothered. More like distracted, now that I thought about it. As if it didn't register that this was where her whole life had changed forever. I wondered if this was more of the Beadford denial at work.

She turned on a table lamp near the bookshelves, and the light cast a warm but meager glow over half the room. The fireplace remained in shadows. I noted the table filled with wedding presents was gone, the Oriental rugs had been removed, and the furniture had been rearranged, but other than that, no evidence of violence lingered—except in my mind.

She gestured to the tapestry wing chairs flanking the lamp table. "Please sit down."

But rather than sit with me, she went to the shelves. Her back was to me, so I couldn't see what she was doing, but seconds later, one set of shelves slid back revealing a wall safe. She pressed a series of numbers on the digital pad first, then turned the conventional dial to open the safe.

When she joined me at the table, she carried a six-inch-high stack of bills with a thousand dollar note on top. Placing the money on the table between us, she said, "I'm only just learning to be a businesswoman, so please bear with me."

"Okay," I said, my confusion evident in my tone.

"I know you're an investigator and that you're working with Megan to solve her father's murder. Whatever she's offered you, I'll double that."

So *she* knew about my real job, too. "She's paying me more than enough, so—"

"You misunderstand. I'll pay you to *stop* investigating. Today. No more questions. No more talks with the chief of police."

Another offer to quit the case. "Did Roxanne tell you about me today after you picked her up at the police station?"

"Yes. And she mentioned that you and Chief Fielder would be sharing information to find the killer. And that's *not* in Megan's best interest, though I genuinely believe you have her best interest at heart." She was sitting rigid, her spine not even touching the back of the chair.

How much did she know? Did Sylvia think her daughter killed James? Was that what this was about? "There is no evidence linking Megan to her father's murder, if that's what's worrying you."

"Certainly there's no evidence," she said derisively. "You think I'm protecting her from a murder charge?"

Gone was the wimpy, weepy woman I'd come to know over the last couple of weeks. This was a different Sylvia. "How much?" she said. "I'll pay you whatever you ask."

"I'm not taking your money."

"Why not?" she said impatiently.

"Did you overhear me talking to Travis tonight?" I asked. "Is that what this is about?"

"I heard enough. You need to stay away from all of us. This has gone too far."

That's when I noticed that though one hand rested in her lap, the other was between the chair arm and her left hip—and out of my sight.

My mouth went dry. Did she have a weapon? Was she that desperate? And for God's sake why?

But what if *she* killed James? What if she recognized Laura Montgomery, confronted her husband, and smacked him with the heaviest object she could find when he told her why the woman was at the wedding?

But I wasn't hankering to learn if she had a gun at her side or just how desperate she was. Not right now. "Listen, Sylvia. If you want me off the case, I'm off the case. You're Megan's mom and you know best."

Her tongue flicked around her lips, and I could tell she wanted to believe me. Her thick makeup had taken on a repulsive sheen in the lamplight, and it was almost as if her newfound assertiveness was melting away with the foundation and blush.

The hand in her lap went to her forehead, and she squeezed the skin between her eyebrows. "Stupid. Stupid. Stupid. I never should have brought you here. You'll go to the police and then this whole thing will crack open like a rotten egg and—"

"She's not going anywhere," came a male voice from the shadowed entry.

I turned. Holt McNabb stood in the doorway.

"I told you to keep your mouth shut, Sylvia," Holt said.

"But I heard her talking with Travis. She knows about Laura. She knows everything."

"And that's why we'll take care of this little problem. Just like I took care of Graham when he figured out what you'd done. And once I fix this mess, what will we do, Sylvia?"

"Keep our mouths shut," she said, eyes downcast.

"Right." He smiled and might as well have added, "That's a good dog."

Sylvia must have still had her doubts, though, because she said, "Roxanne told me Abby and Fielder were sharing information. It may be too late."

"You have that city councilman on your payroll, right? He'll convince Fielder to leave the case alone."

"Yes, but—"

"Money talks. And you have plenty to say. Meanwhile, I'll handle *this* problem right now." He pulled what looked like a Glock from his coat pocket. "Did you know how cold the bay waters get in winter, Abby? You need to be very careful when you walk out on the dock at night because one little slip and BAM!" He slapped the gun against his free hand.

I started, my heart in my throat.

Holt shook his head sadly. "You fall in that water and it's all over but the autopsy."

I looked at Sylvia. "Anyone else dies around here and you'll have cops camping out on your lawn."

"She's right," said Sylvia. "There's been enough killing, Holt."

So I had an ally. A reluctant one, but still an ally. I spoke to her again. "You were so angry the day James died. A jury will understand."

"It was an accident. I never meant—"

"Shut up, Sylvia," said Holt.

"You and I know it wasn't exactly an accident," I said.

"But it was. I never meant to kill him. When he told me he was Megan's real father, that he had a bond with her that I would never have, I just picked up that vase and . . . and . . ." Tears spilled over the mascara on her lower lids.

"You need to shut up, Sylvia," Holt said. He waved the gun at me. "And *you* need to come with me."

Despite the grapefruit-size rock of fear in my gut, despite the big, bad gun pointed my way, I didn't move. Why make it easy for him to kill me? I may be stubborn, impulsive, and foolish on occasion, but I didn't fall off the stupid truck. I wasn't about to jump into the ocean like some trained pig. He could kill me here where he'd leave plenty of evidence.

I looked at Sylvia. "Tell me about the accident. What happened?"

"Don't answer that." Holt marched over and pulled me roughly up by the arm and pressed the gun to my temple. "You shut up. Just shut the fuck up."

"You hit him with the vase, right?" I said as Holt started to drag me away. "And he fell forward. Then what?" She was insisting it was an accident, and my gut told me she believed it.

Sylvia's mouth hung open and her face looked like the dark smudges and teardrops had been painted on.

Holt had me almost to the door, and I wiggled and kicked, even managed to free myself for an instant, but he was far stronger than I. He pulled me back and wrapped an arm around my shoulders and neck, the gun cold against my skull.

Sylvia, sounding like a zombie in some B horror flick, said, "He wouldn't answer me and I knew I'd killed him. So I ran out. And I had to t-take off my shoes. Because of the blood. I had his blood on my shoes. I put them in the caterer's trash bag." Her chest started to heave, and I feared I might lose her to hysteria soon.

We'd reached the door, so I grabbed the frame, braced myself. "You didn't kill him, Sylvia. He would have lived. Holt finished him off."

I wasn't certain of that, but I had a hunch that's why he was so damn anxious to get me out of here.

Holt clamped his hand over my mouth, enough of a switch in our position that I was able to give him a wicked elbow to the gut. He buckled but regained his equilibrium quickly. One finger, however, slipped into my mouth, and I clamped down with all my might.

He hollered with pain and threw me off him. I landed on my butt, facing him.

"You bitch," he said through clenched teeth, the Glock pointed at my heart.

"Leave her be," said Sylvia. She'd stood and her hand wavered with the weight of the gun she'd been concealing since she sat down with me.

Like Laura Montgomery last night, she didn't handle the weapon with the authority born of experience, so I couldn't count on her to save my ass. That was my job.

Anyone who's practiced with weapons knows a moving target is damn hard to hit. So I tucked and rolled, as if a fire was about to consume me. I must have made at least three rolls to reach her.

I heard Holt open fire.

Adrenaline sent my world into slow motion. I heard nothing after his gun went off. And felt nothing. I reached up and grabbed Sylvia's gun. She didn't resist, just fell to the floor and covered her head.

I pointed the gun at Holt, but saw he already had his hands raised in surrender. But not because of me. Laura Montgomery was standing behind him, and I guessed she had her own weapon tucked in his back.

But he still held the Glock and quick as a blink, he swung his free arm around and sent Laura flying. Not good.

So before he could get off a good a shot, I fired.

I didn't miss.

Holt dropped like bricks off a twenty-story building. He began writhing on the floor, holding his thigh, blood leaking through his fingers. No spurting, so I hadn't nicked an artery. Before he could figure out he wasn't hurt all that badly, I hurried over and picked up the gun he'd dropped and stuck it in my waistband. Two guns are always better than one.

Sylvia was still crouched on the floor, her arms covering her head, but when I said, "It's all clear," she unwound and started to get up.

And that's when she saw Laura Montgomery.

"You," she said. "This is all your fault."

Sylvia leaped over the balled-up, whimpering Holt

and ran at Laura like she was attacking a blocking dummy.

They fell to the floor, and Sylvia managed to take off her shoe and wield it at Laura's face.

Laura moved her head in time and the spike heel hit the floor with a sickening *thwack*.

Fortunately Laura's gun had been knocked out of her hand, or she might have used it.

I stepped in to separate them, dragging a flailing Sylvia away. For the first time in weeks, she wasn't crying. She was quivering with rage, the same rage that probably made her pick up that vase and smash it on her husband's skull.

Laura got to her feet and called 911. Meanwhile, I shoved Sylvia into the chair and kept the gun trained on her. Holt had risen to a sitting position and had both hands pressed against his bloody leg. He said nothing, but Sylvia started rocking and repeating, "I didn't kill him." When Laura finished the call, she stood near the library entry, a silhouette in the shadows.

Five long minutes later I heard male voices shouting, "This room clear," several times as they came closer. Then Henderson and another uniformed officer came rushing in, weapons drawn.

Henderson knew how to use his handcuffs almost as well as his mouth, and he had Sylvia restrained in a New York minute. The other cop called for an ambulance on the walkie-talkie pinned to his shoulder while he used plastic bracelets on Holt.

When Fielder showed up not long after, I realized we had a half-dozen guns in the room. A nice number when they're all held by the good guys.

24

After I was questioned at the scene by several cops, I met up with Travis and Megan at the Seacliff Police Station. Fielder had gone to the hospital to question Holt, and Sylvia was transported to the county lockup after she bit Henderson in the arm. She'd tried and failed to get one last kick at Laura on the way out of the room and was now under extra security at the county facility. Bet she had a pretty pair of booties to wear in there.

Kate must have flown from Houston as soon as I called her, because she arrived at the station about the same time as Travis and Megan. They'd been more than a little freaked out when they'd arrived home to find Sylvia being led away in handcuffs, Holt on his way to the hospital and me with paper bags over my hands. That part was plain ridiculous. Everyone knew I'd shot that damn fool Holt.

I had plenty to answer for, what with the gunplay and the catfight, and so did Laura Montgomery, who had been whisked here to the station even before Travis and Megan had arrived. Henderson told me Laura would be held without bail in the small Seacliff jail until the Dallas cops arrived to take custody of her, probably tomorrow.

Megan and Travis had a million questions, but before I could answer even the first one, Quinn arrived and herded us all into her office.

"This has been a difficult time for you, Megan," said Quinn once we were seated around the chief's desk. "And it may not get much easier for a while."

Megan still wore the sweaterdress I'd seen her in at the visitation, but strands of pale hair had come loose from the tie holding her ponytail and her eyes sagged with fatigue.

"Someone said my mother killed my father." She shook her head, her voice filled with confusion and disbelief.

"That's why we need to talk," said Quinn. "You need the facts and not what someone said. Holt is talking, hoping to get a better deal when it comes round to plea bargain time. During the reception, McNabb says he was in the library checking out the wedding gifts when your mother and father came in."

"And don't think for a minute he was interested in toasters and blenders," I said. "Probably looking for cash in the wedding cards."

"I'm betting you're right," said Quinn. "Anyway, your parents were probably so consumed by their argument, they didn't see him. Holt says he hid behind the drapes and got an earful. In his version, Mr. Beadford and Mrs. Beadford argued over Laura Montgomery's appearance at the wedding—seems Mrs. Beadford knew about her husband's affair with the woman way back when. But it was the news about you, Megan, that really got to her, so when your father turned to leave the room, your mother hit him with the vase."

Megan's eyes filled. Kate, who was sitting next to her, put an arm around her.

"So she killed him because of me?" Megan said. "I don't understand."

Travis, seated on her other side, shifted so he could look Megan in the eye. "Meg, there's a lot you don't know. And part of that is my fault."

"We'll deal with the guilt later," said Kate. "First we should let the chief and Abby explain everything."

"Yeah," said Megan, still staring into Travis's eyes. "I want to know everything."

"It's complicated," I said. "But first, let's get one thing straight. Your mother did not kill your father. She knocked him unconscious, but he wouldn't have died from that injury."

"I'm not feeling all warm and fuzzy over that news," said Megan. "But go on. What did happen and why in hell am I to blame?"

Kate said, "You are not to blame for anything."

Quinn said, "Let me give you McNabb's version first—which is filled with self-serving lies, as far as I'm concerned. He says he saw Mrs. Beadford hit your father with the vase, then she checked his pulse after he fell. McNabb claims your mother dragged your father over to the fireplace, lifted his upper body, and let go so he'd hit his head on the bricks."

"No, please God, no," whispered Megan. She covered her mouth with a trembling hand.

"Hang on," Kate said. "Take a deep breath."

A tear slipped down Megan's cheek. "Keep going. I'm listening."

"Holt is lying," I said. "Sylvia would never have had the strength to drag James's body and lift him. The force that it must have taken to kill your father pegs Holt as the killer. But he let Sylvia believe the first blow killed him. He used that lie to control her."

"This can't be the Holt I know," said Travis, shaking his head. "He had an ego, sure, but he was my friend. And a smart guy. Why would he kill Megan's father?"

"He was flat broke," said Quinn. "Had a hundred grand in credit card debt. My guess is, he saw an opportunity to have Sylvia in his hip pocket forever and use her to get control of the company. All his money problems would go away."

"And Graham?" Travis asked, sounding disgusted. "Did Holt kill him, too?"

Quinn said, "Holt admitted he was in the hotel room when Graham fell, but swears up and down it was an accident." She looked at me. "We may never prove any different, you know."

"But he had a *huge* motive to murder Graham," I said. "Graham invited Laura Montgomery to make an appearance at the wedding. He knew everything about James's relationship to her and figured that Sylvia would not want Megan to find out. Graham may have even decided Sylvia killed James and was hoping to cash in. But when Holt rather than Sylvia showed up, Graham lost out big time.

"Hold on," Megan said. "So this Laura Montgomery had the affair with my father?" She faced Travis. "Did you know? Did you and Dad argue about her?"

His earlobes grew red, and if guilt had a name tonight, it was Travis Crane. "I am so sorry, Meg. I should have told you, but . . . I thought you already knew about her. I imagined all sorts of things when I should have just talked to you."

"You didn't trust me," she said, her eyes on the floor. "But I didn't trust you, either. I was sure you didn't argue about money with my dad, even though that's what you said. But I was too scared to confront you. I didn't want to think that maybe Dad knew something about you that I didn't. Some secret. Maybe an ex-wife or—"

"Megan," Kate cut in. "The lies and the assumptions are over. Let Abby tell you what she found out."

I looked at Quinn. "Where is she?"

"In the interrogation room."

"Two-way glass?" I asked.

Quinn nodded.

"You coming with us, Kate?" I asked.

"Nope," she answered. "You and Megan have taken this journey together. You should finish it the same way."

So I was the one who took Megan's cold, mottled hand in mine. Quinn led us to the observation room, let us in, and then left.

Through the smoky glass we saw Laura sitting at a small table, wearing a yellow jail jumpsuit. Her hand-cuffed hands were in front of her and she looked as tired as I felt.

"That's the woman in the composite," Megan said. "The woman you said was at the church. She's Laura Montgomery?"

"Your birth mother made it to your wedding after all," I said quietly.

"Oh my God," whispered Megan.

She never took her eyes off her mother while I told her everything I'd learned when I went to Jamaica and after. After I finished, she pressed her nose against the glass and placed splayed palms on either side of her head.

She stared for a long moment, then turned back to me. "Can I talk to her?"

"I don't know. I'll see if the chief—"

The door opened and Quinn was there. She must have been listening the whole time. "I'll take you to her," she said to Megan.

After Quinn opened the door to the interrogation room, she left Megan with her mother and returned to me. We watched the scene unfold together.

Megan stood by the door and Laura rose slowly. Her cuffed hands hung loose in front of her and her shoulders slumped with the weight of regret and pain.

Megan's chin quivered and tears fell down her pallid cheeks. Finally, she held out her arms.

They walked toward each other, and when they met, Laura lifted her tethered hands and held her daughter's face. They stared into each other's eyes, both of them crying and laughing at the same time. Then Megan put her arms around her mother and held fast.

It was like the best silent movie I'd ever seen.

Epilogue

It took several months for the powers that be to figure out what to do with Sylvia Beadford and Holt McNabb. When the DA finally decided, Jeff and I were in bed—naked, if you want the interesting details. He was asleep, as men tend to do after lovemaking, and I was watching the late news. According to the television reporter, neither McNabb nor Beadford would go to trial. They'd both plea-bargained for twenty to life, which meant they'd get out sooner than later.

Quinn had warned me that's what would happen. Sylvia and Holt had been pointing the finger at each other since the moment they'd been caught. The he said–she said cases tended to end with less than enough jail time for both criminals. And they *were* criminals.

"Those two fell through a toilet hole and came out smelling like Chanel N°5," I said, stabbing the remote to blacken the TV.

"Huh?" Jeff looked up at me through slitted eyes.

"Go back to sleep," I said.

"Sure. Okay." He turned on his side.

I switched off the bedside lamp and curled around Jeff's warm body. I hoped Megan and Travis were cuddled up together, too. They'd bought a little house in Houston and seemed as happy as possums eating persimmons last time I saw them.

Laura Montgomery had fared better than Holt and Sylvia. She'd visited me last week with her brand-new electronic ankle bracelet, provided free of charge by the criminal justice system. She'd done only ninety days in jail, thanks to a compassionate judge who understood that Laura had already done about twenty years of hard time thinking that her child was dead.

She and I had talked for a long time, and she was able to finally answer a few questions that had been bugging me for months.

"When I, uh, *visited* your house," I'd said as we shared coffee at my kitchen table, "I noticed you had a hefty bank account that seemed to disappear. If that was the embezzlement money, where did it go?"

"I gave it back to James. Once he found out I was pregnant with his child and that if I was convicted—as I surely would have been—I'd be having the baby in prison, we made a deal. He got me out of the country with a new identity, and when I was safely established, I gave him back his money."

I rested my chin on my hands. "So that's how his lawyer found you and got the midwife to steal Megan?"

"Yeah. James forgot to mention that part of his grand plan. That's what you get for trusting the devil. Twenty years in hell."

"Okay. Here's another question," I said. "How did you end up at the Beadford place the night Holt nearly made me walk the plank?"

"I had still been following Megan. It gave me such a thrill every glimpse I got of her, even though I knew it would have to end soon. Once I returned to Jamaica, I was certain I'd never see her again."

"But Megan didn't get home until well after the trouble went down, so you certainly didn't follow her there."

"You didn't let me finish. I was out in the funeral home parking lot, waiting for the visitation to end so I could see my daughter. You left with Sylvia. And then not a second later Holt McNabb came out. Call it intuition, but he had this look on his face that was downright evil. I knew in my heart he meant you harm. And after meeting you, I could tell how much you cared for Megan. I had to help if I could."

"And so you did." I smiled.

"Not much. Anyway, the reason I came here was to thank you for all you did for Megan, for bringing us together. I don't have much money, but since my sentence won't allow me to return home to Jamaica, I was hoping you'd accept the profit from the sale of my house as a bonus to whatever Megan has paid you."

"Absolutely not," I said firmly. "But there is something you *could* do."

"You name it." She'd flashed a great smile, so very much like Megan's. And since Laura knew I was no devil, she'd made another deal that morning.

I lifted my arm and pressed the light button on my watch. In about seven hours someone else would be smiling—a wide white smile complemented by shiny brown eyes.

Jug would be opening the overnight mail envelope I'd sent today, the one containing the legal documents and keys to his new house in Kingston.

And he knew exactly where to find the place.

Read on for a preview of another
Yellow Rose Mystery by Leann Sweeney

DEAD GIVEAWAY

Available from Signet

If Daddy were alive and standing beside me tonight, he'd say we've got a "skunk down the well." A situation. I leaned against the driver's-side door of my Camry to wait. Seems I wouldn't be getting near the espresso bar to meet a witness in the case I was working. At least not now. Not with crime scene tape strung in front of the building and red, white, and blue police cruiser lights electrifying the night sky like a patriotic carnival.

Folks from the sports bar farther down in the strip mall had wandered out to see what was going on, too. Then a TV station news van pulled into the parking lot just as the faint mist dampening my hair and bare shoulders turned into a warm June drizzle.

Patches of fluorescent oil from departed cars slicked the blacktop separating me from Verna Mae Olsen, my witness. That's assuming she was inside the coffee place and trapped by whatever event brought the police here. Someone on a caffeine high went postal, maybe? Those five dollar coffees are strong enough to float a wrench, so it wouldn't surprise me. I sure hoped it wasn't anything more serious than that.

I'd interviewed Verna Mae several days ago in Bottlebrush—a town about an hour from here and as different from Houston as a toy poodle is from a wolf. My newest client, Will Knight, hired me to do what the police couldn't accomplish nineteen years ago—learn who had abandoned him on Verna Mae's doorstep. He and his adoptive parents wanted information about his birth family, and since I'm a PI who specializes in adoption issues, I took Will's case.

Verna Mae Olsen seemed the logical starting point and I thought I'd heard all she had to tell the other day, but she surprised me by calling tonight. So I invited her to my house in the West University section of the city, but she insisted we meet here. Why, I don't know, but I agreed.

Hey, I thought, *I could call her.* If she was inside the coffee place or sitting in her car watching like I was, I'd feel a whole lot better if I heard her voice. So I opened the car door, reached across the seat for my phone, and dug in my shorts pocket for her number. When I punched in the digits, it only rang once.

"Why are *you* calling this phone?" said a familiar male voice.

I opened my mouth but nothing came out. It was Jeff. Sergeant Jeff Kline of Houston PD Homicide. My Jeff. The guy I love. He must have read my caller ID.

"Talk to me, Abby," he said.

"You have her phone," I said. "Th-that's not good."

"Whose phone?"

"Verna Mae Olsen. A witness I was supposed to meet. From what I'm seeing in this parking lot, I don't think that's going to happen."

"Where are you?" he asked.

"Not far. If you're inside the coffee shop, look out the window and you'll see me."

"I'll do better than that."

The line went dead and a second later he pushed open the glass door, ducked under the crime scene tape and strode in my direction. He held something in one latex-gloved hand and the badge clipped to his belt glinted in the halogen lights that had been set up to better illuminate the lot and storefront.

My heart was hammering now. Jeff's presence plus his possession of that phone equaled more than skunk trouble. By the time he reached me, my mouth was so dry I wasn't sure I had enough spit to talk.

Jeff wore his cop face—tired and all business. He held up a small black cell phone enclosed in a baggie. "Who is this Olsen woman?"

"I . . . I interviewed her for a case a couple days ago and she asked me to meet her here."

"You can ID her?" he said.

"ID her? You mean . . ."

"I need you to look at a body," he said, his voice tinged with genuine regret.

"Oh no. What happened, Jeff?"

"I'm guessing a robbery that got out of hand. *Guessing.* That could change." He gestured for me to follow and led me toward the coffee bar—a place called The Last Drop. As we walked, he put the cell phone in his pants pocket, removed his gloves, and balled them up. Those went in his other pocket.

The rain had picked up by the time we passed the crew of cops on the sidewalk outside the shop. Several nodded at me in greeting. I'd met them when Jeff and I visited one of Houston PD's favorite watering holes together. Latrell, his new partner, was talking to a tall young woman with spiked hair, low riding capris, and a nose ring. Latrell looked my way and said, "Hey, Abby. What's up?" like it was no big deal I'd show up at a crime scene.

We did not enter The Last Drop as I expected. Instead, Jeff led me around the building to a wide back alley that ran behind the shopping center for delivery truck access. More halogens had been set up and jumpsuited crime scene workers were canvassing the area around the back door of the coffeehouse. On the other side of the alley a huge grassy ditch for flood water collection was illuminated, too. Down in that ditch I saw a heavyset figure kneeling beside a dark mound I assumed was the body.

Telling me to follow exactly behind him so as not to disturb any uncollected evidence, Jeff walked carefully down the bank, taking a path where the grass had already been flattened by footsteps.

"How could you find *anyone* back here?" I asked.

"Pure luck. Guy tied up his dog outside the coffee joint while he went inside. Black lab with a helluva nose. Dog got loose and here we are."

The crouching woman wore a blue oxford shirt, the fabric on her shoulders darkened by rain. As we drew closer, all I could see was the victim's feet. The once white Tommy Hilfiger sneakers were stained brown. Those feet looked to be a size five or six, certainly small enough to belong to Verna Mae, who couldn't have been more than five feet tall. The day we met, it struck me how diminutive she seemed in contrast to my client. The guy checks in at six-foot-ten. Will's a college basketball player and he went with me to Bottlebrush to meet with Verna Mae.

The stocky woman stood and turned with a fluidity that belied her size. She had a chubby face, stringy gray hair and held her gloved hands up like she was ready to do surgery. "What do you want, Sergeant?" she asked, not acknowledging my presence.

Her gruff manner made my neck muscles tighten.

"Dr. Post, this is Abby Rose. She can possibly ID the victim," said Jeff.

The woman smiled at me. Her teeth were yellowed and her eyes were sharp with interest. She refocused on Jeff. "You found family without having any ID? You have skills I didn't know you possessed, Sergeant."

"She's not family," he answered.

"Oh." The detached, cold expression returned. "Well then, have a gander. I've cleaned off her face." She waved a hand at the body.

The dead woman had what looked like fire ant

mounds all over her, but the smell told the truth. They were coffee grounds. *Gheesh.*

I recognized Verna Mae, mostly because of her distinctive gray eyes. They were glassy and wide now, and her face looked like she'd been hammered with a meat mallet. Her broken nose lay against one bruised and swollen cheek and her bottom lip was split. Blood covered her teeth and chin.

I stepped back. Tried to swallow the hot, sour Diet Coke that rocketed into my mouth.

Jeff grabbed my elbow and pulled me back from the body. Good thing, because I bent over and vomited everything but my toenails.

He rested a hand on my back as I rid myself of the last ounce of bile; then he put his mouth to my ear and whispered, "You okay?"

I nodded, wiped my lips with the back of my hand.

When I was upright again, Jeff said, "If you're not able to continue, Ms. Rose, we understand." This formal attitude was apparently for the benefit of the doctor, who was again kneeling by the body.

I made myself take another good look, willing my stomach to behave. "That's her. Verna Mae Olsen."

Dr. Post looked over her shoulder at me. From her expression, puking identifiers were obviously a pain in the ass. She dug into the pile of coffee grounds and lifted one of the dead woman's bruised arms. The wet coffee clung to Verna Mae's skin like dirt. "No rigor or lividity. This corpse is fresher than the grounds the killer or killers dumped on top of her. Why do you think they did that, Sergeant?"

"I can't speculate," Jeff said.

"Made a helluva mess," she muttered. "Murderer probably has the stuff all over his shoes."

"That's been noted," Jeff said.

"Glad you're on your toes, Sergeant, but could you take your witness somewhere else now? I've called the van to remove the body and she'll be in the way. And get one of your police friends to clean up her vomit. I don't want me or my people to step in it."

"I'm really sorry about getting sick," I told Jeff as he guided me back up the incline and across the alley.

His response was to use the walkie-talkie feature on his phone. "Hey, Rick. Jeff here. There's vomit by the body."

I heard Rick say, "You need me to collect it?"

"Nope. Not evidence. A witness lost it. Just wanted you to be aware if you happened to wander up by the body again."

"Gotcha," said Rick.

As we arrived at the back entrance to The Last Drop, Jeff clipped his phone back on his belt. He held open the door and I went inside. By now, my khaki shorts and white blouse were soaked, along with my sandaled feet, so the blast of air-conditioning sent a shiver from bottom to top. I could feel the gritty grounds between my toes and it made me feel sick all over again.

After Jeff pulled the door shut and we were alone in a small hallway, he rested his hands on my cold shoulders. "You did good. Sorry you had to go through that, but it really helps us out."

"I feel so bad for her, Jeff. She must have been terrified before . . . b-before she died." I blinked back unexpected tears and glanced around. There was a restroom on the right and a storage room filled with huge, clear bags of coffee beans on our left. The aroma was so strong it could have knocked me flat. I wasn't sure I'd ever love coffee as much as I used to after tonight. "What could she have possibly done to deserve that beating?"

"That's what I have to find out. Let's go sit down, talk about what you know about the victim," he said.

"Can I rinse my mouth first?"

"Sure. Want some gum, too?" He patted his shirt pocket.

"No. I don't want anything even marginally connected to the food pyramid."

"Okay. I'll meet you up front."

I stepped inside the lavatory, closed the door and then leaned against it. I closed my eyes but that only made me see Verna Mae's battered face again, the face that had been so happy when I'd brought Will to see her.

I looked in the smudged oval mirror across from me. My skin was the color of concrete and my hair was so wet it looked black rather than auburn. I stepped over to a sink that resembled the bottom of a dirty coffeepot, turned on the faucet and splashed my face. After I rinsed away the taste of bile, I stared again in the mirror, ran my fingers through my hair and pushed back my bangs. I looked like I'd been through a carwash without a car, but this was as good as it was gonna get. I went back out into the hallway and walked the short distance into the coffee shop to give my statement, thinking about Verna Mae lying dead so close by and knowing in my gut her death had some sad connection to my client.